PERFECT WORLD

The First Chapters

Gerry Hines

Copyright © 2009 by Gerry Hines

ISBN 0-7414-5333-9

Published by:

PUBLISHING.COM

1094 New DeHaven Street, Suite 100
West Conshohocken, PA 19428-2713
Info@buybooksontheweb.com
www.buybooksontheweb.com
Toll-free (877) BUY BOOK
Local Phone (610) 941-9999
Fax (610) 941-9959

Printed in the United States of America

Published June 2009

IN MEMORY OF

NANNY

CHAPTER ONE

My eyes moved across the room, scanning every one of its small details for the umpteenth time. The sun was beginning to rise. After lying in my bed all night, the sheets and blanket were warm and comforting to me as I tried to become familiar with my new home. All of my belongings were neatly dusted and put away, soon to become unorganized and covered in a new layer of dust after a while.

The sound of the door opening caught my attention as Laura entered my room.

"Breakfast is almost ready, Krystal," she said sweetly. "Come down whenever you're ready." Her smile was soft and gentle.

I returned a small smile of my own, then Laura turned around and walked out to go back to the kitchen. Sliding out of bed, I stood up and stretched. The clean carpet felt nice under my feet as I made my way out of my room and across the hallway into the bathroom. After using it, I checked myself out in the mirror. My face was completely blemish-free, except for the scar just above my right eyebrow. I'd had it for years, and couldn't remember how I got it. I looked at the palm of my left hand, examining the long scar that spread from my index finger to my wrist. I didn't remember how I got that scar either.

I opened the medicine cabinet and removed my five different prescribed medications. I was told that if I didn't take them, I'd go completely insane. They were the best things I had, until the doctors could find out what was truly wrong with me and find a better treatment, or if possible, a cure, but I wasn't very hopeful.

The shower I took washed away the pain of the sleepless night. However, it was a brief shower, just like every other happy moment in my life.

As usual, my long blonde hair wasn't very messy, so it was easy to brush. Walking slowly down the stairs to the living room, I ran my fingers along the wood grain railing, taking note of its smoothness. Before I reached the bottom of the stairs and into the living room, I took a small sniff of air. The smell of the new house and the smell of our furniture hadn't mixed quite perfectly yet, creating an oddly uneven scent that would take a few more weeks to blend.

When I entered the kitchen, Laura was serving up a big mound of pancakes onto a plate and setting it on the table for me. Jack had already seated himself and was reading the newspaper. He folded it up and put it aside when he saw me walk in.

"Well, if it isn't our beautiful daughter on her first morning in our new house," he announced. "How'd you sleep last night?"

"Good," I replied quietly. Of course, that was a lie. I hadn't had a good night's sleep in about three years, but no one needed to know that.

I sat down in the chair that Laura had placed my plate in front of, drowned the heap of pancakes in syrup, and started digging in. I was always a big eater and could eat all I wanted and not gain a pound. At least I had something to be thankful for.

Laura took a seat next to Jack, and they started discussing their usual business plans. After all, our move was centered on their job. I was told that by moving from Michigan to this small town in Florida, the two of them would be able to become more efficient. Whatever was truly meant by that, I wasn't sure.

Most people consider Jack and Laura to be my parents. However, I see them as merely guardians. They adopted me a few years ago, but I had never been able to connect with them completely. Every time I felt myself become closer to them, it was as if I was trying to form a bond with empty shells. Maybe it was just me.

When breakfast was over, I stood up and took my dishes to the sink. Morning sunlight was beaming into the kitchen, beckoning me to go out into it. The pool in our backyard seemed to be an appropriate place to go and relax outside. To get to it I had to go through the big glass sliding door in the living room.

Right when I opened the door and stepped out, warm air rushed around me. Jack had set up lounge chairs the previous day. I took a seat in one, then leaned back to look into the sky and watch the white fluffy clouds as they floated slowly across the blue. Even though there were plenty of houses around, our home had an isolated tranquility because of the high fences, shrubs, and palm trees everywhere. Florida was much different than Michigan.

I began to wonder about the new neighborhood. Summer had just started, and school was still far off. What would it be like? Would I make any new friends? My old school wasn't very big, and I really didn't have friends. Most of the popular people seemed to avoid me. Sometimes they were forced to interact with me in some way, such as a group project with randomly chosen members, but at least they treated me with respect. One could say that I just got along with everyone, even if they didn't want to.

About half an hour passed when I thought about getting a nice glass of lemonade. I walked back into the kitchen where Jack was still reading the paper and Laura was clipping coupons out of a magazine. As soon as I finished pouring the lemonade into a glass, the doorbell rang throughout the house. Jack got up quickly, looking excited.

"Our first visitors!" he said cheerfully. "I'll go get it!" He rushed to answer the door, Laura right behind him, leaving me alone in the kitchen. I was always hesitant to meet new people, especially over the past few years, so I didn't want to draw attention to myself.

They came back with three people following them. Two of them were boys, and one was a girl. One of the boys had dark hair and a gentle face, and he looked a little like the girl who followed behind him. The other boy was taller and had light brown hair that came down to his shoulders. They all looked to be about the same age as me.

"This is our daughter, Krystal," Laura introduced. The dark-haired boy came up to me and shook my hand.

"Hi," he said, looking a little nervous. "Uh, my name's Gary. This is my older sister, Abby," he pointed at the dark-haired girl behind him, who smiled at me, "and this is my best friend—"

"James is the name!" Gary was interrupted by the taller boy, who thrust out his hand and firmly grabbed mine. "It's a pleasure to meet such a wondrous girl as yourself!" I watched as his eyes slid quickly up and down my body. For some reason, I didn't really care.

"We saw the moving van yesterday," said Abby, "so we thought we'd pay a visit and meet the new people."

"I'm glad we did!" said James. "Meeting new people can be really cool." He looked around the kitchen before his eyes flickered over me again. I looked at Gary, who instantly smiled. I couldn't help but smile back.

"Well, I'm sure Krystal will make some great friends here," said Jack.

"It hasn't even been twenty-four hours yet, and she's already met some nice teenagers her age to hang around with," Laura added.

"We were thinking about going into town today," said Gary to Jack and Laura. "If it's okay with you, we can show Krystal around."

"That sounds good," Jack agreed. "Is that all right with you, Krystal?"

"Sure," I said.

"Man, something smells good." James turned his attention to the leftover pile of pancakes on the counter. "Hey, can I have some of these?"

"Help yourself," Laura told him.

"Cool, thanks!" He grabbed the top one and immediately stuffed it in his mouth. Abby looked a little disgusted, and Gary seemed somewhat embarrassed. I thought it was a little funny.

"Um, should we go now?" said Abby, trying to ignore James as he slurped down another pancake. I followed her and Gary to the door with James bringing up the rear.

"Have fun!" Laura called to me on the way out. I waved to her and Jack as I headed down the street with Gary, James, and Abby.

"You're gonna love this place!" James told me. "We hang out in town all the time!"

"Now that summer's just started," said Gary, "we'll be going into town almost every day. You can come with us if you want."

"It's about a ten minute walk into town from the neighborhood," said Abby. "Before we get there, I'll let you in on the geography of the area."

"She doesn't want to hear you drone on and on about stupid stuff!" James blurted out.

"Hey!" Abby barked. "It's important to learn the geography of an area!" She turned back to me. "Let's see, right now we're in the neighborhood. If you take the road we're on now, it'll lead into the town. On the way there you can see the ocean from the road."

"The view of the ocean is great at sunset," said Gary. "You'll have to see it."

"After we get into town," Abby continued, "you can get to the city. There's only one road that leads directly to the city from here, and it's about a fifteen minute drive. I'd drive you over there, but I don't have my own car yet."

4

"It's only a little over five minutes if you drive fast enough," James whispered to me. I giggled softly, and Abby shot James a dirty look.

"So, Krystal," Gary looked a little nervous while he spoke, "w-where are you from?"

"Michigan," I said quietly.

"Wow, that's far!" said James. "Did you have any cactuses in your yard?"

"Michigan isn't a desert," Gary told him. "At least, I don't think…"

"No, it's not," said Abby, "and it's 'cacti', moron."

"Well, sorry, miss know-it-all," said James irritably.

"Hey, guys," said Gary. "Knock it off."

As the road came to the top of the last hill, Gary pointed out the view.

"You can see the town from here," he said.

"And over on the right," said Abby, "you can see the ocean now."

I gazed down at the town we were heading into, then looked over and saw the ocean for the first time in my life. Since the sun was over land, there wasn't any glare on the water, so it looked blue and sparkly. It was one of the most amazing things I had ever seen.

"It's so pretty," I said.

"Like I said," said Gary, "you should see it at sunset."

"I really would like to," I replied softly. He smiled at me again, and I felt my lips curve up into a smile automatically. Something about Gary could make me smile.

The rest of the way down, James talked mainly about sports and surfing, Abby talked about things such as the area's weather patterns and good places for sightseeing, and Gary mainly was interested in what I liked to do and where I used to live. Of the three, Gary seemed to be the most easygoing. However, when it came to being carefree and happy-go-lucky, James took the cake.

Not much longer, we made it into town. There was a moderate amount of traffic, and the atmosphere was lively. Unlike in Michigan, an occasional palm tree was planted in the sidewalk, giving the town a tropical feel. I was in Florida, after all.

"Well, this is it," said Abby. "I don't come here as often as the boys, so I'll let them be your guides."

"Just follow us!" said James. "We'll give ya the grand tour. This way!" He strutted down the street, and the rest of us tagged along.

A few blocks down, we stopped at a restaurant located on the corner of a somewhat busy intersection.

"Normally, we come here first," James told me. "This is the Shady Palm Café, best diner in town! Or at least the best one we can afford."

"We'll bring you back here sometime if you want," said Gary.

"Okay," I replied. "Sounds great!"

We followed James a little ways through town until he came to an arcade.

"This is the arcade," he said. "Like video games?"

I felt a small urge of excitement deep inside me.

"Yeah."

"Awesome!" said James loudly. "I'm just liking you more and more!"

"James is the champion of one of the games here," said Gary. "He has a high score that nobody else has even come close to." He then leaned closer to my ear and whispered, "It's kinda gone to his head, so be careful when discussing it with him."

"Um, where are we going next?" Abby asked James, pulling him away from the arcade window he was peering through.

"Look at those poor fools try to beat my score," he mumbled menacingly. As soon as he saw the look on Abby's face, he quickly added, "Oh yeah, the tour! Let's get going! We can show her the beach!"

James took off down the sidewalk again. I began to wonder if he could ever act seriously if need be. While following him to the next destination, I looked over at Gary again, who was walking next to me on my right.

"He's a strange one, isn't he?" said Gary.

"Who?" I asked. "James?"

"Yeah, well," Gary scratched his head, "don't you think so?"

"Come on, just admit it," said Abby, who was walking on the other side of me. "We all know he's a totally moronic screwball. Isn't that right, little bro?"

"I don't know if that's exactly what he is," said Gary. "There aren't too many out there quite like him…"

"Hey, hurry up ya'll!" James was already way ahead of us. He stopped to turn around and beckon us to pick up the pace.

"Yes, master," Abby replied.

"What's taking you guys so long?" James asked us when we caught up to him.

"We're moving at our own comfortable pace, thank you," said Abby.

"I'm sure Krystal wants to take her time," said Gary. "There's a lot more to this town than specific places of interest. She might even come across something she wants to check out that we wouldn't think much of."

James looked a little aggravated at first, but thought it over and said, "Yeah, that's cool. She's the new person, after all."

Right after he had said that, I noticed a small building across the street. There was a welcoming sensation to it. Eventually, my curiosity got the best of me.

"Hey," I said quietly.

"Hmm?" Gary turned to me. "See something you want to check out?"

"What's that place?" I asked, pointing at the small building across the street.

"Oh, that's the antique store," said Abby. "I've never been in it, but they probably have some neat stuff in there."

"Like what?" said James. "Antiques are boring."

"We'll go over there for Krystal, okay?" said Gary.

"I thought we were going to the beach!" James sounded confused and irritated.

"We are," said Gary. "After we do this."

"Fine," James groaned.

The four of us walked across the street to the front of the antique store. Inside, the place looked dark and empty, but for some reason, I still felt welcomed by it.

"Oh, they're closed," said Abby. The lights were all turned off, making it hard to see inside. James made a small noise of satisfaction.

"Today's Sunday," said Gary. "They probably don't open on Sunday. We can come back tomorrow. Sorry about that, Krystal."

"It's no big deal," I said, smiling.

"Beach, anyone?" said James, wearing a big grin.

"Oh, hush," Abby told him.

Walking to the beach took about twenty minutes, but I took the time to check out the town and enjoy the weather. The sun was out, and it wasn't too hot, making it a perfect day to get to know everything. I began to feel as if Jack and Laura had done something good by moving. Deep down, I knew that I was making a connection with the new town.

As the air began to have a fresh, salty smell, I knew that we were getting closer to the ocean. James was blabbering on and on, but I really wasn't paying much attention to him. Some of my attention was focused on Abby, who kept making funny little side remarks on things that James would say. The rest of my attention was directed at Gary. Although he didn't say much, I couldn't help but notice him.

"We're here!" James announced. Those were the first words from him I actually listened to since we left the antique store. "This is our major attraction in the area."

My eyes were pulled over the sand and across the ocean. Without a doubt, it was one of the most beautiful things I'd ever seen. Even as we made our way up to the sand, I was amazed by how much better my new home was than what I had expected.

"Judging by Krystal's stare," said Gary, "coming back here is on our list of things to do!"

"So, what do you think?" Abby asked me.

Words failed me. "It's…cool."

"Is that all you can say?" James laughed. "Oh well, you can tell that she's not from around here. We're gonna turn you into one of us, you just wait!"

"We'd prefer you turn into either Abby or me," said Gary. Abby and I found that remark somewhat funny.

"Ha ha," said James indignantly, "you're a hoot, Gary."

After they showed me the beach, Gary, James, and Abby showed me the rest of the town. There was a lot more to see than I had expected, including a movie theater, bowling alley, and a handful of restaurants. They even showed me the high school where they went to, and where I'd be going once summer ended.

"It's a nice school," I said.

"Well, it's not the biggest school around," said Abby. "It's mostly for kids who live in the residential area around the town, but a handful come from the city."

"It's the only big city nearby," Gary added. "We don't go there often. There's a huge mall we go to around the holidays to find gifts and stuff. Other than that and the hospital, there's really no reason for us to go there."

"Everything we ever need is right here!" said James loudly, stretching out his arms.

"It's a beautiful town," I told them. That was no lie. Everything seemed just right. Maybe even…perfect.

"Yeah, it's nice around here," said Gary. "It took a lot of hard work from the area's officials to get it the way it is now. Crime rates aren't bad, either."

"Do you want to stay here after graduating?" I asked him.

"Probably," he replied. "It's a big world out there, though."

"I might stay remotely in the area," said Abby, "but I really don't know what I want to do. I like it here, but like Gary said, it's a big world to explore."

"Heh, I'm outta here after graduation," said James. "I was thinking about moving somewhere west of here. I'm gonna be an adventurer!"

"You said Arizona, right?" Gary asked. "Doesn't it get hot there?"

"I don't care!" James declared. "It gets hot here, too! We live in Florida! Did you think I wouldn't buy a house without air conditioning?"

"I didn't say that," said Gary.

"He was just asking," Abby muttered. "But if you do move out there, just be careful not to fall into any 'cactuses'."

"Anyway," James continued, ignoring Abby's comment (or not hearing it), "I would stay out there for a while, get a little R & R, then maybe come back here. I like it here, but I might go and see what's out there, ya know? Like you said, Gary, it's a big world out there!"

"Will you guys quit stealing my lines?" Gary looked cute when he got irritated like that.

"Well, what now?" Abby asked. "We just about showed her everything."

"Uh, I don't know," said James. "What time is it?"

"About a quarter after one," Abby replied, looking at her watch.

"Let's go get something to eat," said Gary. "We can take Krystal to the Shady Palm Café."

"Yeah, that's great!" said James excitedly. "I'll even pay for her food."

"That's an awfully nice thing for you to do." Abby was looking at James kind of suspiciously.

"What are you talking about?" he asked defensively. "I'm just being nice to our new friend here."

Gary and Abby looked at each other, then at me, then back at each other.

"I wasn't trying to infer anything," Abby told him. "I was just saying that it's not something you do very often."

"Oh." James almost immediately dropped his defensive position. "I just felt like doing something nice for a change. Now let's go, I'm hungry!" He took off again, and as usual, I followed behind him along with Gary and Abby.

The walk back to the Shady Palm Café wasn't very long. When I stepped inside, I took a good look around. The smell of hamburgers and fries filled my nose, making my mouth water a little. The place wasn't crowded, but it still had a good share of customers. We made our way over to the counter, and I studied the menu.

"Hey there, kids." A fairly chubby guy with glasses and a balding head greeted us from the other side of the register.

"Oh, hi Bernie," said Gary. "This is our new friend, Krystal. She just moved here yesterday."

"Well, welcome to our town!" said Bernie happily. He reached over and shook my hand.

"Thanks," I replied. "I really like this place."

"That's good!" he said. "If they're going to be your closest friends, this restaurant is going to be one of your more familiar places. Let's see, since it's your first time here, how about I make your meal on the house?"

"Really? Thank you!" I said cheerfully.

"That's…cool…," said James flatly. He was obviously disappointed that he couldn't perform his act of kindness of paying for my food.

"I wouldn't go around telling anyone this," said Bernie quietly, leaning over the counter. "Now, what can I get ya?"

I looked back up the menu, studied a little longer, and then came to my decision.

"I'll have the number one," I said. "The deluxe size."

Bernie hesitated to punch the order into the register. Gary, James, and Abby exchanged glances.

"That's a lot of food," Gary told me. "Are you sure?" I smiled and nodded at him.

"Well," Bernie chuckled, "it looks like we've got a good

eater here! If that's what you want, no problem!" He punched in the order. "What about you three? The usual?"

"Yep," they said in unison.

Bernie rang up the orders, collected their money, and a few moments later, handed us our trays.

"I've gotta go to the bathroom," I said to them.

Abby pointed it out. "Over there in the back."

"We can get your stuff for you," said Gary.

After using the bathroom, I went to the sink and washed my hands. As I was using the hand dryer, I was caught off guard by something that flashed in front of my eyes. Since it was so fast, I couldn't make out what it was.

Ever since I was twelve, strange visions flickered in front of me every now and then. I remembered what all of the adults had told me; during my teenage years weird things would be happening within my body. Therefore, I always assumed that the visions were just a part of puberty, caused by random hormones going crazy, and that most people had them. Thinking nothing of it, I walked out of the bathroom and sat down at the table with Gary, James, and Abby, and started eating.

"Cool place, huh?" James asked me.

"This place is never packed," said Gary. "Then again, it's never empty, either. There's always someone else in here besides us."

"You're already almost done with that burger?" Abby asked James in disgusted awe.

James swallowed the mammoth-sized bite he was chewing on, took a drink to wash it down, and then attempted to stifle a burp. When he did, I thought his eyes were going to pop out.

"I was hungry," he said innocently. He glanced over at me, and then had to double take. "Look at Krystal! She's almost done with hers, too!"

I got caught with the three of them looking at me with my cheeks stuffed with my deluxe hamburger like a chipmunk as I attempted to somehow suck out some more soda with my straw. Abby, who was disgusted by James stuffing his face, giggled as she watched me.

"She eats faster than you, James!" Gary laughed. After swallowing all of the contents in my mouth, I smiled and joined in with a little laughter myself. James, however, just looked completely blown away.

"How did you…? You didn't even choke…that's the coolest thing ever…"

When I was finished eating, the three of them seemed amused that I had finished eating before them, even though they started before me and I had the most food. I waited for them to finish and then we headed back to the residential area. On our way back to the neighborhood, our next plans were discussed.

"What are we going to do now?" Abby asked.

"I think Krystal should go home now," said Gary. "We don't want her parents to think we abducted her."

"Yeah," said James, "that would suck. They probably wouldn't let her hang out with us again."

We walked all the way back to my house. I was feeling a little disappointed that our day together was soon to be over, but I knew that tomorrow was going to be a whole new day.

"See ya tomorrow?" said Gary when we made it back.

"Sure, okay," I replied, smiling.

"Yeah, we'll come get you," said James. "Make sure you're ready!"

"I will," I said. James and Abby turned around first, then Gary and I looked and smiled at each other briefly before he followed them.

"Hi sweetie!" Laura greeted as I came into the house. "Did you have a good time?"

"Yeah," I said somewhat dreamily.

"You look happy," said Jack. "How was it?"

"Good," I said.

"Did you already have lunch?" Laura asked. "I can make you something."

"No, I'm fine," I replied languorously, heading up the stairs into my room. When I plopped down on my bed, my eyes once again scanned the room. Everything was just the way it was before I had left, but it felt different. It felt better. While looking around, I realized just how good I was feeling. Maybe it was because I had found such good friends. Perhaps it was the town, as it was just right for me. Either way, it seemed as if I had found my perfect world. Nothing was going to stand in my way of living in this new perfect world.

Nothing at all.

CHAPTER TWO

"Good morning!" said Laura as I reached the bottom of the stairs. She was in the living room, sorting through some catalogs. Another long night, another morning started with Laura. I had grown quite used the routine, as most people do. "I'm about to make some bacon and eggs."

Normally breakfast is the thing I look forward to in the morning. However, this time I was more excited about my friends coming to see me.

"My friends are coming back today," I told Laura as she was walking into the kitchen.

Her face lit up. "That's nice, dear! Just as long as you stay out of trouble."

"I will," I said. Looking over at the television, I decided to see what was on. I didn't watch TV a lot, but it still was useful to kill time. I sat down on the couch and used the remote to turn the TV on, then started flipping through channels. Finally, I found some cartoons and watched that. I was still a little kid at heart. Actually, a lot of people my age still watch cartoons. Some just don't like to admit it.

The smell of bacon began to float through the house, tormenting me with its nearly hypnotic aroma. My mouth began to water as I imagined the taste of the bacon and eggs being washed down with an ice-cold glass of orange juice. The worst part about food is the agonizing wait just before it's ready.

"Krystal, breakfast is ready!" Laura's voice was like a leash around my neck that yanked me off that couch and into the kitchen. When I sat down, Laura put my plate down in front of me. The food practically lifted itself from the plate and into my mouth.

"Your eating never ceases to amaze me," said Jack amusingly.

"She's a growing girl," Laura commented.

"With the way she eats," said Jack, "you'd figure she was growing into a mammoth." He chuckled as I finished off the bacon on my plate.

After breakfast, I went out to the backyard by the pool again. Standing inches away from the water, I looked at the sunlight reflecting off its surface. A breeze came through the trees and rustled my hair a bit. I sat down on the edge of the pool and gently splashed my feet in the water, watching the ripples spread slowly outward. The water reminded me of the ocean I saw the day before.

Another quick vision flashed in front of me. Blinking it away, I tried to make out what it was, but no luck. Puberty was so weird.

I heard the sliding glass door open, and I turned to see Laura step through it.

"Ever think you'll get in it?" she asked.

"I don't know," I replied flatly.

"Feel free to take a dip at any time," she said. "I came out to tell you that your friends are here."

I quickly stood up, feeling excited to see Gary and James appear behind Laura.

"Hey, Krystal!" said James. "Whoa, I didn't know you guys had a pool!"

"Come on out, boys," said Laura. "Krystal, I'll be in the kitchen with Jack getting our things together for work, okay?"

"Okay," I said.

As soon as Laura was out of the way, James burst out of the doorway and started checking out the pool with wild excitement in his eyes. Gary followed him slowly, took a quick look around, and then looked at me, smiling.

"Hi," he said.

"Hi," I repeated. My face started to feel warmer, and I immediately looked away. James continued to check out every inch of the pool as Gary and I spoke.

"So," he said, "how are you doing?"

"Good," I replied, daringly turning to look at him. "How about you?"

"Oh, I'm doing fine," he told me. There was a short pause. "Nice day, isn't it?"

"Yeah. Um…where's Abby?"

"She's back home. Yesterday was really the only day she spent with us. All she wanted to do was get to know you. It's usually just me and James always hanging out."

"Yo, Krystal!" James had finished scoping out the pool area and came rushing up to us. "What're we gonna do today? We'll let you choose."

"She might want to go back to the antique store," said Gary.

"Oh." James didn't look very motivated at first, but that

quickly changed. "Alright, then we can go to the arcade after that!" The thought of being in a video game environment sparked something in my enthusiasm compartment.

"Let's go, then!" Gary opened the sliding glass door open for me (and James), then closed it behind us. We saw Jack and Laura walking out the front door to go to work just as we came in.

"Bye, sweetie!" said Laura.

"We have stuff in there for you to make if you get hungry," Jack told me. "See you tonight. Have fun."

"Okay," I said. "Bye."

"See ya," said James. As soon as the door closed, he headed straight into the kitchen.

"What are you doing?" Gary asked irritably. "Didn't you eat this morning?"

"Yeah," James replied distractedly, "but I'm still hungry. Ask Krystal, she understands."

I felt a little amused, but Gary looked slightly embarrassed.

"You can't just raid people's kitchens!"

"I don't mind," I said. "If you're hungry, you're hungry."

Gary seemed shocked by my reply. I thought it was cute whenever he had that look on his face.

"See?" I heard James say. "She doesn't care!"

"Well, uh…just hurry up." Gary looked at me, and then he smiled and shook his head. "What a guy," he said. I laughed.

James had found a box of crackers with a few left in it and indulged himself until it was empty. He threw the box away, and then we headed out the door. I saw our car heading down the road into town. Jack and Laura had to go through the town to get to work in the city Gary and James had told me about.

"Man, it's hot out today," said James. "It's definitely summer now!"

"After we go the antique store and arcade," Gary told me on our way to town, "we'll get some lunch at the Shady Palm Café. Then me and James were going back to his house for a while. You can come if you want."

"Sure," I said. "I'd like to meet your family, James."

"Actually," said James, "my parents will be at work."

"You don't have a brother or sister?" I asked.

"Nope," he replied delightedly. "When the parents are gone, it's just me!"

"Same with me," I said. "Jack and Laura are hardly home

on weekdays."

"Who?" James asked.

"My parents," I said.

"Why aren't they ever home?" Gary asked. "Are they that busy?"

"Yeah," I said dully. "They always have these business meetings and trips. I only see them a lot on weekends."

"Must be nice," James muttered. "I wish my parents would go on a trip and leave me behind. I'd throw a party or something! Have you ever done that?"

"Done what?" I asked.

"Thrown a party when your parents aren't home?"

"No," I replied. "I never had enough friends to have a party."

"You've never had a party?" James was in total awe. "Have you ever been to someone else's party?"

"No." James was beginning to make me feel unhappy with his questions.

"You don't know what you're missing!" he said. "What about a sleepover?"

"We could invite her to one of our birthday parties," said Gary before I could answer, which was going to be another no. I started to feel a little bit better after he said that.

"Yeah, that'd be cool!" said James. "Mine's coming up in November. I'll have a birthday party, and you're invited, Krystal!"

"Thanks," I said happily.

"When's your birthday?" Gary asked me.

"April," I told him.

"My birthday's in March."

"I'm older than Gary is," said James.

"Only by a few months!"

James calculated the exact number on his fingers. "Four months, to be exact. I was born the year before."

"Come on," Gary chuckled, "we're in high school. Don't you think we're a little old to care about that?"

"Ha," James replied victoriously, "the words of an inferior."

All the way into town, the two of them goofed off like that. They made me feel very comfortable to be with. Something about James's childlike behavior and Gary's tactful attitude drew me like a magnet to them. I followed them down the sidewalks and up to the front of the antique store.

"We're here," said Gary, peering in through the window. "They're open, too."

"Let's make this quick," said James, sounding bored.

Gary pushed the door open and James and I followed right behind him. I looked around at all of the old items up for sale. There were shelves full of old books and countless trinkets. I walked behind Gary as he slowly made his way down the aisles. Shortly after, an old man walked out of the backroom. He was tall and skinny, but had the appearance of a strong war veteran.

"Hello there!" he called from behind the counter. "I don't see too many of you kids in here often."

"Ya don't say," James muttered quietly.

"We were just looking around," said Gary. "Our new friend wanted to check the place out."

"Oh, is that so?" the old man said. "Well, have a look around!"

"Hey, what's in here?" James walked up to the glass display case next to the counter where the old man was standing. "Whoa, hey guys! Come check this out!"

Gary and I walked over to James to see what he was looking at. Inside the display case was an assortment of glistening swords. Each one was polished and looked brand new.

"You like those, eh?" the old man chuckled. "Some of those are hundreds of years old. Would you care to take a closer look?"

"Uh, sure," said Gary.

The old man opened the display case and removed one of them, then handed it to Gary.

"Ever held one of these before?" he asked as Gary grabbed it.

"I don't think so," said Gary.

Those words were the last things I heard just before another quick vision popped in front of me. I wasn't sure what it was, but it certainly made me jump a little. For some reason, that particular vision hit me more forcefully than the others.

"Umm…" I looked at Gary's face as he examined the sword. He seemed surprised about something. Perhaps the sword was so interesting to him that words failed him. After looking at it for bit longer he said, "Pretty cool."

James was looking at him eagerly.

"Hey, let me see it," he said impatiently. Gary handed the weapon over to him, and as soon as James's fingers touched it, another quick vision flashed in front of me. This second one was just as forceful as the first. I started to get a little worried. Two visions had never occurred so close together before.

James had the same reaction as Gary. He looked at it for a few moments.

"It's...neat. I wish I had one. Do you want see it, Krystal?"

I hesitated a little. "Sure."

When I touched the sword, I was expecting another vision. Nothing happened. The other two were watching me a little closer than normal. I examined the blade closely, looking at its curves and angles as I ran my finger along it. Just I was about to say how much I liked it, a third vision flashed in front of me.

"Hey, don't we have somewhere to go now?" said James quickly.

"Uh, yeah," Gary replied. Maybe it was just my imagination, but they both sounded a little nervous.

"Good to see you three," the old man told us. "The name's Tyler. Feel free to stop by whenever."

The three of us quickly gave him our names. Something wasn't feeling right at all. We walked out of the store, trying to look as casual as possible. The funny part was that I had no clue as to why we were acting so strange. As soon as we made it outside, James immediately opened his mouth.

"Did you two notice anything when you touched that thing?" he asked almost in a whisper.

"Actually, I did," Gary responded just as quietly. "Have I ever held a sword before? I can't remember."

"Do you think he jinxed us?" James asked, sounding really worried.

"What?" said Gary loudly. "No...I...maybe. But why would he?"

"I don't know. Just to be mean, or have a little fun."

Gary and I gave James a puzzled look. Then we started laughing.

"Don't tell me you're afraid of witchcraft and magic," Gary told him.

"You never know!" said James. "It might exist!"

A strange feeling boiled in my stomach. For a moment, I was actually going to *agree* with him. Those visions...

"What, now you're going say aliens live in your attic," said Gary. "Come on! We aren't cursed or jinxed or whatever. Let's just get to the arcade. Maybe the heat is getting to us or something."

"Yeah, maybe you're right," said James. "Let's go."

The walk to the arcade was much quieter than the one to the antique store. We didn't say much, but continued silently. I was still trying to figure out what had just happened at the antique store. After a while, I began to concentrate more on the heat than anything else. It's hard to concentrate on something while your brains are being baked.

"Finally," said James tiredly as we approached the arcade, "we made it!"

When we walked in, the cool air conditioning blasted me in the face, instantly refreshing me. The sounds of video games swarmed around me, and I quickly felt better about the day. Kids of all ages filled the room as they excitedly played around.

"Isn't this place sweet?" James asked me. "Here, we got you some quarters."

"Thanks," I replied as he handed them to me, which I stuffed into my pocket.

"Hey, it's Nick." Gary pointed across the room at a tall boy with dark hair. When the boy saw us, he came over to greet us.

"What's happening, guys?" he said in a laid-back voice. "Hey, who's this?"

"This is Krystal," said Gary. "She moved here a couple days ago."

"I'm Nick," the boy said, shaking my hand. His grip was firm and gentle at the same time. "Hope you like it here." I felt really flattered and smiled as he spoke. "Where are you from?"

"Michigan," I replied.

"Really? I heard it was really nice up there." I could tell right off the bat that Nick was a romanticist, a kind word for a player.

"We're in charge of watching out for her," James told him, sounding important.

"That's cool, man," Nick replied. "You three wanna hang with me a bit?"

"Yeah," said James. "I wanted to show her my favorite game!"

"Nobody can beat his score," Nick told me. "James is the best at it."

We followed James over to his favorite game, located near the back of the arcade. Determined on defending his high score, he put some quarters into it and started blasting alien after alien. A small crowd had already gathered as kids watched their high scores get knocked off the charts. While James was busy blowing up aliens, I was having a conversation with Gary and Nick.

"Well," said Nick as he watched James. "I see that some people just never change."

"Heh, it's the coolest thing he can do," said Gary. "I've never seen anything like it. So, what have you been up to, Nick?"

"I was on my way to see my dad at work. It's his birthday, so I'm going to swing by the sports store and pick him up some new golf balls later on."

"Oh, that's cool," said Gary. "Yeah, we brought Krystal here to show her around. She said she liked video games."

"Is that so?" Nick replied, sounding interested. "A girl gamer, huh?"

I giggled a little. "Yup!"

We continued to talk until James interrupted.

"Oh yeah!" James pumped his fist into the air. "A new record, baby!" The small group of people around us cheered. Others who were in the arcade looked curiously over to see what the commotion was about. "Hey Nick, I bet you can't beat my high score!" James boasted.

"What are you, crazy?" Nick laughed. "No way, dude. You're too good."

"Can I try?" I asked.

"Go ahead," Gary told me. I took some change from my pocket and dropped the coins into the slot.

"Use this to move your spaceship," said James, pointing out the controls, "and use this button to shoot the aliens. Just don't get hit, and you'll be fine." James stood and watched over my shoulder. Gary and Nick continued talking.

"So," said Nick, "How's your summer been?"

"Oh, it's awesome!" said Gary.

"Any luck with…well, you know."

"Well…uh…I…"

"Don't worry about her," said Nick. "I'm sure things will go okay."

"Yeah," said Gary hopefully.

"Hey, you're pretty good," James told me.

"I wonder how school's going to be next year," said Gary to Nick. "Man, I hope it's not too hard."

"You know," said Nick, "it shouldn't be that hard. It shouldn't be much different than last year. Just new stuff, ya know?"

"Hey, guys!" A kid watching me playing the game called his friends over. "Look at this!"

I didn't even notice how good I was doing. Everything on the screen was being blown up. Not only that, I hadn't lost a single life. Another group gathered around the game to watch me get closer and closer to James's high score.

"She's doing better than I thought!" said James, scratching his head. He seemed a little nervous that he might have his high score beat.

About five minutes passed, and a large crowd had already gathered around me as I made my way up the ranks. Shortly after, my final life was taken just as I broke the high score. Everyone cheered and applauded as James looked completely awestruck.

"Holy crap!" he yelled. "You must have played this game a lot!"

I smiled weakly. "I've never played it before." James looked as if he had just swallowed a spider, but didn't want to make a face.

"Nice shooting!" said Nick. "No one's ever beaten him before. I can't believe you actually did it!"

"Wow," said Gary, "that was crazy!"

"Uh, yeah," said James quietly. "You're really good."

"It's nothing," I said, giving a small smile. "Really."

"What are you talking about?" said Nick. "That was sweet! You've got skill." Nick glanced at his watch. "I think I've spent enough time around here already. Catch y'all later!" We all said good-bye as he hurried out of the arcade, removed his bike from the rack, and took off.

The three of us stayed in the arcade for about another two and a half hours or so. When it got close to lunch we were starting to get hungry.

"So," said Gary, "what now?"

James shrugged. "I don't know. I'm out of money."

"Me too." Gary dug through his pockets. "I only have change for here. I guess we'll just go to your place now. We shouldn't have spent all of our money for lunch."

"Yeah, okay," said James. "That way we can hang out there until…uh, what time was your thing?"

"Three," Gary replied. "Yeah, we can do that."

"Alright!" said James excitedly. "Let's go!"

As we reached the edge of the town, curiosity was reaching the best of me. Not much longer, as we were walking up the road into the neighborhood, I had to ask.

"Gary," I said, "what do you have at three o'clock?"

"Uh, well," he said.

"He's got a date!" James announced.

"You do?" I became all ears. "With who?"

"Her name's Stephanie," said James before Gary could answer. "He had a crush on her since last year. Isn't that right?"

Gary looked a little embarrassed. "Do you have to go around telling people that?"

"That's nice," I said happily.

"I think that I should go along with you two," James told Gary.

"No!" said Gary. "It's only going to be the two of us. You'll mess it up!"

"Oh, get real," said James. "Wait, I thought she had a boyfriend. That Brandon guy. Did she dump him?"

"Who cares?" said Gary. "I'm going out with Stephanie. In your face!"

"Maybe I should tag along, just in case," James suggested.

"Just in case what?" Gary asked confidently. "What could go wrong?"

"You could say something stupid," said James. "I don't know. Just in case you need my help for something. You did say you're the cautious type."

"I'll be fine," Gary assured. "Don't worry."

"Are you gonna kiss her?" James asked, looking directly at Gary.

"No! Well…maybe…"

"Since I can't come along," said James, "good luck, then."

"Nothing should go wrong," Gary argued. I could tell that Gary was getting a little aggravated.

"Just remember this," said James. He put one hand on his hip and the other behind his head, then made some kind of little dance move.

Gary just looked at him like James was on drugs.

"What was that?" he asked.

"You know," said James, doing it again, "make a move."

"Make a move?" Gary squinted his eyes. "I'm not doing some stupid dance like that!"

"No, not like that," said James. "You gotta make a move on her!"

"I'll do whatever I feel like," said Gary. "Let's just get back to your house."

When we got to James's house I was really hungry. There was a box of cereal sitting on the coffee table in the living room. James hurried over to it, picked it up, and poured the rest of the cereal into his mouth.

"I'm hungry," said Gary. "What do you have to eat?"

"I just ate the last of the cereal," said James as he tipped the box upside down. A few crumbs fell out and bounced off the table. "You might find something in the kitchen. Mom won't be back from shopping until after work this evening. Just make yourself at home!"

Gary and I rummaged through the refrigerator, but couldn't find anything. As I looked in the cupboards, all I could find was a bag of nacho chips. Thinking it would have to do, I ripped it open and took a bite of one, just to spit it out. Gary tried some, but he spit it out, too.

"Hey James," Gary called. "How old are these nachos?"

"What nachos?" he replied, coming to see. "Wow, I forgot about those. Dude, they must be over three years old."

"Why do you have something that old in your kitchen?" Gary asked, tossing the entire bag into the trash.

"I guess we just forget about them," said James with a chuckle. "Oh well. My dad found a ten-year-old bowl of sauerkraut in his car while he—"

"Maybe I shouldn't be eating anyway," said Gary, trying to prevent James from making him sick. "It would spoil my appetite for Stephanie."

"We could watch TV instead!" said James. He ran over to the couch and turned the TV on. Knowing that he didn't have anything else to do, Gary followed. I immediately joined them.

After a few brainless reality shows, Gary looked at the clock again.

"Well, it's almost three o'clock," he said, standing up. "I guess I should be going."

"Okay," said James. "Good luck."

"What're you going to do, Krystal?" Gary asked.

"I think I'll stay here a little longer," I replied.

"Yeah, that's it!" James cheered. "Ahem, I mean, uh, cool. We'll just chill here."

Shortly after Gary left, James looked over at me with a mischievous look.

"Wanna follow him?"

I felt a little mischievous myself as I cracked a small smile. "Sure."

We went over to the door and slowly pushed it open. James peeked out to see if Gary was far enough down the road. He crept outside with me right behind him. I could see Gary, who was about a good fifty yards away.

"Follow me!" James whispered excitedly.

After closing the door as silently as possible, the two of us scurried down the street, making sure not to be too loud or Gary would discover us and blow our cover. I felt kind of like a spy sneaking around and it felt pretty good.

Gary rounded the corner and we stayed as close behind him as we dared. He was completely oblivious to us as our pursuit continued. Not much farther down Gary stopped in front of a house. I slammed into James as he came to an abrupt halt. We ducked behind a car parked on the side of the street in front of the neighboring house. Both of us watched Gary through the car's windows as he slowly made his way up to the house's front door. James was trying to force back a laugh and had to bite his hand to prevent himself from making any noise.

A few seconds after ringing the doorbell, Gary was greeted by a girl with hair almost as dark as his. From where I was watching I could see that she was very pretty. James and I were just in range of earshot and I could hear what they were saying.

"Hi!" the girl said, smiling brightly. "Ready?"

"Uh, yeah," Gary responded. "So, where do you, uh…want to go, Stephanie?" He sounded a little nervous.

"I don't know," Stephanie replied. "Where do you want to go?"

"Well, how about the Shady Palm Café?" he suggested.

"Yeah, okay!" said Stephanie.

"The Shady Palm, eh?" James whispered. "Heh, he's a natural! Oh, there they go!"

Gary and Stephanie walked back to the street, so James and I moved around the car to make sure that we were still hidden. They turned their backs to us and started walking in the direction towards town. We came out from hiding and followed some more.

At last, we made it all the way to the restaurant without giving ourselves away. We stood on the opposite corner of the intersection and watched Gary open the door for Stephanie. James chuckled when he saw it.

"Such a gentleman," he said mockingly. "Let's go pay 'em a visit now!"

"Okay," I replied.

Both of us casually walked through the doors of the Shady Palm Café as Gary and Stephanie were ordering. We stood right behind them in line, acting as if they knew we were even there.

"You can find us a table," Gary told Stephanie, "and I'll get the drinks and food. You want a root beer, right?"

"Yes," said Stephanie. She turned around to head for a table and saw us behind them. "Hi, James!" she greeted as she kept going.

Gary whirled around. His face instantly turned white, and then quickly to red.

"What're you doing here?" he hissed quietly.

"Just having lunch," James answered, trying to sound falsely innocent on purpose. "Ain't that right, Krystal?"

I giggled quietly. Gary looked exasperated more than ever.

"Did James drag you into this?" he asked me coolly.

"Hey, don't pin this all on me!" said James. "Besides, I had to make sure that you didn't screw up."

"Man," Gary groaned, "you're gonna blow this whole thing! Why don't you just let me be?"

"I had to come just to make sure," he said. "I was worried."

"What about Krystal?" Gary glanced at me. "What's her role in your scheme?"

"Just company," James replied bluntly.

Gary's expression went from angry to puzzled.

"Is everything all right?" Stephanie was standing right behind James. She was wondering what the commotion was about.

"Everything's fine," said James.

Gary's order came up, which he picked up and took over to the soda machine to get the drinks, mumbling something the whole time while James continued talking to Stephanie.

"This is Krystal, our new friend. She just moved here, and we're in charge of watching out for her!"

"Nice to meet you," she said to me with a smile.

"Thanks," I said quietly while smiling back, "same here."

"Let's go sit down," said Gary when he came back with their food.

"I'll get us something," James told me. "You want that mega meal you had last time?"

"Yeah," I said.

After getting our food, James and I sat down with Gary and Stephanie. During the entire meal, James kept talking to Stephanie about sports, who found it interesting. Gary quietly sat and ate, and I could tell that he was mad at James for ruining his date. I began to feel bad for going along with James.

On the way back to the neighborhood, James kept talking to Stephanie. When we reached her house James finally shut up.

"I had a good time," she said. "We should do that again some other time."

"Yeah," Gary replied.

"Oh, you bet!" said James. "Catch ya later!"

"Bye," she said. "Hope you like it here, Krystal."

"I do," I replied.

"See you later, Stephanie," said Gary.

"Bye, Gary." She gave him another big smile, and it looked as if he had forgotten James was on the same planet. As soon as Stephanie closed the door, Gary turned and glared at James.

"What?" he asked defensively.

"You know what!" Gary barked. "I told you not to come, but you had to! You ruined it!"

"I was just making sure nothing went wrong," said James. "That's all."

"The only thing that went wrong was you," Gary mumbled. "Oh well, I guess you didn't screw things up that badly."

"I didn't screw things up at all!" said James. "What's the big deal?"

"You're missing the concept," said Gary. "The idea of a date is for two people to spend quality time together and try and get to know each other. You messed up that concept."

"I was just trying to help," said James. "I didn't mean to make such a big deal out of everything. I'm sorry."

"I know," said Gary, cooling off. "I was just a little pissed off, that's all. It doesn't matter that much, I guess."

"Yeah, no hard feelings!" James put his arm around Gary and pulled him close. "We're buds, after all!"

"Hey, get off me!"

"Yo, is it okay if I hang out at your place for a while?" James asked Gary. "I don't want to go back home yet."

"That's fine with me," Gary replied. "We'll just ask my parents."

"Cool," said James. "I can call mine after they get home." He looked over and saw me standing next to him, then quickly added, "What about Krystal?"

"I don't mind if she comes over, too," said Gary. He looked at me and smiled. "It'd be great if you did."

"Sure," I said happily.

"Do you have to ask your parents if it's okay for you to come over?" Gary asked.

"No," I replied, "they're not too strict like that. They aren't home, anyway."

"Alright!" said James. "The three of us are gonna have a blast!"

"Doing what?" Gary asked. "There isn't much to do at my place."

"Of course there is!" said James. "You've got a bunch of video games that I don't have, and we both know that Krystal likes video games! C'mon!" He took off down the street as fast as he could go without running.

"I don't have that many…" Gary said to himself. "Ready to go, Krystal?"

"Yup," I said.

We ran to catch up with James. He slowed down when we finally caught up to him.

"Is your sister home?" James asked Gary.

"Abby's at her friend's house," Gary answered.

"Which one?"

"Jessica."

"Ooh!" James got a bright gleam in his eye. "The hot one!"

"Humph." Gary looked a little disgusted.

"Oh yeah," said James, "you don't like her, do you?"

"Not really," Gary told him. "She's annoying."

James chuckled. "Isn't she the one who almost ran you over with her bike a few years ago?"

"That's the one," said Gary flatly. "It wasn't just one time she tried doing that, either."

Thinking about what James had just said, I suddenly realized something.

"Don't you two have bikes?" I asked.

"We did," said Gary, "but a few months ago this kid named Brandon stole James's and tossed it into a trash compactor. Actually, it was the same Brandon who used to be Stephanie's boyfriend."

"I still want to beat his face in for that!" James blurt angrily.

"In order to buy him a new bike," Gary continued, "the two of us started doing odd jobs around the neighborhood trying to collect enough money for one."

"And being the awesome guy Gary is," said James, "he promised not to ride his bike at all until I got my new one. That way I wouldn't have to suffer alone, right, pal?"

"You bet," said Gary. "Too bad we usually end up spending our earnings on food and the arcade…"

"That's really sweet of you, Gary," I said. His face turned a little red.

"Yeah, well…uh, it was nothing."

"Man," James groaned. "Brandon really gets on my nerves."

"Yeah," said Gary, "but what can we do about it? He's a year older than us and he plays defense on the football team. He could tear us in half if he wanted to."

"I don't know about you," said James, "but I'd put up a fight. I play sports too."

"You play basketball," said Gary. "You're not exactly muscular and you're the worst at getting the ball in."

"What's that have to do with anything?" James asked.

"I'm just saying that Brandon is a better athlete," said Gary, "and the sport he plays is more of a contact sport."

"You're saying that I couldn't take him?" said James. He thought it over for a little bit. "Yeah, you're right. He'd probably kill me in a fight. But I still wanna get back at him for destroying my bike."

We made it to Gary's house when James was still talking about how he would get his revenge on Brandon. The front door was locked, so Gary had to lift up the welcome mat and use the key underneath it.

"Such a clichéd hiding place for a key," he said as he put the key into his pocket. He looked up at me and smiled, making me smile. When he pushed the door open I followed him in with James. Once inside, we took off our shoes and placed them aside.

"I'll go get the game set up!" said James excitedly, taking off through the living room and up the stairs.

"There's stuff in the fridge if you want anything," Gary offered to me.

"Okay," I replied. I went to the kitchen and opened the refrigerator, then browsed its contents. A sandwich sounded good, so I took out all the different deli meats I could find and put it on the counter. After I found the bread, I made my sandwich. Then I decided to make another one. Then I made a third one, just for the heck of it.

"You're an eating machine," I heard Gary say from behind. "Let's go up to my room. I know James is getting impatient."

I put my three sandwiches on a paper plate and followed Gary up the stairs to his room where James was waiting for us. We all sat down on Gary's bed as James handed us each a controller.

"Hope you like racing games, Krystal," said James, sitting down next to me.

"Not this one again!" Gary groaned. "Can't we play something else for once?"

"Gary hates racing against me," James told me. "He's terrible at it."

"I'm not that bad," said Gary. "I only do really bad against James."

"Because I'm the champ!" James beamed proudly as if he were in front of a million people.

"That's what he said in the arcade," said Gary quietly to me.

"I heard that!" James snapped. "Alright, Krystal. You and me, one-on-one!"

James set up the race that the two of us were going to compete in. We both chose the same car to make it fair, then he chose the most technical track he could find. When the race started, we were alongside each other, but I passed him on the first turn. He never managed to make it back into first place. Before long, the race was over.

"Hey, James," said Gary, "I think you lost."

"Whoa…" James stared at the screen for a few seconds

with his mouth open. "You're the coolest chick I ever met!"

I wasn't quite sure what to say, so I just smiled a little.

"Nobody's ever come close to beating me!" said James, his eyes bugged out with excitement, "and you smoked me! First in the arcade, and now here! I can't believe that I actually met a girl like you!"

"Getting a little crazed, aren't we?" said Gary.

James started to speak faster. "I mean, you can't find too many chicks who play video games and are actually good at them! This is some kinda breakthrough! I bet that if she continues to do this, then—"

"Okay!" said Gary loudly. "I think we get the picture."

After that, James kept going on and on about how I'll be the world's best female gamer, and he didn't stop until I left to go back home later that afternoon.

CHAPTER THREE

"Hey, check this out!" James was reading the newspaper when I was with him and Gary in the Shady Palm Café the next day for lunch. "It says that there were more weird sightings around that secret military base in the desert yesterday."

"You and your sci-fi stories," said Gary, dipping his fry in ketchup.

"Three people saw this one," James continued. "They said it was black and looked like it had wings or something. How do you explain that one?"

"Simple," said Gary as he took a sip of his drink, "three people out in the desert were smoking a little grass and started seeing things."

I giggled a little bit, and James got irritated.

"Ha ha, very funny," James replied indignantly. "Then how do you explain that three people saw the same hallucination?"

"I don't know," said Gary, sounding a little amused. "Maybe they all smoked from the same plant."

"Well, I think it wasn't a hallucination," said James, folding up the paper. "These kinds of things could happen. So, okay, here's my theory."

"Here we go," Gary muttered.

"I say that this recent sighting has some kind of connection to the destruction of the secret Military Base 15," James began.

"Man, I don't think so," said Gary. "Base 15 was destroyed a few years ago. That's old news."

"Would you just listen to me?" James snapped.

"Fine, fine," said Gary, "go on."

"Anyway, this sighting might have something to do with that," James repeated.

There was a short pause with the exchanging of looks.

"Is that it?" Gary asked.

"That's it!" said James, looking satisfied. "What do you think of my theory?"

"You didn't even back up your theory with any evidence," said Gary, trying hard to keep a straight face.

"Ah, you just wait," James told him with a confident smile. "You just wait."

Gary couldn't help himself from laughing.

"Listen to yourself," he said. "You sound like one of those crazy people who air their own radio shows from a van and talk about aliens and government conspiracies!"

"Man, come on!" said James. "Why don't you ever take me seriously?"

"Because I'd rather keep my sanity, that's why," Gary replied curtly.

James raised one eyebrow at Gary, then muttered something under his breath. He picked up his hamburger and took a big bite out of it and gazed out the window.

Something deep inside me began to stir. The mentioning of Base 15 bubbled up some weird feelings in my stomach.

"What happened to Base 15?" I asked Gary and James. "I know it was destroyed, but that's it."

"Well," said Gary, "that's about all everyone else knows, too. They didn't even give an explanation about it."

"Yeah," said James. "Normally those government guys come up with something to try and cover up the truth, but they didn't say anything about this one."

"Kinda makes you wonder if anyone really knows what happened," said Gary. "They didn't find any survivors."

We continued to sit and eat for a little longer. James went back to his newspaper as he clutched his food in his other hand. He looked strangely professional as he read. I slowly ate my food, thinking more about Base 15.

"It sure did get dark really fast," said James through a mouthful of his hamburger. "It's not even three o'clock."

He was right. I looked up at the sky through the window, and ominous clouds seemed to have come out of nowhere. There wasn't a single cloud in the sky as we walked through town earlier. Thunder rumbled in the distance.

"I think we should hurry up," said Gary. "We might get caught in a storm on the way back."

"Too late," said James.

Rain had already started coming down heavily. Everyone in the restaurant groaned. By this time, it was so dark outside that I could hardly see across the street.

As I was about to finish my fourth cheeseburger, there was a bright flash of lightning and a loud clap of thunder just as the front doors burst open. Everyone in the café stopped what they were doing to see a man with scraggly black hair slowly walk inside. His eyes were hidden, so I really couldn't see his expression too well. He was wearing a worn out black trench coat that was dripping water.

"What's with that guy?" James whispered.

"Shh!" Gary hissed.

His thick shoes clopped as he ever so slowly worked his way to the counter. I saw that Bernie was giving him a curious face. Something about the man didn't feel right. There was an uneasy feeling that lingered in the air as the man made his way through the restaurant. All eyes were on him.

When the man reached the counter, it was obvious that everybody was holding their breath to hear what he was going to order.

"Give me a hamburger." His voice was deep and demanding. Something about his voice made the hair on the back of my neck stand on end.

"Will that be all, sir?" Bernie asked casually.

"Did I ask for anything else?" the man asked darkly. Without taking his eyes off the stranger, Bernie rang up the price. Everyone watched as the man thrust his hand into his pocket.

"He's got a gun," James whispered frantically. "He's gonna shoot Bernie!"

"Shut up," Gary muttered nervously.

It turned out the man didn't have a gun. He pulled the money out of his pocket with a tight fist, then dropped it on the counter. The clinging of the coins was as loud as firecrackers in the dead quiet restaurant. More thunder broke the silence as Bernie gave the order to the kitchen. All of the employees in the back were watching the man very carefully through the window.

While the stranger waited for his order, he just stood over the counter and supported his weight on his arms. He didn't budge a single inch. I felt very uncomfortable about the situation. I looked over at James, and he seemed scared. Too scared to say anything. Gary just watched the man very closely as if studying his every move.

The rain was coming down heavier than before. Thunder rolled over the town like a giant bowling ball. Lightning split the sky like a hatchet striking dried wood. The man had to have been very tired to have walked through such weather just to arrive at a small restaurant like this one. What was he doing out in the rain anyway?

Without warning, those annoying visions returned to my head. They were flashing frantically this time. I had a feeling that they were trying to tell me something about the man that was giving everyone the creeps. I wanted to know what they were trying to tell me, but I couldn't make them out at all. There were too many of them and they were appearing too fast. I could tell Gary and James were both witnessing the same thing as they grabbed their heads.

They stopped. I looked to see what Gary and James were thinking. Why did they see visions at the same time as me? Even if they were a part of puberty it would seem highly coincidental for us to have them simultaneously.

Nobody seemed to want to move from their spot as the man received his food tray. Everyone seemed too afraid he'd shoot someone if anyone moved wrong. Instead, we all watched as he examined his hamburger. First he held it up to nose and sniffed deeply. Then he grasped the bun firmly and removed it, revealing a blob of spit that stretched between the top bun and the meat. The tension in the restaurant grew as he let out a rattled breath, then slammed the bun back onto the hamburger, making everyone jump.

The stranger slowly walked up to Bernie with the hamburger in hand. Then he thrust the burger into his face.

"What is this?" he demanded threateningly, slamming the food onto the floor. When Bernie didn't answer, the man reached across the counter and lifted him off the ground by his collar. "Well?"

"Leave him alone!" Every soul in the café turned their attention to Gary as he stood up. A flash of lightning followed by a shout of thunder made the lights flicker. "Put him down now!"

"What are you doing?" James choked.

The man released Bernie, then turned to face Gary. With the different angle of light, I saw his eyes were stern and frightening. For some reason, I didn't seem very scared, but I was still very uncomfortable.

The man walked up to Gary and stopped right in front of him. Gary was significantly shorter than the man. I could see his face up close, and it was strong and had a solid look. More thunder shook the restaurant.

"If you were smart," he said as he stood over Gary, "then you wouldn't mess with me."

"If *you* were smart," Gary shot back, "then you wouldn't

have come here in the first place. You had no right to—"

The stranger thrust out his hand with his palm facing Gary. As soon as he did, the lights flickered and Gary was sent flying backward through the air. The floor beneath the man imploded like a trampoline with a huge weight in the middle. James and I were knocked to the floor by a burst of energy that felt like a hot gust of air.

"Gary!" James shouted, jumping up.

Before I could get back up, I felt a brief, but very strong rush of pure hatred. My head throbbed once and there was a sharp pain in my chest. In an instant, it vanished. I clutched my chest wondering what that feeling was.

Everyone started to panic as Gary hit the window, causing it to crack. I saw the man flee out the door as James and a few others tried to help Gary up. Bernie ran after the man, bursting out through the doors into the rain as lightning lit the sky. He walked back in, looking as if he had come out of a swimming pool.

"Damn, he's gone," he said, shrugging his shoulders.

One of the employees had called the police, and they arrived on the scene shortly after. Everyone who was in the restaurant at the time was being interviewed by different officers.

"So, what you're saying is you were standing here," the officer said to Gary, pointing to the spot next to the table we were sitting at, "and he punched you across the room and into that window way over there?"

"For the last time," said Gary, "it wasn't a punch. He didn't physically touch me. I didn't feel any actual contact. It felt more like a super powerful gust of wind."

The cop scratched his chin, then said, "Well, I think this is going to need a lot more investigation." He turned to Bernie. "Until then, we'll just have to close the restaurant."

"Do whatever it takes," said Bernie. "Just find that creep."

"Alright kids," the cop told us, "let's wrap it up for tonight. We have to get back to the station soon before this rain floods the streets too badly. I'll give you three a ride home."

The three of us got into the police car just as the other officers started to close off the Shady Palm Café. When we arrived at Gary's house, the rain hadn't lightened up at all. Gary's dad opened the door for us.

"What happened?" he asked. The cop told Gary's parents about everything that happened. Before dropping James off at his house the cop told James he would call later that night to talk to his parents. When I was taken back home I was told the same thing.

"Okay," I said.

"I want you kids to look after yourselves," the cop told me. "We'll catch this guy."

"Okay," I said again.

Once back to my room I sat on my bed to think about what had just happened. To relieve the stress I turned on my stereo and played some metal music. The heaviest music always calmed me down, although Jack and Laura weren't too fond of it.

Leaning back onto my bed, I spent the rest of my day wondering about Gary. He took that hit really hard and I was worried if he was badly hurt. He didn't seem like it, but I was still concerned. Just what kind of attack did that man use? I had heard of chi waves in martial arts, but I didn't know much about them.

I sat down at my desk and took out my sketchbook. Drawing was my favorite hobby and I hadn't drawn at all since I moved to the new house. My pencil always seemed to move across the page by itself. I was told by my parents that my family had good artistic abilities. My real parents, that is.

Later that night Laura came up into my room. I turned down my stereo to hear what she had to say.

"Hey," she said quietly, "we heard a message on the answering machine from the police." She came over and rubbed my face with her hand. "We called them back and they told us the story. Are you alright?"

"Yeah," I said.

"It's kind of unfortunate for something like this to happen just after we moved here," said Jack as he walked into my room.

"We're here if you need anything," said Laura.

"I'm okay," I said, smiling weakly.

"That's good," said Laura, kissing me on the cheek. "Dinner will be done in an hour."

"Okay," I said.

When Jack and Laura went back downstairs I turned my music back up and continued drawing. The empty shells were concerned for me…

After the incident at the Shady Palm Café, things got extremely weird. I kept my thoughts from Jack and Laura, knowing that they would probably overreact and take me to a hospital to have all kinds of tests done on me. Either that, or they'd tell me that my imagination was getting to me.

It was a couple days later when I was walking with Gary and James around our neighborhood, trying to find something to do. It was a dreary day, with dark clouds hinting at rain. We eventually walked past Stephanie's house, who happened to be on her way out the door.

"Hey, Stephanie!" Gary called. She walked up to the sidewalk to meet us.

"Hi there!" she answered. "I have to pick up some ricotta cheese for my mom. She's making lasagna later tonight."

"But the market's all the way across town." said Gary. "Why can't your parents drive there instead?"

"My mom's car is at the shop," she said. "It stalled on her the other day, so my uncle came and towed it for her."

"What about your dad's car?" James asked.

Stephanie lowered her head a little, then replied quietly, "My dad was killed in a car accident almost a year ago."

"Bummer," said James. "I'm sorry, dude."

"Oh, I'm really sorry," said Gary sympathetically. "I didn't know about that."

"Yeah, oh well," Stephanie sighed. "I guess I'd better get going if I want to beat the rain."

"Mind if we come with you?" Gary asked. James looked at him and raised his one eyebrow. Gary tried to ignore him.

"Sure," she said with a smile.

As we walked into town, the wind started to pick up and the temperature dropped. I shivered as Stephanie got closer to Gary.

"I wonder how Bernie's doing?" Gary asked as we walked by the Shady Palm Café. It still had the yellow DO NOT CROSS strips around it.

"I don't know," said Stephanie. "I hope he's okay." She pressed herself against Gary as a gust of wind blew past us.

"Man, it's getting cold," said James, rubbing his arms. "It feels like winter."

"I don't think it's that cold," I said.

"That's because you're from Michigan," said James. "I'm not, so I think it's cold!"

"It's just really windy," said Gary, pressing on. "If it wasn't for the wind, it wouldn't be so bad."

After a long walk through the wind, we finally made it to the supermarket. Once inside, it was warm and cozy. We walked to the dairy section and found some ricotta cheese for Stephanie. As Stephanie was paying for it at the checkout, a voice sounded over the loudspeaker.

"Ladies and gentlemen, it has come to our attention that a powerful tropical storm has hit. We recommend that everyone stay inside until further notice. Thank you."

"What?" Gary groaned. "No way. What's with this weather?"

"Well," James huffed, thrusting his hands angrily into his pockets. "This really sucks. How are we supposed to get home?"

We walked up to the front of the supermarket, and looked outside the windows. Rain was coming down heavily as the wind blew it across the roads.

"Why do we always get stuck in these storms when we leave the house?" James asked irritably. "I wonder if some weirdo's going to walk in right now and threaten the employees."

"Man, it's really blowing out there," said Gary. "This is just as bad that other night."

"I should call my mom," said Stephanie, getting out her cell phone. "I'll tell her we won't be back for awhile."

"Ugh," James moaned. "I'm gonna get wet again. This sucks."

"A shower would do you some good every now and then," Gary chortled.

"Gah, I don't have any service," said Stephanie as she held up her phone looking for a signal. "It must be this storm. I'll just use the payphone."

Gary dug in his pockets and took out some change, giving it to Stephanie. She smiled and walked over to the payphones.

"Hey, Gary," said James. When Gary looked at him, James did his little dance move again.

"Come on!" said Gary, glancing at Stephanie. Her back was turned so she couldn't see what was going on. "You can't be serious."

James chuckled right as Stephanie moaned.

"The phones just died," she muttered.

"Don't worry about it," said Gary. "I'm sure that every-thing's going to be all—"

A huge flash of lightning and roar of thunder drowned his words. The glass windows at the front of the store shattered and blew in. Rain gushed inside the store, and the wind pushed the four of us on to the ground. I shielded my eyes from the glass as it blew over us. When we got to our feet, we scrambled with all of the other customers to the back of the store. The whole time, visions flashed in front of me. Then the lights flickered, going out along with the visions. What was going on?

When the generator kicked in, the storm had calmed down a lot. Slowly, the crowd in the back of the store moved to the front, then we all made our way out into the parking lot. The rain had become a light drizzle and the wind had died down almost completely.

"That was a crazy tropical storm," said James.

"Yeah," said Gary, "it was more like a brief hurricane. But I've never heard of a hurricane that comes and goes that fast."

"I think we should go back now," Stephanie breathed. "It looks like it's over."

We all took off at a brisk pace back into the suburbs. Gary's house was the first on the way, so we stopped there. Gary was about to say good-bye when he noticed the living room light wasn't on.

"What does it matter?" James asked. "It's only a light."

"The only time we turn it off is when we leave the house," said Gary. "Wait here."

I waited on the sidewalk with James and Stephanie as Gary ran up to the front door. When he found it locked he tried knocking. No answer. He peered into the window, but saw absolutely no movement. The rain started to come down harder again.

"I'm going to check the garage real quick," he said. A few moments later he returned. "The sedan is gone, so nobody's home. They must have gotten worried and went out to look for me. Why didn't I put the key back under the mat from the other day?"

"You can't get in?" James asked.

"Nope. That key was the only one I had. I really should carry it with me from now on."

"You could come to my house," Stephanie offered. "You all could, since your houses are too far to walk in the rain. I could have my mom drive you home when my uncle brings the car back tomorrow morning if the weather doesn't get better."

We took off at practically a run to Stephanie's. Thunder rumbled far off in the distance as we turned onto her street. Puddles splashed underneath us as the rain continued to come down heavier than before.

Stephanie opened the door, and we made our way into the

dry, warm house. Her house was very nice and clean.

"Stay here, and I'll get you some towels," Stephanie told us. "I'll tell Mom that you're here." She hurried off, leaving James, Gary, and I dripping on the floor mat.

"This is a nice place," said James, looking around. He flipped his hair out of his face, splattering Gary with water. "I wonder where her mom works."

"I don't know," I said. A loud roar of thunder made us jump. "Isn't it weird how fast that storm came and went?"

"I'll say," James responded. "It sounds like it's coming back, too." He reached into his pocket and pulled out a dollar bill, then wrung it out. "Dude, I'm soaked. It was like I got attacked by Poseidon or something."

Stephanie came back and handed us each a towel.

"Mom says you can stay for dinner if you want," she told us as we dried off.

"Cool!" said Gary, trying to soak up as much of the water out of his clothes as possible.

We followed Stephanie into the living room. It was huge and filled with expensive-looking furniture.

"Can I use your phone?" Gary asked Stephanie. "I need to call my house to see if anyone's there."

"Sure, use my cell. I'll be in the kitchen, guys. Make yourselves at home."

She walked off into the kitchen as Gary dialed his phone number. After it rang a few times, the answering machine kicked in.

"Yeah, it's me, Gary," he said into the recorder. "I'm over at a friend's house to stay out of the storm. I tried going home already, but no one was there and I was locked out. I'll be staying for dinner, too, and I have a ride back in the morning. Okay, bye."

"You didn't leave her phone number?" James asked, lounging back in a big recliner. "What if they want to call you back?"

"Oh, I guess I forgot." He looked at the phone, deciding if he should call back. "I don't think they'll need to."

We all took a seat. Gary sat there, looking around, then noticed James looking at him.

"How does it feel?" James asked with a grin.

"What?" Gary asked. "Being in her house?"

James nodded.

"Uh, I'm gonna see if they need my help in the kitchen."

Gary stood up and walked off, leaving me with James in the living room.

"Heh," James chuckled, "I bet he didn't leave her number so he'd have an excuse to stay longer." I didn't know if James was right, but it was obvious Gary really liked being in Stephanie's house.

James and I went into the kitchen. Stephanie was helping her mom make the lasagna as Gary was talking to them.

"Hello," Stephanie's mom greeted. "You three look terrible. Why don't you help yourself to a drink or something? I still have to bake this, so it'll be a while."

James immediately started rummaging through the refrigerator. I got myself a glass and filled it up with water.

"If you wanted water, you should've just gone outside," Stephanie told me with a giggle. I heard the sound of a soda can opening, and looked over in time to see James chugging down an entire can of cola. That's just what he needed. More sugar. He let out a stifled burp, then blinked some tears out his eyes. Then he looked up with an amused face.

"Well, since you're all here," Stephanie told us, "I guess I should show you around the house."

We followed her out of the kitchen, and she showed us around the house, ending up in her room. It was well kept, which wasn't too surprising. She seemed like the organized type, completely the opposite of me. The only reason why my room was clean at the time was because I hadn't been there long enough to wreck it.

"It's really raining out there now," said Gary, looking out her window. Rain pounded against the glass. "I don't think it's going to let up soon."

"Speaking of rain," James announced, "I have to go to the bathroom. I'll be right back. Come on, Krystal."

I followed James out of Stephanie's room and down the hall.

"Why'd you want me?" I asked, wondering what on Earth James would need me for if he was going to the bathroom.

"To leave them alone," James replied with a smile. "Let's go back down to the living room."

We went down the stairs and sat on a big couch, which I sank down into. It was very comfortable. I could smell the lasagna baking, and my mouth started to water. I love Italian food.

41

"Haven't things been getting eerie around here?" James asked. "Ever since that day at the restaurant, this neighborhood lost some of its feeling of security."

"Yeah," I said. At least I knew it wasn't my imagination.

"I mean, just think about it," he said. "That cheery atmosphere around this time of year is…gone. Now that I think about it, I haven't heard a single bird since that incident. The sun hasn't been shining as much. Nothing's the way it used to be." He ran his hands through his hair and sighed. "This place was perfect, man. What's happening to our perfect world?"

He had called our town a 'perfect world'. That's exactly what I called it, but I never told anyone.

"I don't know," I said quietly, looking away. At that time, Gary and Stephanie came downstairs.

"Oh yeah!" James blurted. "I gotta go to the bathroom really bad! Then I'll come back and check what's on TV." He took off out of the room, immediately returning. "Which way's the bathroom, Stef?"

"That way," said Stephanie, pointing the way.

"A lot of things have gotten weird around here," said Gary, "but at least James is still the same."

We watched some TV until the lasagna was done. During dinner, I couldn't help thinking that Stephanie purposely sat next to Gary. James sat across from them and kept looking at them. However, I wasn't sure if he sat next to me to silently harass Gary or if he only wanted to be by me.

"This is really good," Gary told Stephanie's mom. "I haven't had lasagna in a long time, and when I do, it's not very good."

"Well, thank you," she responded. "It's an old family recipe that my mom taught me. I'm glad you like it. More breadsticks anyone?"

"I'll take some," said James, taking the plate from Stephanie's mom. As James ate his sixth breadstick, I wondered where he put it all. He was always an eater, but didn't have hardly any body fat on him. Just like me.

After we were done, Gary called home again, but no one answered the phone. He left another message with Stephanie's phone number. I could see he was getting worried. He must have began to think that something bad might have happened to them.

"I'm sure they're all right," said Stephanie. "They must still be out looking for you, or out to dinner."

"I hope you're right," said Gary.

Thunder continued to shake the house. Rain pummeled the roof, and the wind was howling again.

"Well," said Stephanie, looking out the window, "it looks like you all might be spending the night here. I should see if there are any extra pillows and blankets you could use. Wait in the living room."

I stretched out on one of the couches, which was a lot more comfortable than the one at my house.

"You know," said Gary quietly, "it would have been wonderful to spend the night with Stephanie, but I'm only doing it because I don't know where my family is."

"Don't worry, bro," said James. "They're fine. I'm sure of it."

As I was lying on the couch, Stephanie came back carrying a mound of blankets.

"It's kind of early to go to bed now, isn't it?" she asked me as I was stretched out on the couch.

"I've had a long day," I told her. "I'm feeling kind of tired."

"Yeah, I know." She sat down on the floor next to me. "Let's just try and get some sleep."

I took a blanket and made myself comfortable on the couch. Gary made a little bed on the floor and James leaned back in a recliner.

"James," said Stephanie, "shouldn't you call your parents, too?"

"Huh? Nah," he said. "They'll just think I'm at Gary's. Technically, that's not entirely incorrect."

"I guess I should call my house," I said. Stephanie handed me the phone and I called Laura's cell. I told her I was staying at a friend's house, and although she sounded hesitant, she said I could.

"Well?" James asked after I handed the phone back to Stephanie.

"It's okay," I said.

"Goodnight," said Stephanie, going back upstairs. "Goodnight, Gary."

"Uh, goodnight." I could see Gary blush just before James reached over and turned off the lamp on the table next to him.

After the others had fallen asleep, I continued to lie awake. Surprisingly, James was a very quiet sleeper. For someone as loud as him I figured he would wake the neighbors with his snoring. My mind wondered around a bit, thinking about the past few days. That deep feeling of hatred I felt when the man attacked Gary at the restaurant…what was that? I never felt that way in my entire life.

Then I remembered my medication. I needed to take it in the morning. I thought about going out and facing the storm to get my pills, but Stephanie said her mom would get the car back in the morning. Deciding I would be fine if I got my medication in the morning, I rolled over on the couch and fell asleep.

I woke up to the sound of Stephanie's mom. She told us that Stephanie's uncle had just brought the car back.

"I can take you all back home before I go to work," she said.

Looking at the clock, I saw that I only got three hours of sleep; more than I've had in a long time. James stretched and yawned, stumbling when he stood up from the chair he was sleeping in. I smiled, thinking he looked funny.

Stephanie told us good-bye as I got into her mom's car with Gary and James. When I got dropped off at my house I immediately went straight to the bathroom for my medication. Jack and Laura had already left so it was very quiet. Maybe too quiet. With nothing else to do for the time being I went back to my room and continued drawing in my sketchbook. I finished a lot of pictures that day.

CHAPTER FOUR

Two weeks after the incident at the Shady Palm Café I was walking around town with Gary and James again. We were checking out all the small stores they didn't go to very often, including a candy store located near the beach.

"I haven't had those in years," said James, pointing at some chocolates. "Oh, those are heavenly." He looked up at me with his childishly excited expression. "They have this weird, soft, gushy thing in the middle that explodes with the titanic love of a million symphonies of flavor in your mouth when you eat them."

"I have no idea what you just said," said Gary from behind, "but I like those things too."

James hurried over to the jelly beans and gazed up at the wall filled with assorted colors and flavors. I stood next to him and looked at all the different jelly beans.

"Isn't it beautiful?" James asked dreamily. "A wall of food. I'm sure you'd understand how I feel, Krystal, not like Gary."

"I'm not sure if I wanna feel anything you do," Gary replied.

"You don't have an appreciation for food, my good friend," James told him. "You're one of those people who only see food as a necessity."

"What do you mean?" Gary asked. "It *is* a necessity."

"But you have to see it from another angle," James explained. He was getting very deep into his words. "Food can also be enjoyed as an art! You have to take time to enjoy the, uh, *sophistication* behind it. There are culinary masters out there who turn food into works of art, and I'm one of the people who appreciate the artistic value of it."

Gary gave James a quizzical look. "Since when were you artistic?"

"I'm not the artist," said James, "I'm the one who appreciates."

"How can you appreciate anything you eat when it doesn't stay in your mouth for more than one second?" Gary asked bluntly.

James looked as if his speech had run into a brick wall.

"Well, um." He struggled to think of something to say. "Hey, Krystal, help me out here!"

"This place is making me hungry," I said.

"Whole lot of help you are," James muttered.

"Well, why don't you buy something?" Gary asked me. "They have all kinds of stuff here you'd probably like."

"I don't know," I said. "I'm not in the mood for candy."

"Ah, I know what she wants," said James, putting his hand on my shoulder. "And it's the same thing we always want."

"But the Shady Palm's on the other side of town," said Gary. "Are you sure you won't starve to death by the time we get there, James?"

"The smell of candy temporarily fueled me," said James. "I'll make it."

"Okay, we can go," said Gary. "We can check to see what Bernie's been up to."

The walk to the restaurant was a somewhat dreary one. The weather had been cold, cloudy, and rainy. Once inside, we noticed that they had fixed the window, but the one thing that stood out the most was that we were the only three customers in there.

"Hello kids," said Bernie. He didn't seem quite as cheerful as he usually did. "How are you? Can I get you anything?"

We placed our orders, then continued talking with Bernie as we waited.

"How's business going?" Gary asked.

"Slower than usual," he replied. "I think this is the first day I've seen without a single customer in here."

"Things have been kinda screwed up lately," James told him. "This whole town is making me depressed."

"You know," said Bernie quietly, leaning over the counter, "things just haven't been the same around here since that stranger blew into town. It was like he brought a little rain cloud over this place."

"More like an entire army of little rain clouds," James added.

Our food came up, which we ate in almost complete silence. No matter what I did, it was hard for me to shake the uneasy feeling that followed me everywhere. While we were in the restaurant, not a single other customer came in. Except for us, the restaurant was completely dead.

"Well, we'd better get going," said Gary. "We'll see ya later, Bernie."

"Watch out for yourselves now," he called to us as we

walked out the door. There weren't as many cars or pedestrians as usual. The entire town was slower than it was when I had first moved here. Not to mention it was in the middle of summer. A Florida town like that should have been bustling like mad. I walked quietly with Gary and James until we saw someone wearing a black trench coat go into an alley just up ahead. When we passed by, it happened to be the same man that was in the restaurant that stormy night.

"What are you looking at?" he asked as we walked by. James tried to keep Gary from stopping, but failed.

"I'm looking at whatever I want," said Gary. The stranger let out a deep chuckle.

"You're a tough little runt," he muttered. "You'd better watch yourself, or you might end up in big trouble."

None of us spoke for a few seconds. James fidgeted as his eyes darted back and forth between the stranger and Gary.

"Who are you?" I asked.

The stranger stuffed his hands into his pockets and leaned up against the building. For a while, he didn't speak. Thunder rumbled, then it started to drizzle.

"I'm someone who discovered my secret," he told me. "There's a handful of people out there who have done the same thing. I want to find them. You shouldn't worry about me. Just stay out of my business, or die."

James grabbed Gary's shirtsleeve and tugged. I followed them away from the alley, glancing back at the man.

"Isn't it obvious, Gary?" James whispered. "He's a psycho, man. Cuckoo in the head. I suggest you stop trying to act like Mr. Brave and stay away from him! He said he'd kill you if you don't, so take my advice!"

"Wait," said Gary, grabbing James by the arm. "I want to ask him some more questions. He could have the answers to the visions we've been seeing!"

"What do you mean?" James asked irritably.

"He said something about finding out his secret," said Gary. "I want to know what he meant!"

"Are you insane?" said James, trying to restrain him. "We both see those stupid visions! Krystal, too! If we need help with hallucinations we can see a certified psychiatrist, not some mental killer! Hey, what the…oh no…"

"What is it?" Gary asked.

"It's Brandon," James squeaked. "Stephanie's old boy-friend."

"Huh?"

We looked across the street to see the very large and muscular Brandon come stomping towards us. He was rolling up his sleeves and squeezing his fist. Then he walked right up to Gary and got directly in his face.

"Look who it is," he said, grabbing Gary's collar and picking him up a foot in the air to become eye-level with him. "Who do you think you are, stealing my girl?"

"It's not his fault!" James shouted. "She asked him!"

"I don't know why she'd want to be your girlfriend," said Gary angrily. "You're a brainless idiot!"

Brandon's face turned red with rage. He punched Gary square in the stomach, then tossed him to the ground. He was about to stomp on his face with his foot when Stephanie practically came out of nowhere.

"Stop it right now!" she ordered.

"I'm saving you from the loser," Brandon told her. "Isn't that what you want?"

"You're the loser!" Stephanie yelled. Several people who were walking by stopped to watch. "He didn't do anything to you!"

"How dare you talk to me like that!" Brandon pushed Stephanie forcefully back, almost making her fall to the ground. Gary sprung to his feet and grabbed Brandon around the waist and tackled him. Brandon, who was much stronger and bigger, flung Gary off of him.

"Is that all you've got?" he growled.

James ran up and punched him directly in the face. Un-fazed, Brandon returned the attack, hitting James in the mouth. He fell to his hands and knees, then spit out a mouthful of blood. All the while Stephanie was yelling at Brandon, and I just watched helplessly.

Then it happened again. That quick surge of absolute rage pulsed through my body. My head throbbed, my chest hurt...then it disappeared. I stepped back, holding my chest. What was going on?

Brandon scrambled to grab Gary, then shoved him into the middle of the road. Gary was about to get a shoe to his head when he grabbed Brandon's leg and tripped him. He landed facedown on the road. When Brandon tried to get back up, a car hydroplaned on the wet road, then slid directly into Brandon's head. When the driver stopped his car he immediately got out and raced over to Brandon. To my surprise, it was Tyler, the old man who was the owner of the antique store.

"Oh my!" he cried, supporting Brandon's bleeding head in his arm. "He's unconscious. Someone, call the ambulance!" One of the pedestrians who witnessed the accident pulled out his cell phone and called 911. All I could do was stand on the side of the road with Gary, James, and Stephanie and watch.

The ambulance arrived shortly after. The paramedics put Brandon on a stretcher and placed him in the back of the ambulance. Then they hurried off to the hospital. I felt really bad, but it wasn't my fault.

"I can't believe I would hit my dear Brandon," Tyler moaned. "Of all people, it had to be Brandon."

"You knew him?" James asked, wiping his mouth and smearing blood across his face.

"He's my grandson," Tyler told him grimly.

"Oh, that's right," said Stephanie. "You must be his grandpa who owns that antique store he's always talking about."

"That's me." Tyler looked at me, Gary, and James. "What were you three doing here?"

"He tried to kill me," said Gary. Blood trickled down his forehead. He tried to rub it off. "We were just defending ourselves."

"Why would he do that?" Tyler asked, sounding astounded.

"He was jealous," said Stephanie huffily. "He found out that I was hanging out with Gary and his friends."

"That's strange," said Tyler. "Brandon never struck me as the jealous type."

"He's an idiot," James added. "No offense, Mr. Tyler sir. It's just that he had no right to attack us."

"Well, I guess I'd better get home and call my son about this," said Tyler, sighing loudly. "He would probably like to know that I ran his kid over."

When the police came we told them the story. They asked if we'd like a ride back, but Gary decided that walking would help us cool off.

"This isn't cool," James whined as the three of us headed back into the suburbs. "I'm all beat up. My mom's going to have a fit when I get home."

"I'm not exactly in the best shape of my life either," Gary muttered.

"Gary," said Stephanie, "I'm sorry about what had happened."

"It's not your fault," said Gary. "There wasn't anything you could do about it."

"I guess you're right," Stephanie replied. "I'm just a little upset."

"I can't believe you actually were his girlfriend," said James. "What did you possibly see in him?"

"He didn't seem so bad at first," said Stephanie. "Then, after a while, he seemed to get more and more protective of me. Before long, he was so protective that he would beat anyone up who decided to get anywhere near me."

"We can see that," said James, rubbing his face. "He could pack a wallop."

"So he was trying to protect you?" I asked. "That would mean that he wasn't jealous, but concerned for your safety."

"That's right, I guess," said Stephanie. "He's really not a bad person."

"But why would he get all crazy like that?" James asked. "Why is he so protective?"

"I don't know," Stephanie replied thoughtfully. "Hey, who's that?"

We immediately stopped in our tracks. In front of us was the guy from the café walking across the street. My heart began to beat a little faster when I noticed he was wielding a sword. I wondered what it was for.

"What do you want?" James demanded. "Why are you here? What's that you've got in your hand?"

"There's something about this little town," the man said, slowly advancing towards us. "Something is here for me, but I'm not sure what it is. That is why I am here. I want to find it."

"Look here," said Gary, "I'm sure that you're looking for something, but what was the point of what you did at the restaurant?"

"Point?" The man smiled a sinisterly. "Does everything have to have a reason?"

"Well, yeah," said James. "You nearly knocked the crap out of my friend!"

"You mean…" Stephanie looked confused.

"This is the guy," Gary told her. "You saw the news. That's him."

"I felt like it," the man said. "That was the reason."

"It wasn't a very good one!" Stephanie yelled. "You could have seriously hurt someone back there!"

"Oh, too bad." The man ran his finger along his sword.

"What's that sword for?" James asked. "If you're going to be a murderous lunatic then get a gun. Go to school much?"

"James!" Gary hissed. "Don't give him advice, even if it's obvious!"

"Guns?" the man croaked. "You really don't know anything, do you?"

"Why don't you just tell us who you are?" Gary asked angrily. "What's your name?"

"My name's not important," the man responded. "What I do is none of your business."

"Then I'll make it my business," said Gary.

"And I'm sure the police would like to make it their business as well," Stephanie added.

"That goes double for me," James mumbled. The man cackled a high pitched laugh. It was a very disturbing laugh.

"What are the police going to do?" the stranger laughed. "Try and shoot me? Let them try, but it won't do them any good."

"I'm tired of your rambling!" James shouted, rolling up his sleeves. "Let me give you a piece of my mind. I've already been in one brawl today and I'm pumped to rumble with your ass any day!"

"Stop." I stood in front of James to stop him. "He'll destroy you."

"What?" James asked. I didn't really know how to explain it, but I gave James a hopeful look. He retreated, and the man laughed again.

"What's the matter?" he teased. "Too scared to fight? Is the little baby afraid of the big bad man?"

"Just leave us alone," said Gary hotly. "We weren't doing anything to you."

"Fine then." The man stepped off the road and onto the sidewalk. "I will see you around, maybe." He held up his hand, and a pure black, very futuristic-looking sports car came zooming pass us from behind, scaring us all half to death. It stopped next to the man and opened its door, taking off as soon as he got inside. Oddly enough, I really liked the car. It was my favorite car when I was younger.

Or did I ever see that car before? I had no idea what kind it was.

"Whoa!" James exclaimed. "What was that?"

"I don't know," said Gary quietly. He paused for a little. "Let's get out of here."

"Man, I hate that guy!" James growled angrily. "Just who does he think he is?"

"Who cares?" said Stephanie. "Whoever he is, he just needs to die."

Shortly before reaching Gary's house, a car coming from the other direction stopped next to us. It looked very familiar, then I saw it was Tyler.

"Hey, Tyler," Gary greeted. "What's up?"

"Get in," he said sternly. "I have to tell you all something."

"What is it?" Stephanie asked. "Is it something we did?"

"No, no. It's nothing like that." Tyler looked up and down the street. "Quickly now, before we get caught."

Curious to see what was going to happen, we all got into Tyler's car. He drove us into town to his antique store. When we got there, he took us into the backroom and locked the door.

"Sit down, everyone," he said. We all took a seat around an old table. "I have to tell you all something," he said, "and you all have to swear not to tell a single person outside this room about it."

CHAPTER FIVE

"What is it?" James asked eagerly.

"Don't get all excited about it," Tyler told him. "It's not good."

"What's wrong?" Stephanie asked. "Is it about us?"

"Not you," he told Stephanie, "but them." He nodded towards Gary and James.

"Us?" Gary asked. "It's about us?"

"That's right." Tyler looked nervous. His hands were shaking. "I never thought I'd have to tell anyone this."

"Well, spill the beans!" said James. "What's up?"

"I was sensing something between you two boys," Tyler began. "Ever since you walked into this store a few weeks ago I sensed something about you."

"Yeah," said James, "we're best friends."

"Please," said Tyler, holding up his hand, "let me finish. I was given a gift to be able to sense this kind of thing."

"What's that supposed to mean?" James blurted out.

"James!" said Gary angrily. "Just listen."

"It means that you two were given a gift," said Tyler. He paused for a moment, and there was a complete silence. "Everything that I say from this point on will seem completely and utterly preposterous. All I ask is to follow along with me and save all questions until I'm finished."

"Okay," Gary added quickly before James could open his mouth.

"There is a type of energy that exists in this world. Everyone has it, but only a small percent of people can use it, and an even smaller percent actually learn how to control it. This energy is called Soulpower, and gives anyone who uses it special abilities. Is everyone with me?"

We all nodded.

"Since someone's Soulpower has nothing to do with their physical body," Tyler continued, "they're able to do things that would normally rip their body to shreds. A ninety year-old could lift a city bus without breaking a sweat. Someone with asthma could run for miles without getting short-winded." He stopped talking for a little bit.

"What's this got to do with us?" Gary asked.

"I'm getting to that. Anyway, recently I began to sense Soulpower nearby, but I couldn't figure out who it was coming from. Apparently, it's coming from you boys."

"So does that mean we have superpowers?" James asked, his eyes bugging out. "Wait, you're full of it! I don't believe this."

"Shut up!" Gary barked. "Let's just hear everything he has to say."

"Well," said Tyler, "there's someone else in this town who has it besides you two. I never would have told you boys about your Soulpower if it wasn't for this third person."

"You don't mean…" Gary looked very disturbed. "Not that guy we just saw."

"Don't tell me you believe this," James groaned. "How do we know this old guy isn't senile?"

"How do you explain your visions?" said Tyler.

James looked like he was about to say something, but stopped.

"Those with special souls are given special abilities to foresee danger," said Tyler quietly. "These visions are a result of your Soulpower wanting to take form."

I sat in my seat, not saying a single word. If I saw visions, wouldn't that mean I have Soulpower too? Couldn't Tyler sense it in me as well?

"Hold it!" Stephanie looked as if she didn't know what emotion to feel. "What are you trying to say?"

"There's someone going around using their Soulpower for evil, and only these two can do something about it."

I looked over at the other three. No way could Tyler be serious.

"What?" James was completely awestruck. "Dude, that's a bunch of crap on a sesame seed bun!"

"I'm sorry you don't believe me," said Tyler. He looked at us all directly in the eye. "I really wish I could prove it to you."

"No, it's not like that," said James. "I just can't believe…those visions. Is that what they really are?"

"That's what it seems like," said Gary.

James looked over at Tyler, who just nodded. All this time I believed it was just puberty doing its things.

"Man," said James, scratching his head, "this is too weird, but those visions…"

"How do you know all this?" I asked.

"He's old," said James. "What'd you expect?"

"I read a lot," said Tyler.

"What kind of books told you all this stuff?" Stephanie asked.

"A very special one," said Tyler with a smile.

"This is nuts," James muttered. "This really is nuts. Nuts! Not the good kind of nuts you can eat, but the crappy nuts."

"Is it possible that people could see the same vision at the same exact time?" Gary asked.

"Hmm...that's likely." Tyler thought it over for a few seconds. "It seems logical. I guess it could happen. Souls have a habit to connect with each other, and if two people with Soulpower are very close, then it seems likely."

That didn't make much sense to me. I had only just met Gary and James, but I was sharing visions with them. Tyler said people had to be close to share visions. Everything he was saying didn't explain my situation at all.

"This is too much." Stephanie put her hands on her head. "I can't believe what I'm hearing."

"I understand," Gary said, getting close to her. "This is crazy, I know."

"Man, what a world!" James exclaimed. "How can this happen to us? I thought we were normal! I never would've dreamed of something like this! So how do we beat this guy? If what you said is true, then I really want to get back at him."

"Now that you know about your Soulpower," said Tyler, "it should be very easy for you to use it. Just practice fighting or something. I'm sure that'll be no problem for you boys."

"I sure wish we would've known about this before Brandon beat us up," James mumbled. "Why didn't you say anything then?"

"I was too concerned about my grandson," Tyler replied. "And I wanted to make sure you two truly had the gift to use Soulpower. After your tangle with Brandon I could sense the energy in your souls heighten."

"How can you sense Soulpower?" Stephanie asked. "Do you have Soulpower too?"

"Everyone has Soulpower," said Tyler, "but not everyone can use it. I'm not one of the gifted ones who can use my Soulpower, but after reading about it I had to see what I could do. With years of meditation and concentration, I've gained the ability to sense the levels of Soulpower in others."

"Nuts, nuts, nuts…," James repeated, holding his head.

"Okay," said Gary. "We'll do our best to get rid of this guy."

My stomach quickly became the focus of my attention.

"I'm hungry," I said timidly.

"Good idea!" James announced, seeming overly eager to forget everything he just heard. "Let's just all go and get something to eat."

"How can you think of food at a time like this?" Stephanie asked. "You all just found out that you're a part of some fantasy fairytale!"

"And we just ate," said Gary.

"Hey, I'm a guy." James looked over and gave me a cheesy smile. I giggled softly. "Dudes need food."

"You all do understand that this is a very serious situation," said Tyler.

"Don't worry about it," Gary assured. "We've got this thing under control. We're going to find this guy and stop him."

"And there's one more thing I need to tell you two," said Tyler. "If you want to use a weapon guns are ineffective against Soulpower."

"Why?" James asked.

"Because the bullet is the actual weapon," Tyler explained. "Once it leaves the gun it disconnects itself from your soul. Only weapons that come into direct contact with your body can connect with your soul."

"Okay," said Gary, "thanks for telling us."

"Very good," said Tyler, patting Gary on the back. "You kids hurry along, and try not to think too much about what I just told you."

"Um, sir?" said Stephanie hesitantly. "How's Brandon?"

"Oh, he's doing fine," Tyler replied. "He was just knocked out. In a few days he should be heading home."

I actually felt sorry for Brandon. Even though he tried to pound Gary into oatmeal, I still felt a little bad for him. He did get hit by a car after all.

Tyler unlocked the door for us.

"Take care now," he said.

"You okay?" Gary asked Stephanie.

"Yeah," she said, "I'm just a little shocked. I can't believe…"

"Kind of crazy, isn't it?" James told her. "Now that I had it explained to me, I know it's true. I think I can feel that Soulpower stuff inside me! But I want something to eat, so let's go already!"

"Food is first priority for you," said Gary, rolling his eyes.

I tried to leave my worries behind by getting something to eat, but I was reminded of the stranger as soon as I saw the Shady Palm Café. I couldn't get over that fact that he attacked Gary without even touching him. That must have been Soulpower.

The restaurant was a little busier than it was earlier that day. When Bernie saw us he perked up a little.

"You kids back?" he asked.

"You guys must put something in your food to make it so addicting," said James. We ordered our food and found a table for the four of us.

"Hey," said Gary as we sat down, "what if that weird guy we met is the guy Tyler told us about?" James stopped chewing for a little bit, then swallowed.

"Who knows?" he replied. "Just because he's weird doesn't mean he's the one."

"No, he might be right," said Stephanie. "It makes sense. Gary, you said he hit you without actually touching you."

Gary leaned forward onto the table and dropped his voice.

"That would mean this town is in trouble. We have to find this guy as soon as possible."

"But how do we find him?" Stephanie asked. "He could be anywhere."

"If anything," said Gary, "he'll find us. I'm sure of it."

"But what if it's not him?" James asked, taking a drink and swallowing hard. "Then what would we do?"

"Like Gary said," said Stephanie, "he should find you if you can't find him."

"We can't wait that long," I said quietly.

"She's right," said Gary. "If we wait too long, more innocent people might get hurt."

"Or killed," said James through a mouthful of fries.

"So," said Gary, "we'll have to start looking for him."

"Yeah, after we eat." James took another drink and let out a stifled burp.

"How are we going to find him?" Stephanie asked. "Where do we start?"

"First of all," said Gary, eating a fry, "you're not a part of this. It's too dangerous."

"Oh, come on," Stephanie pleaded. "You don't know that."

"Believe me," said Gary. "It's bad enough that you already know what you know. Unless you find a way to use your Soulpower, I can't let you get involved in this. We don't know exactly what we're dealing with. Besides—"

Gary quit talking as soon as I noticed who had just walked in the doors. A man dressed completely in black had entered the restaurant. We all turned our heads and looked at him. Looking closer, I noticed it wasn't our man. He was wearing a leather jacket, not a trench coat. His black hair was longer too. When Gary saw that it was someone else he continued talking.

"Besides, you shouldn't even be a part of this situation."

Stephanie sighed. "Okay, you win."

The four of us continued eating without saying anything. For some reason, I looked over to where the man in the black jacket was. I saw he was sitting across the restaurant, reading a newspaper. Although his face was completely hidden behind the newspaper, I still had the feeling that he was watching us. James slurped his drink loudly, getting my attention.

"Whatcha looking at?" he asked. Gary and Stephanie both looked at me, eager to hear what I had to say.

"Nothing," I replied. "Just him." I nodded my head towards the man, and the three of them glanced over at him.

"The guy with the newspaper?" Stephanie asked.

"Yeah," I said.

"What about him?" James asked. "It doesn't look like him."

"I think he's watching us," I said.

"Oh, so it's not just me, then," said James. "Ow!" James grabbed his forehead.

"What's wrong?" Gary asked.

"My head hurt for a little bit," said James, "but it's gone now. Back to food!"

"Who is that person?" Stephanie asked. "I can't see his face, so I don't know if I've seen him around."

"I didn't recognize him," said Gary.

"What if this is the guy?" James whispered.

"Don't go pointing your finger at everyone," said Gary. "Just because he's different doesn't mean he's a maniac who wants to kill us."

"He's got a bad vibe," said James. "I'm telling you, I don't like him."

"A bad vibe?" Gary glanced back over at him. "I don't feel anything bad."

"Let's just go," said Stephanie, standing up. "We've had a weird day, so our minds are a little messed up." The rest of us stood up and we left the restaurant.

"What a day," said James. "I just want to go home and play video games."

"I'm not going home alone," said Stephanie nervously. "I still feel a little bit freaked out about everything."

"How do you think we feel?" James asked. "This guy wants us, not you."

"He's right," Gary told her. "You don't have anything to worry about. Besides, hanging around us is dangerous. If we have a run-in with him, I don't want you involved."

Stephanie bit her lip, then heaved a sigh. "Yeah, you're right. I'll go home now, so don't get yourselves killed." She headed out of the town into the suburbs. A few minutes later I left the Shady Palm Café with Gary and James. The three of us walked aimlessly around town, wondering what to do next.

"Krystal," said Gary, "I think you should go home, too."

"I don't want to," I said.

"Really, it's dangerous," said James. "You might get hurt."

"I don't want to go home," I repeated. "Please don't make me go home."

"Well, I don't know," said Gary. I looked straight into his eyes. After a moment he said, "Fine, just stay close to us. But if anything goes down, you hightail it outta here."

"Thanks," I said, giving him a big smile. Gary blushed a little.

"Uh, don't mention it," he said.

I continued walking around town with Gary and James, who talked about what they were going to do. The reason why I didn't want to go home was unclear to me. Maybe it was because I wanted to know why I still had those visions if Tyler didn't sense any Soulpower in me. I should have asked him, but I wasn't sure if I really wanted to know the answer.

"You know what's crazy?" said James as we were going past the beach. "I'm not sure if I want to find this guy, or not. If we find him, then we'll have to fight him, but as long as we wander around, I keep getting more anxious."

"Let's just try and find him," said Gary. "If we stop him, then it's over. The sooner, the better."

"Yeah," said James. "That would suck if we spent our whole summer wondering if this guy's going to jump out from behind a bush at you."

Suddenly I felt eyes burning into the back of my head. I turned around to see what it was.

"He's watching us again," I said.

Gary and James stopped walking and turned around. The man from the restaurant wearing the black leather jacket was standing across the street, looking right at us. He was right in the middle of the sidewalk, and people walking by were giving him curious looks.

"I have a bad feeling about this," said Gary. "We're in the middle of a crowded public area. If we fight here, then someone could get hurt."

"Ugh." James swallowed hard enough for me to hear. "You mean someone besides us? Uh, shouldn't we get weapons or something? I don't know if this Soulpower stuff will work right. We haven't trained, and I don't wanna die in the street."

At that instant, the man walked straight at us, directly into traffic. We backed up, keeping a close eye on him as cars screeched their tires trying to avoid hitting him. A truck swerved out of control and slammed into an oncoming car. A series of accidents occurred after that, and the man continued coming towards us. He seemed completely oblivious to what he was causing.

"Run!" Gary shouted before he made it to our side of the street. The three of us took off towards Tyler's shop.

"We need to get swords!" Gary yelled at the others as we were running. "Go back to Tyler's!"

We burst through the door of the antique shop. Gary and James each immediately grabbed a sword.

"What's going on here?" Tyler walked in from the back-room and gave us all a puzzled look. "Is something the matter? What're you doing with those?"

"Someone's trying to kill us, man!" said James hysteri-cally. "We had to run back here for these!"

"I wonder if he followed us here?" said Gary. He walked over and peered out the window. A few cars casually drove by.

Nothing unusual was outside.

"If who followed you here?" Tyler asked sternly. "I don't mean…"

"That weird guy," I said. "Yeah, we think we saw him."

"Well, for God's sake," said Tyler shortly, "don't lure him over here!"

"He's right," said Gary. "Let's go. We've got what we came for. Krystal, you stay here where it's safe."

"I don't want to," I said.

"Krystal, listen to us!" James grabbed my shoulder. "We don't want you in the middle when this goes down, got it?"

"They're right," Tyler said to me. "You need to stay back."

Gary and James ran out the door, leaving me with Tyler in his shop. Deciding that I didn't care what they thought, I followed after them. Tyler yelled at me to stop, but I ignored him as I left his shop and followed the others into the suburbs. I could see them up ahead of me, but it was hard for me to catch up. After we had made it back to the neighborhood Gary and James stopped running and I caught up with them.

"What are you doing here?" Gary demanded. It was the first time I had ever seen him mad at me. "We told you to stay in the store!"

I had nothing to say. All I wanted was to be with them.

"She doesn't want to listen to you." A voice came from the trees. We looked up to see the new mystery man jump off a branch and land on his feet in front of us. He must've fell twenty feet and made it look as if he had only jumped three inches.

"Stop right there!" Gary demanded, brandishing his sword. "Don't make a move!"

The stranger had a gentle face and looked as if he was in his early twenties; he was much younger than the other guy. His long black hair was shiny and didn't look scraggly like the other man. In fact, I thought he was quite handsome. He didn't move, nor speak. Instead, he gave the three of us a dark, ominous smile. It was a smile so sinister that it made me shiver.

"Who do you think you are?" James barked. "I bet you're the one using his Soulpower like a jerk!"

The man's grin grew broader as he crossed his arms, signifying that he didn't take us as a threat.

"No," he answered. "I do not use Soulpower."

"Oh," said Gary. The three of us looked at each other.

"Then how'd you jump down from so high up?"

"That's not important, is it?" he replied, keeping his grin. "What's important is that you haven't taken care of Dexter yet."

The three of us looked at each other again.

"Who?" Gary asked.

"His name is Dexter," the man told us.

"Is that other guy Dexter?" James asked. "The guy who attacked Gary at the restaurant was Dexter, wasn't he?"

"That is correct," the man said. "You have to kill him."

"We're looking for him," said James. "Can you help?"

"He is your concern, not mine."

I could tell Gary and James were getting completely creeped out. However, the man really didn't bother me. I looked over at Gary, who was watching the man closely.

"But he'll be your concern if he destroys the world!" James shouted. "Then it'll be your fault because you didn't help us look for him!"

"Just let him be, James," said Gary. "He doesn't look like he's against us, so let's not bother him."

Some kind of energy seemed to radiate from the man. I could feel it as it slithered around us. It felt cold and frightening...and I was familiar with it...

"Your power," I said quietly. The stranger looked at me. "What is your power? I've felt it somewhere before..."

I stared hopefully at the man, but all he did was grin.

"I must be going now," he said, walking past us. "And by the way...," he held out both his hands, and the swords that Gary and James were holding flew out of their grasps and into the stranger's hands, "...you won't be needing these. Just use your Soulpower."

We watched him as he made his way into town, then we slowly continued on our way. I stopped and turned around again. Not to my surprise, the stranger was gone. Gary and James also stopped walking and stood on each side of me as the three of us gazed down upon the town that needed us.

James heaved a heavy sigh. "How are we going to do this?"

Gary thought it over for a moment. "I...I don't know. We just have to find Dexter."

"Well, I know that," said James. "But how? What if we don't find him in time?"

"We will," said Gary. "I'm certain we'll find him soon

enough."

"Yeah, but…" James scratched his head. "What if we can't beat him? I don't know how strong he is."

I looked up at the sky as if looking for an answer. That cold power…I had felt it before. It crawled around inside me.

"What'd you see?" Gary asked me.

"Nothing," I said. "Just looking…at the clouds."

We moved off the road and sat under a palm tree. I could see the ocean from afar, dull and gray as it reflected the cloudy sky. A vision flickered in front of me. I knew the other two saw it.

"I'm going home," said James grimly, getting up. "See you tomorrow. That is, if we don't die." I watched James head back to his house, looking like a drunk as he tried to walk straight. Gary and I continued sitting for a little longer.

"Hey," said Gary, "sorry about all this. I know you just moved here. It must be hard on you."

"Don't feel bad," I said timidly with a weak smile. "I know that I'm…" I looked down at the ground.

"That you're what?" Gary asked.

I looked up at him. "That I'm a loser. Everywhere I go it's just the same."

"No, don't say that." He scooted closer to me. "Me and James really like having you around."

"Yeah," I said. "But no one really loves me. No one really cares for me…"

"What about your parents?" said Gary. "I'm sure they care about you."

"They care about me," I said quietly, "but they don't love me."

"What makes you say that?" he asked.

"They aren't my real parents," I said. "I was adopted."

"Oh." Gary looked down at the ground. "What happened to your real parents?"

I let out a sigh.

"I don't want to talk about them."

"Sorry," said Gary, scooting closer to comfort me. "Look, I'm sure that you'll do fine here. This is a nice neighborhood. If anything, I'll be your friend."

I looked up at him and smiled.

"Thanks," I said. "I feel I can trust you."

I looked back up at the sky.

"What do you see?" he asked curiously, also looking up.

"Nothing," I said. "Just looking at the sky. It's something I started doing when I was a little girl. Hey, Jack and Laura aren't going to be home Friday evening. Want to come over? I can make a pasta dinner."

Gary looked a little surprised.

"You don't have to," I said, "because of Stephanie."

"I'll come over!" he said. "It's not official with me and Stephanie, so I can still pretty much do whatever I want."

"Okay," I said. "They won't be back until the next morning, so we can do whatever we want."

"Uh…" Gary looked a little funny. Was it something I said?

"Will you take me into downtown?" I asked timidly. "You can show me around again because I wasn't paying attention to James when he gave me the tour my first day here. We could get to know each other better then."

Gary's mouth opened a little as if lost in thought. Then he seemed to snap back.

"Of course," he said.

The two of us went into town together. Gary gave me a nice tour of the entire town. Half of it I didn't remember because James wasn't a very good tour guide, but I was much more comfortable with Gary.

"I used to come here with James," he said as we stood in front of the movie theater. "We used to watch movies all the time."

"Maybe we should come here," I said. "I'd have fun."

"That sounds like a good plan," said Gary. "We could also go the carnival that comes here to the beach at the end of summer."

"Yeah, I'd like that," I said. "I like carnivals."

He looked at me and smiled. Naturally, I smiled back. We walked around town for a little longer, getting my mind off Dexter. As long as I was with Gary, I felt safe. After the sun went down we decided to head back.

"I had fun," I said. "You're a good tour guide."

"Well, uh," said Gary, blushing. "Guess we'll go back now. It's getting dark."

"Okay," I said with a big smile.

Gary's face reddened even more.

CHAPTER SIX

The rest of the week was uneventful up until Friday. I felt as if Dexter wasn't a threat at the time, so I spent my time enjoying summer as any kid my age would. Gary and James had gotten over the shock about everything Tyler told us, so we just decided to kick back and plan our next move. On top of that, ever since Tyler told us about Dexter, those visions I had were gone. He said it was probably because we had become aware of our souls and capabilities.

I spent that Friday morning in town at the arcade with Gary, James, and Nick. James had made it a lifelong project to beat my high score, but wasn't having any such luck. Gary and I left James to his obsession to hang out with Nick for a bit.

"He's really determined, isn't he?" said Nick.

"Oh, James?" Gary looked back at James who was staring at the game's screen with a strange hypnotic look in his eyes. "Yeah, it gives him something to do, I guess."

"So," said Nick, giving me and Gary a smile, "you two going out yet?"

Gary's face instantly turned bright red.

"No!" he said quickly. He looked so embarrassed I couldn't help but smile.

"Okay, take it easy!" Nick chuckled. "I was just asking, man. Wow, you got really red. Look at how red he is, Krystal."

If Gary's face had gotten any redder it would've glowed in the dark.

"He's coming over to my house tonight," I said to Nick.

Nick's eyes lit up and a big grin spread across his face.

"Ooh," he said, "have a long night ahead of you, eh Gary?"

"It's, uh, just for dinner," said Gary. "That's all, really."

"Sure, alright," said Nick, still grinning. He looked back and forth between us. "You two look great together, even if you are just friends."

I looked at Gary. Did I really look good with him? I did think he was cute, though. He looked back at me, and we made eye contact. We held it for a few seconds, and I began to feel a little warm in the face.

"Gah!" James had lost his last life on the game and apparently hadn't reached my high score. He walked over to us scratching his head.

"Did you beat it?" Gary asked.

"Not even close!" said James. "Krystal, I swear your score is even higher than what it was because now I can't even get close to it!"

"It is," I said. "I played it again the other day and beat my last score."

James's jaw almost hit the floor. Gary and Nick laughed.

"Looks like you've got a long way to go, man," said Nick.

"Shut up," James grumbled.

"What do you guys wanna do now?" Gary asked.

"I spent all the money I had on me," said James.

"Guess we're not going to the Shady Palm Café for lunch," said Gary.

"Ugh," James groaned, "I hope my mom bought some more groceries. I'm sick of frozen waffles and chicken noodle soup."

"Let's all just go home for a while," Gary suggested, "then meet back at my house to do something. My parents are both at work today, so I've got to make my own food, so it'll take a little while. I'm a lousy cook, and I want something more than just a stupid sandwich."

"Yeah, alright," said James. "Let's go."

"I'll see ya guys around," said Nick. "I'm gonna chill here for a little longer."

"Alright," said Gary. "See ya."

"Take it easy, Nick," said James.

We were on our way out when we were stopped by someone who had a knack for ruining a good day. Gary and James immediately took offensive positions in front of me as if I was in danger.

"What is it now, Brandon?" said James irritably. Brandon's arm was in a cast.

"Does it matter?" he asked, grinning stupidly. When he saw me, he said, "Who are you? I think I saw you before. You new or something?"

"She's a friend," Gary replied quickly. "Now let us through."

"Fine, fine." Brandon moved aside, and the three of us left the arcade easier than we expected.

"At least he didn't want to fight," said James as we were walking out of town.

"His arm was in a cast," said Gary. "If it wasn't for that, he probably would've tried to pick a fight with us again."

"Do you think he'll want to get back at us?" James asked.

"I don't know," said Gary. "Maybe. It wasn't my fault he was hit by a car."

"He might not look at it like that," said James. "To him, it's always someone else's fault."

"I guess you're right," said Gary quietly. "That seems like him."

Our walk was just like every other normal walk with Gary and James goofing off about stupid stuff. I took time to notice the flowers and how they added a nice touch to the neighborhood. It was amazing how much a little color can make a difference. I kept a mental note of it to use in my artwork.

"Hey, guys," said Gary as we got close to his house. He sounded serious, so James and I stopped walking to see what he had to say. "I know we're enjoying ourselves, and I don't want to ruin our day or anything, but shouldn't we be thinking about Dexter a little? He is our responsibility, you know?"

James took a deep breath and looked at the ground.

"Yeah," he said, "but what can we really do?"

"Tomorrow," said Gary, "we should find a nice place somewhere to see what we can do with our Soulpower. Nothing major has come up on the news, so Dexter probably isn't doing too much right now."

"Okay," said James, "we'll do that. But right now, let's enjoy the rest of the day! It's beautiful, and we don't wanna stress ourselves out, right? We haven't had too many days like this yet."

"Yeah," said Gary, smiling.

When we got back to the suburbs the three of us headed home for lunch. I didn't have much to eat at my place so I just made a few cans of ravioli to hold me over. When I finished scarfing it down I walked out to the backyard where the pool was. The water was clear and sparkly. I lied down on one of the pool chairs and stared into the sky. Watching the clouds float by made me a little sleepy, so I closed my eyes for a bit and began to drift off. The nice summer breeze was so relaxing.

I snapped back awake. Looking around I realized the sun had nearly gone down. What time was it? Gary and James were probably waiting for me. When I stood up my eyes caught the water in the pool. It was perfectly calm.

I kneeled down next to the water and looked at my reflection. It was just like looking into a mirror. There wasn't a single ripple in the water at all. With one hand I swished the surface a little, but I immediately jerked it back. The water was freezing. In fact, everything was freezing. The sun had just set, and it was so cold I could see my breath.

I turned around to go back into the house, but the sliding glass door was locked. As I struggled to open it I tried to remember if I had locked it myself. I didn't think I did. No, I didn't lock it. Something else did.

The backyard was fenced in, so that meant I would have to climb over a fence to get around the house. When I looked around I saw everything was covered in an icy, silver light. The blood in my veins ran cold as I looked up at the moon that was looming over the world. It took my parents, and now it was looking back down at me. Watching me…waiting…

Something on the other side of the pool caught my attention. I peered across the frozen water to see a little girl with blonde hair standing on the other side. She was staring right at me. It was too dark to see her face, but her eyes were piercing my soul. My head began to hurt, and with every pulsing throb the moon's silver light grew brighter.

I fell to my knees. The world was spinning. I felt so weak. An angel was here with me, but not a real angel. The little girl on the other side of the pool was watching me. I knew her. But I didn't see her face. Her white, lifeless wings fanned out as I fell into a swirling darkness.

Darknae had found me again.

"Krystal!"

A hand grabbed my arm and pulled me out of the water. The warm sun shone in my eyes as I coughed the water out of my lungs. Gary and James dragged me out of the pool and carried me into the grass.

"Krystal, are you all right?" Gary's face was still blurry. I gasped for air as he and James helped me back onto my feet.

"We waited around at Gary's house for you," said James, "but you never showed up, so we came looking for you."

"I must've fallen asleep," I said weakly, forcing myself to smile, "that's all."

"That's all?" said Gary, unsatisfied with my answer. "We found you floating facedown in the pool! What were you doing?"

"I just had a dream," I said.

"Must've been a hell of a dream," said James, scratching his head.

"We were going to go to the park," Gary told me, "but if you're not feeling good you don't have to go."

"No, I'm okay," I said.

"Well, alright," said Gary. "We should go there now before it gets too late. Are you sure you're okay?"

"I'm fine," I said innocently. "Let me dry off real quick."

The three of us walked together into the heart of the town. Gary and James kept asking if I was okay, and it was assuring to know they really cared. I thought more about the dream I had. I felt Darknae again, but I had no idea what that meant. I couldn't remember what Darknae was, or why I recognized it.

The park was mainly where parents brought their little kids to play. It had the area's biggest playground, a lake that made a popular fishing spot, and was also just a good place to hang around.

As we walked through the park a small group of teenagers caught our attention. There were five of them sitting under a tree listening to some music. I instantly recognized one of the teenagers as Nick, who we had seen earlier that day at the arcade.

"Hey guys," Nick greeted as we approached them. "What're you guys up to?"

"Not much," said James. "We were bored so we came here."

"How's everyone doing?" Gary asked. Everyone smiled and said they were doing good. They were apparently kids they went to school with.

"Why don't ya hang here for a while," Nick offered. "We're just gonna stay here until we feel like doing something else."

The three of us sat in the soft grass under the tree with the others.

"Hey, guys," Nick announced to the others, "this is Krystal. She just moved here earlier this summer and she'll be going to school with us, so let's make her love it here."

Everyone smiled and shook my hand. They all seemed like really nice people.

"So, tell me," said Nick to Gary, "how's it going with you

and Stephanie?"

"It's alright," he said, "but I'm not sure how it'll work out. She seems like a really nice girl and I've liked her for a long time, but I don't know if I really feel that special connection with her."

"Ah, I see." Nick quickly thought it over. "What are you gonna do?"

"I don't know," Gary replied. "We never officially dated, so I'll just leave it at that, I guess. At least I got to spend time with her."

"Why don't you and Krystal go out?" asked one of the girls with us. "You two look kinda cute sitting next to each other like that."

"I thought the same thing," said Nick.

"Well, um…" Gary turned red. I just giggled, thinking it was funny.

"Man, what are you guys listening to?" James asked, completely oblivious to the world around him. "This music sounds kinda old."

"It's classic, man," Nick replied. "He's a legend. He wrote songs about living in a perfect world."

I thought it had to be a coincidence. Another reference about a perfect world. Just what exactly was a perfect world, anyway?

"Well, it's been cool," said Gary, standing up, "but I think we should get going and see if we wanna do anything."

"Alright," said Nick. "I'll see ya around."

James and I also stood up. We said goodbye to the others and started walking through the park some more.

"So now what?" James asked, lying down on a bench on the other side of the park.

"What do you guys wanna do?" Gary asked.

"I don't care," said James lazily.

"Me neither," I said.

"Let's just stay here for a while," said Gary, sitting on the ground under another tree next to the bench. "We should just enjoy the weather."

"I know," said James. "But I'd rather enjoy the weather while doing stuff in it."

"Like what?" Gary asked. "We can't always do stuff all the time."

"Wanna get some ice cream?" James suggested.

"Not really," said Gary. "I'm kinda not in the mood for ice cream. And we're broke, remember?"

"How about the beach?" I asked as I took a seat on the bench next to James. "I haven't been there."

"No way," James quickly answered. "It's too crowded there. You want to go at night, otherwise you'll get caught in the insanity."

We eventually continued to stay underneath the tree for a few hours. I could hear James snoring on the bench. I took the time to walk around and smell some of the flowers blooming around us. I looked over at Gary who was sitting quietly under the tree, and I started thinking about all of the things that happened so far this summer. My mind eventually wandered over to Dexter, and my heart sank a little. We still had to worry about him. As much as we were enjoying the weather, he was still a problem. He was a little black speck in my perfect world.

James grunted and rolled over off the bench. As he stood up an elderly man who was walking his dog gave James a confused look.

"I think I dozed off," James yawned. He dusted himself off, then asked, "What time is it?"

"It's a quarter to four," said the man with the dog, looking at his watch.

"I think I should be going home," said James. "It's a long walk back."

"Yeah, okay." Gary stood up and brushed the leaves off himself, then called over to me. "We're getting ready to go now."

The three of us headed out of town back onto the street that leads into the suburbs. The sun was beating down on us; it felt nice and warm. We made it to Gary's house and told each other good-bye. James started to walk away, but I stayed behind.

"Are you still coming over tonight?" I asked Gary without James hearing.

"Sure will," said Gary with a smile. "What's a good time to show up?"

"How about eight?" I said.

"Sounds good," he said. "I'll see you tonight."

I walked back to my house and began the preparations. I invited him over for a pasta dinner, so looked through the kitchen for stuff to make it with. Since I didn't really know how to cook fettuccine alfredo or spaghetti I took out the macaroni and cheese. It was one of my favorites, and since it was pasta I thought it'd make a really good pasta dinner. I wasn't very sure how much to make, so I set five boxes on the counter.

There were still a few hours left before Gary's arrival. To pass the time, I worked on a few crossword puzzles. All of my video games didn't seem to be of any interest to me for some reason. Even though I never was any good at crossword puzzles, I was doing pretty well.

After a while, crossword puzzles didn't entertain me anymore, so I went up to my room, turned on my stereo, and stretched out on my bed. Nothing was more relaxing to me than blasting metal, and I had no idea why.

Another vision flashed in front of me. That was the first one I had since I learned about Dexter. What did it mean? Ever since I learned of Dexter, all the visions except for that one disappeared. I thought I had seen an angel in that vision. A little girl with wings…

Perhaps it was coincidence, and the visions didn't stop. Since the visions appeared to be completely random it was simply the first one that came back. That seemed logical, but at the same time, unlikely. A feeling way down inside of me was saying that it was more than just coincidence.

I listened to music until it was time to make the macaroni and cheese. I rummaged around the cabinets for the biggest pot I could find and put it on the stove, filled it with boiling water, and dumped all five boxes of macaroni into it. As I stirred it around I hoped it would be enough.

When the noodles were strained, I began to make the special cheese sauce from an old recipe my mother had told me about. Laura said the packets of cheese in the box was good enough, but nothing could beat our family recipe. It was actually pretty easy to make.

Since this was a special occasion I thought it'd be best to use the dining room table instead of the kitchen. After I had set the table and evenly distributed two heaps of macaroni and cheese onto our plates the doorbell rang. I placed the pot in the sink and went over to the door. Gary was waiting outside, wearing a nice flannel shirt and tan khakis.

"Oh, hi!" I said. "Come on in. I'm almost done with dinner."

Gary smiled and stepped inside. I watched him take off his shoes.

"You look good," he said with a smile. His face was red.

I smiled gently. "Thanks, you too. Sit down in the dining room. I'll bring the food out."

Gary sat down at the table and I went to fetch our plates from the kitchen.

"Macaroni and cheese?" Gary looked over the table. "Uh, this is great! I haven't had this in a while."

"Want something to drink?" I asked.

"Sure."

I went back to the kitchen and looked in the fridge. There was a 2-liter of cola, so I grabbed that, a couple cups, and brought it back. I filled one up for Gary and set it down in front of him.

"Thanks," he said.

I sat down across from Gary. Everything was going great. Macaroni and cheese the hardest thing I could make, and I was glad he really liked it.

"This is good," he said.

A big smile spread across my face. He had complimented my dinner.

"Thanks," I said. "I normally don't have to cook, so I didn't know if it would be good."

"I like it." he said. "It's different, but really good."

"It's a family recipe," I said. "This is the first time I made it by myself."

We both smiled across the table at each other. We held each other's gazes for a few seconds until Gary quickly looked away.

"Hey, Gary," I said, noticing his nice clothes again, "how come you're dressed in such nice clothes?"

"Uh, um..." Gary looked a little embarrassed. "I just wanted to look good when I went to someone else's house."

"Oh." I felt a little confused. "But you've been over here before and you've never dressed nicely."

Gary looked a little lost for words. His face began to glow again.

"I thought it'd be different this time," he said quietly.

"You look good," I said, smiling. "I wasn't aware that I had to dress nicely. I'm sorry."

"No, it's okay," said Gary. "I don't mind. You look good anyway."

"Thanks," I said, my smile getting bigger.

Gary and I continued eating for a few more minutes. It

made me feel good to have a guest at my house to eat dinner with.

"Well," said Gary after dinner, "thanks for inviting me over. I had a good time."

"Are you leaving?" I asked, putting the dishes in the sink. "There's one more thing I want to show you."

"What's that?" Gary looked a little unsure about the situation.

"I got something just in case you or James would come over," I said. "Follow me."

Jack had bought me something the other day, saying he thought I could use it in case Gary or James came over. I led Gary upstairs to my room. He looked around and was acting a little strange.

"Look over in the top drawer next to the bed." I said. "I've got something we can use tonight."

"Uh, what is it?"

"Aren't you going to look?" I asked with a big smile. "I think you'll really like it."

Gary looked over at the drawer, over at me, and back at the drawer. He slowly reached out, opened it, put his hand inside, and pulled out what was in it.

"Movie tickets?"

"It's to that movie you said you wanted to see," I said happily. "I thought that we'd go see it tonight."

"Well, this is great!" He wiped off his forehead. I don't know why he was so warm, I thought it was fine in my room. "You want to go see a movie with me?"

"Yup," I replied.

"Wow, that's cool!" said Gary. "We can get popcorn and stuff and sit next to each other and everything!"

I giggled, then walked out of the room.

"Hey Krystal," he called while I was in the hall. "What's this third ticket for?"

"Isn't this so cool?" James asked excitedly as he walked to the theater with Gary and I. "The three of us going to a movie together? This is going to be so awesome! Krystal, you're the best!"

"You're welcome," I said. "It's the least I could do for you two."

"Hey, Gary," said James, "what's wrong, man? You look

kind of bummed."

"What? Oh, no, I'm fine." he said. "I'm probably just a little bit tired, that's all. I'll probably wake up when I have some popcorn and soda."

While we were on our way to the theater I kept looking up at the sky. The moon was peeking through the clouds. As long as it was concealed I was fine.

"See anything?" Gary asked curiously.

"The moon is behind the clouds," I said quietly.

"It's a full moon tonight," he said. "I saw it on the way to your house."

"Oh." I looked down at the ground as we walked and started fidgeting.

"Is something wrong?" Gary asked.

"No, nothing," I said, trying to hide my shaky voice.

"You're not afraid of werewolves, are you?" James teased. "AWOOO! Ha ha!"

"Dude, shut up," Gary mumbled.

"I'm just playing," said James. "Sheesh."

"It's okay," I said quietly. "Don't worry about it. The moon…it just…never mind."

"Are you sure you're fine?" Gary asked. "If not, we can do this some other time."

"Really, it's okay." I smiled gently. "Let's go, or we'll miss the start of the movie."

After walking for a while longer, we made it to the movie theater, then the three of us handed our tickets to the person behind the booth. As soon as we walked in, cool air conditioning and the buttery smell of popcorn hit my face.

"I'll pay for the food," I said as we made our way to the concession bar. I bought everyone a large popcorn and large drink.

"You didn't need to get me a large," said Gary. "We just ate." I smiled, thinking how dumb I was, but he smiled back and said, "Nah, don't worry about it. I'll try to eat it all so your money won't go to waste."

"Aw, nuts!" James accidentally let the bubbles overflow the side of his cup at the drink machine. "Pass me a napkin, will ya?" Laughing out loud, Gary grabbed a napkin and gave it him.

"Just make a huge mess, why don't ya?" said Gary. I giggled.

"It's genetic," said James, shrugging and wiping off his

cup. "C'mon, let's go!"

We found our seats in the middle of the theater. I sat on one side of Gary and James sat on his other side. There were quite a bit of people there. As more people came in, Gary took a sip of his drink, looked over at the entrance, and about drowned in his root beer. Abby and another girl had just walked in.

"Aw, crap!" Gary slouched down in his seat.

"What's wrong?" James asked through a mouthful of popcorn.

"My sister and her friend are here," Gary muttered. "I can't let them see me!"

"Oh, you mean Jessica!" said James loudly, looking around. "The hot one!"

"Get down!" Gary hissed, pushing James down into his seat. "I can't stand Jessica, and if they see me they'll just harass me."

Luckily, Abby and Jessica took their seats in the front of the theater without even looking in our direction. Gary would only have to deal with avoiding them after the movie.

When the movie started, James reached over and started eating out of Gary's popcorn. He quickly pulled it away.

"What are you doing?" Gary whispered. "Don't you have your own?"

"I ate it all," he said.

"Already?"

"Well, I spilled about half of it on the floor,"

We looked down at the floor in front of James. A carpet of popcorn was under him. Gary rolled his eyes, then offered to share his popcorn.

The movie was actually pretty good. It was about an hour in when I had to go to the bathroom. Drinking all that root beer wasn't a smart thing to do. I decided to hold it in as long as I could. A few minutes later, though, it was too much to bear.

"I'm going to the bathroom," I whispered to Gary. I stood up and hurried out of the theater. Once out in the hall, I ran as fast as I could to the restrooms without wetting my pants. Why did they have to have only one restroom? Not only that, it was on the opposite side of the building, and we were in the biggest theater in the area. I heard that even the nearby city's theater wasn't as big.

Finally being able to use the bathroom was a huge relief. While I was washing my hands, it happened again. That same vision. I blinked a few times, then quickly dried off my hands and made it back to the movie.

As I sat back down I looked over at Gary and James. They didn't seem to notice the vision at all. I wondered if I was the only one who saw it.

When the movie ended, James and I both stood up and stretched. Gary remained seated, making sure that Abby and Jessica were gone. When he saw the coast was clear, he stood up and the three of us left.

"That was crazy!" said James. "I didn't expect it to end like that!"

"Me neither," said Gary. "It was really cool."

We followed the crowd of people out of the theater. Gary and James were talking about the movie the entire time, but I kept thinking about the vision. Surely they would've mentioned it if they'd seen it. As soon as we walked outside, I immediately looked up. The moon was out and shining. I started to tremble. What had happened to the clouds?

"What are you doing?" Gary asked, looking up at the moon, then back to me.

I didn't say anything. I was too scared.

"What's wrong?" Gary asked, leaning close to me. "Are you alright?"

"The moon," I said quietly. My voice was too shaky to hide anymore. "It sees us."

"Huh?" James looked up at it. "How can it see us?"

"Come on," said Gary firmly, grabbing my arm, "let's go."

"I hate the moon," I said, looking down. "I want to kill it."

"What are you talking about?" Gary asked. "You want to kill the moon?"

"This doesn't feel right," said James. "Something isn't right about her."

"Why do you want to kill the moon?"

I looked back up at the moon.

"It killed my parents." I was trembling so badly now I thought I was going to start having convulsions. My heart pounded and my head throbbed. That vision flashed in front of me again as a cold pain burst through my chest.

Gary tried to get me to look at him. "Krystal? What are you talking about?"

"*It killed them!*" I shouted. My chest felt heavy and I

couldn't breathe. Sweat was pouring down my face. People were looking over at us, and Gary tried to act as calm as possible.

"Just settle down," he said calmly, firmly gripping my shoulders. "It's going to be just fine."

I closed my eyes, then took a series of deep breaths. I could feel the moon staring at me. It was laughing at me. I tried as hard as I could to ignore it. I opened my eyes, and Gary took his hands off my shoulders.

"I'm sorry," I apologized. "I don't know what came over me."

"You had us a little freaked out there," said James, letting out a sigh of relief.

"It's going to be okay," said Gary. "Let's just take you back home now."

We took off at a swift pace from the theater, not saying a word. I felt bad for ruining the night. It was supposed to be a fun time, and I was going crazy.

"Hey," said James as we were walking, "what was that about the moon killing your parents? That was really creepy."

"Oh, that," I said flatly. "I don't want to talk about it."

I could feel the energy draining from my body. I did my best to keep my strength up, but it wasn't long before I started feeling too weak. Gary and James caught me just before I collapsed onto the sidewalk.

"You'd better let us help you," said Gary.

"Okay," I said.

We walked back to the neighborhood in complete silence. The moon continued to flood everything in its silver glow. I kept my cool, trying not to think about it. Gary and James held me up on my feet the entire time by letting me put my arms around their shoulders. However, it was just a matter of time before my legs didn't want to move anymore.

"Hey, c'mon," Gary told me when I stopped walking. "We're almost there. Just a few more blocks."

My head started to feel heavy and it was increasingly difficult to keep my eyes open. I tried to keep walking, but it just made me more tired. Eventually, my body didn't want to respond at all, and I passed out from the exhaustion. The last thing I remembered was the moon's frozen, silver light covering me.

CHAPTER SEVEN

I woke up in my bed to the sound of Laura's voice. She was sitting next to me, dabbing my face with a wet washcloth. Jack was standing behind her and they were both relieved to see me open my eyes.

"Good morning," said Laura, only this time her voice was lacking its happy singsong tone. "How are you feeling?"

"Better," I said.

"Your friends were here when we got back late last night," said Jack. "They told us you fainted and they brought you back here."

"Both of them stayed here until we got back," said Laura. "You have really good friends."

"They did that?" I asked. My heart was lifted to know that Gary and James actually cared for me so much.

"We told them they were welcome to use our pool if you were feeling better," said Laura, "so they said they'd stop by later today. Is that alright?"

"Yeah," I said, smiling. "I'd love it."

"You should stay in bed a little longer," said Laura, handing me a glass of water and my medication. "Be sure to drink plenty of fluids."

"Okay," I said.

"Well, we should be going now," said Jack, checking his watch.

"Right," said Laura. "We're leaving for work now, sweetie. You have our cell numbers if you need anything, okay?"

Laura kissed me on the cheek before she and Jack walked out of my room. I stared up at the ceiling. Gary and James stayed with me all night. I was so lucky to have them as friends.

The moon. What was it doing? I thought about how it killed my parents. Christmas was supposed to be the best time of year for a six-year-old, but that day left a haunting scar in my mind for the rest of my life. I could still remember the blood. I could still remember the song I heard that night as the moon sang them their final lullaby. That song; the moon's lullaby.

It was so beautiful, and it killed them.

Hours went past as I waited for Gary and James to show up.

My bed was very soft, but it felt hard and cold. So many sleepless nights in that bed. There didn't seem to be any explanation to my sleeplessness. Was it simply insomnia, like the doctors said? No, it had to be something else. Something else was keeping me awake. It was that empty feeling I felt deep inside my heart, like a part of me was missing. I just hoped that I would someday find a way to fill that emptiness.

I heard footsteps coming down the hall. When I saw Gary and James standing in the doorway a smile spread across my face.

"Hey," said Gary quietly.

"Hi," I said.

The two boys walked into my room. James stumbled over a pile of clothes on the floor, causing him to hit my desk and knock over my lamp.

"Oh, crap," he muttered, fixing the lamp. When I giggled, he looked up and smiled. "Still giggly, I see. That's good."

"We asked your parents if we could use the pool today," said Gary. "Do you think you'd want to use it too?"

"Yeah," I said.

"Gary thought it'd be a good idea not to practice using our Soulpower today," said James. "We don't want to push you after that stuff last night."

"And that reminds me," said Gary, taking a seat on my bed next to me. "We have to talk about last night."

"It was kinda creepy," said James. "You freaked us out a little bit."

"After you passed out," Gary began, "we had to bring you back here. When we got you back, you kept talking in your sleep."

"Oh," I said, thinking it over. I never remembered anyone saying I talked in my sleep.

"You said something about the moon," Gary continued, "and how it killed your parents. But you also kept repeating yourself, saying you didn't want anymore tranquilizers. You sounded really scared, and me and James couldn't figure out what you were really talking about."

"Yeah," said James. "Then it was like you were asking someone why they looked like you, and you just kept saying the same thing over and over."

"Do you know what you were talking about?" Gary asked.

I looked at him, then over at James. Both of them looked like they really wanted to know. Unfortunately, I had no idea what they were talking about.

"I don't know," I said timidly. "Sorry."

"You don't know anything at all?" said James disappointedly. "Nothing?"

"No," I said. They were both quiet for a little bit.

"Okay," said Gary. "Just thought we'd tell you."

"There are too many things," I said. "I can't understand what they mean or why I know them, but they haunt me."

"Like what?" Gary asked.

"Darknae," I said, "and a little girl who looks like me. I have dreams about an angel, tranquilizers and operating rooms, black horses with wings, and an old piano that plays the moon's lullaby."

"Just try not to think about it," said Gary. "You don't have to talk about it if you don't want to."

"Yeah," said James. "Let's just have fun in the pool!"

The rest of the afternoon was spent with Gary and James in the pool. It was extremely relaxing and it took a load off my mind. I floated on my back most of the time and stared up at the sky.

"You're always just looking at the sky, huh?" Gary said to me as I drifted past him.

"Yeah," I said.

"Ever try to see what the clouds look like?" Gary gazed up and pointed one out. "What do you think that one looks like?"

"A cannonball!" James splashed into the water right next to Gary, spraying both of us. After surfacing he shook his shoulder-length hair, splattering more water everywhere. "Isn't that what that cloud looked like?" he said with a grin.

"How about I show you what the bottom of the pool looks like?" Gary jumped up and tackled James, dragging him underwater. I could see the two of them wrestling near the bottom of the pool. Finally, they both came up, laughing.

After hanging around in the water for a little longer we just sat around outside on the pool chairs, letting the sun dry us off. We snacked on chips and lemonade as Gary and James told me about their school.

"Last year," James told me, "I secretly memorized Gary's lock combination on his locker. So when he wasn't looking I switched my lock with his, and he went all day carrying all his stuff to every class 'cuz he couldn't open his locker. It was great!"

"Yeah, I remember that," said Gary with a chuckle. "But

one time James had diarrhea really bad after lunch, and he didn't realize there was no more toilet paper until he was done. That was priceless!"

"That sucked so much!" said James, holding his head. "I had to use the hand dryers so it wouldn't be all wet, then clean the rest when I got back home."

Gary started cracking up as he remembered the incident.

"But the best part was when Jason and Jon walked in and saw you!" Gary laughed.

"Dude, that was horrible!" said James, grabbing his forehead. "They just kinda stared at me with my butt up to the dryer, and all I could do was say, 'Wassup?' Then they turned and walked out without saying anything. Talk about embarrassing!"

By that time, Gary was rolling on the ground, busting up with laughter. A few moments later he caught his breath and wiped the tears from his eyes.

"Priceless," he said. "Just priceless."

A few hours had passed, and we were still sitting outside. When I noticed the sun was going down I looked up at the sky again. Gary looked over and saw me looking up.

"Worried about the moon?" he asked.

I didn't answer, but just looked down at the water in the pool. Gary and James both stood up.

"We should go inside," said Gary.

"Yeah," I said.

We walked back inside and put our clothes back on over our swimsuits. The three of us took a seat in the living room. As soon as we got situated, James had to break the silence.

"Hey, Krystal," he said. "Do you think you can tell us about this moon thing? It's been really bugging us."

"Don't ask her that!" said Gary angrily. "She doesn't want to talk about it."

"It's okay," I said. "I guess I can tell you."

They both leaned forward in their seats intently. I thought about it for a second, then took a deep breath.

"It started when I was six," I told them. "It was Christmas Eve, and I had already gone to bed. In the middle of the night I woke up. I could hear a song being sang. It was a woman's voice, and it was a very beautiful song. I got out of bed to see what it was. It sounded like it was coming from my parents' room, so I followed it in there."

I paused. My throat became tight as I thought about the next part of the story. I swallowed hard and continued.

"My parents' bed was all ripped up. There was blood everywhere. My parents were dead. The window was broken and the moon was shining directly onto their bed. I could hear its lullaby."

I stared at the floor. Gary bit his lower lip and James scratched his head. Both of them just sat silently.

"The moon killed them," I said. Then I looked up at them both, and they looked back at me. "When the moon sings, Darknae takes your soul."

Gary looked up as if trying to read me.

"What's that mean?" he asked.

I shook my head. "I don't know. I just remembered hearing it, but I don't know what it means."

"Wait," said James, "when the moon sings? I've never heard it sing. Can you really believe what she's telling us, Gary?"

"After what Tyler told us," said Gary dully, "it's hard not to believe anything." He rubbed his chest wear Dexter's energy blast hit him. "Especially after experiencing it first hand. But," he said to me, "I really don't understand what you're talking about, Krystal, and I have to agree with James that I've never heard the moon sing."

"Yeah," I said quietly, "I know how you feel."

"So," said Gary, "you said when the moon sings, something takes your soul?"

"Darknae," I told him. "I don't know who said it, but that's what I've heard."

"What's Darknae?" he asked.

"I don't know," I said. "I just remember hearing it."

"Do you think that's what killed your parents?" Gary asked. "Darknae?"

I nodded a little. Gary and James remained silent for a few seconds. They must've thought I was crazy for telling them the moon killed my parents. Gary looked over at me and opened his mouth as if to say something, but a knock at the door interrupted him. I stood up and walked over to the door. I opened it and was confronted by the last person I'd expect to see.

"Hello," he said. It was the stranger in the black leather jacket who we mistook for Dexter at the Shady Palm Café. He had that same creepy grin as last time.

Gary and James quickly came over to the door.

"What do you want?" James demanded.

"The name's Zenox," the man said. "Thought I'd tell you that."

"Okay," said Gary, "what do you want, Zenox?"

"You three," he said.

"Why do you want us?" Gary asked. "Is it about Dexter?"

"Yes," he replied. "You might want to go to the park."

He turned around and started to walk away. Gary, James and I followed him outside.

"Why?" Gary ran up to Zenox and turned him around. "What's at the park?"

"Better go quickly," he said. "Wouldn't want something bad to happen, would we now?" He chuckled slightly, then disappeared in a black cloud of smoke.

"He v-vanished!" James stammered, sounding panicked. "How'd he do that? What's going on? What's at the park?"

"I don't know," said Gary. I could tell he was frightened. "He said to hurry, so let's go!"

"Take me with you," I said to Gary.

"No, you stay here!" he told me. "It's too dangerous! Dexter could be there!"

Before I could resist, he and James took off running down the street in the direction of the town. My head throbbed, and I felt that feeling of pure rage and hatred surge through me, but only for a second. After it was over I felt empowered. I hesitated at first, but I ran after them. No way was I going to let them do anything crazy by themselves. Even if I didn't have Soulpower, they were my friends, so I was willing to do anything to help them.

All the way to the park I stayed a ways behind them. If they saw me they would just tell me to go home. My heart was racing from running, but also from anxiety. I had no idea what was going to happen once we got there.

Finally we made it to the park in the middle of town. Gary and James stopped to catch their breath. It was amazing that they were able to run that fast for so long, but it was even more amazing that I could keep up with them. I couldn't use Soulpower, but how did I manage to run all that way? Nobody I knew could sprint that far for that long.

"Krystal?" Gary looked furious when he saw me. "What are you doing here? I told you to stay back!"

"I didn't want to," I said quietly. "I wanted to help."

"You can't really do too much!" said James. "You don't have Soulpower, so you might not be able do anything."

"Did somebody say the magic word?"

All three of us then saw the man with the black trench coat walking over to us, carrying his sword. Everything inside of me cringed up.

"I believe you said something about Soulpower, correct?" he said coldly.

"That's right," said Gary sternly. "We know who you are, Dexter."

Dexter cackled menacingly. "You three are smarter than you look!"

"We came to end this crap," said James, "and we'll beat your ass into the ground!"

"Are you serious?" Dexter asked amusingly. "Do you truly think you can defeat me? Do you little boys even know how to use your Soulpower?"

"Of course," Gary told him, putting up his fists. I could tell he was lying. Gary and James were going to practice for the first time today, but went swimming instead.

"Oh yeah?" Dexter chuckled. "We'll just see about that!"

Instantly, Dexter thrust out his hand and did the same exact thing he did to Gary in the restaurant, except with a lot more energy. Gary went flying back and slammed against a tree. James ran up to Dexter and attempted to punch him, but Dexter dodged it and pushed James onto the ground. Gary ran to join in, but Dexter let out a big wave of energy that sent Gary and James flying back. I watched from a distance as the shockwave rippled across the ground towards me. It felt like a huge gust of hot air when it went past me.

"Take this!" Dexter shouted. He held up his sword, and a maelstrom of lightning bolts shot down out of the sky, blasting small craters in the ground. Gary managed to avoid them, and lunged at Dexter, who dodged every attack. Then James came from behind and tackled Dexter. I could see James trying to punch him in the face, but Dexter used an energy attack to blow James off of him.

Gary saw what happened to James, and somehow created a fireball in his hand. He looked a little surprised at first, but immediately pitched it at Dexter, striking him directly in the face. It exploded on impact, and Dexter stumbled back and angrily sent down another storm of lightning. Gary got hit by a bolt and staggered to his knees as the surge of electricity flowed through him.

As the battle raged I hid behind a tree. People were running for their lives as stray energy blasts and fireballs were flying everywhere. As I could see, Gary was the only one doing most of the successful damage to Dexter. James seemed to stumble around a lot, and Gary had to constantly protect him. Maybe it would take longer for James to learn how to unlock his Soulpower.

An energy ball from Dexter flew in my direction, hitting the tree I was hiding behind. I could hear the wood splinter and explode, and I ran away before it fell on me. Keeping an eye out for anymore danger, I took cover behind a bush. It wouldn't serve as very good protection, but at least I was hidden.

James tried to tackle Dexter again, but Dexter grabbed him and slammed him hard onto the ground. My heart started to pound as I saw Dexter lift his sword high over his head and point it directly at James.

"You good for nothing vermin!" he spat. "I'll kill you all!"

Before he could bring his sword down, Gary ran up and hit Dexter across the face with a flaming punch. Dexter fell to the ground, his sword coming out of his hand. Gary quickly picked it up before Dexter could get back to his feet. He glared at Gary, wiping the blood off his face. His cheek was burnt from Gary's fire.

"Give up, Dexter," said Gary. "You've lost."

Dexter growled angrily, and Gary pointed his sword at him, threatening him not to move. Knowing better, Dexter stayed where he was. He looked around, then spotted me in my hiding spot. Using another energy wave, Dexter caught Gary off guard and knocked him backward, then used the opportunity to jump back to his feet. I readied myself for the worst as Dexter charged at me faster than I've ever seen anyone run.

"Krystal, run!" Gary shouted. I took off as fast as I could. I could hear Dexter's feet pounding the ground behind me as I tried to get away from him. Just as it sounded like he was going to catch me, I saw a bright flash of light that erupted from behind me.

I turned around to see Dexter hunched over on the ground. His trench coat was burnt and smoldering. James was standing in a position about fifty yards back that suggested he had just used some sort of long range energy attack.

"Leave her alone!" James yelled angrily.

Dexter slowly stood back up, and James fired a bright beam of light out of his hands that struck Dexter in the back. It exploded with another brilliant flash, and Dexter fell to the ground. Gary, James, and I stood in our spots and watched him. After a few moments, we slowly walked over and stood around him. He groaned and twitched on the ground, but didn't show any signs of getting back up.

"I think we did it," said Gary.

"It's over," said James quietly. Then he pumped his fists into the air. "Yeah, rock on, baby! Oh yeah! Who's bad? *Who's bad*? We are! That's right!"

"That was it?" said Gary. "That seemed a little easier than what I expected."

"You did it!" I said happily. I hugged them both, feeling so glad that Dexter was done for.

"I can't believe it," said Gary. "We didn't even practice, and we beat him."

"Maybe he didn't practice much either," said James, prodding Dexter with his foot. "Tough talk for a wimp!"

"Okay," said Gary, looking around, "we'd better get out of here now, before the cops or something get here. We don't need this kind of attention."

I looked at Gary and smiled, and he smiled back. I gave him another hug.

"I'm so happy," I said. "Everything's going to be all right now, right?"

"I think so," said Gary.

"Hey, guys." James was rubbing his stomach. "I feel kind of funky."

Before any of us could react, James began to give off a bright golden glow. He slowly raised into the air, giving off a brilliant light like a second sun. His hair was flowing like he was underwater, and I could feel warmth radiating from him. Whatever was going on, I didn't feel threatened by it at all. In fact, it made me feel even better.

"What's going on?" said Gary in awe.

"I don't know," I replied quietly. "He's giving off good energy. It's…comforting, isn't it?"

James soon became completely engulfed in light. My whole body was filling with warmth and good feelings. Something was telling me that a very good thing was happening to James.

After a few seconds, he stopped glowing, and floated gently to the ground, holding an incredibly beautiful sword. The pearly white blade was polished to perfection. The gold handle was encased in a diamond coating and filled with glistening jewels. I'd never seen a more brilliant weapon, not even in the movies.

"What is this thing?" he said, examining it closely. "What just happened? Wait a minute. This sword is…Flare Blade."

Our time of confusion was interrupted by the sound of unenthusiastic clapping from one person. Zenox had come out of nowhere and was walking up to us.

"Very good," he said darkly, his creepy smile spreading across his face. "You have finally succeeded in becoming strong enough to defeat Dexter."

"You'd better believe it!" James cheered. "Check out this sword! It's awesome!" He instantly stopped smiling and stared at Zenox uncomfortably. He, too, felt the same thing I was feeling.

"What's wrong?" Zenox asked, advancing closer to us. A feeling of pure evil was flowing from him.

"Get back!" Gary warned, holding Dexter's sword out.

"Who are you?" I asked quietly. "That feeling…I've felt it before. Not just the other day when we met, but before that."

"Oh, really?" Zenox let out a dark, quiet laugh. "And where did you feel it before, my little sunshine?"

I thought it over. My mind searched every memory trying to find out where I had felt it. That haunting feeling of darkness and despair that filled my dreams. Suddenly, a cold feeling brewed in the pit of my stomach. I looked up at Zenox as he gave me his sinister smile.

"When my parents were killed…"

"What?" Gary gave me a very unsure look. "Krystal, what do you mean?"

"Darknae," said James quietly. "I can feel it."

"I remember it," I choked. "Darknae was there when they died."

"What are you two talking about?" Gary asked, sounding frightened.

"It's a long story, really," said Zenox, taking another step closer as we took another step back. "Do any of you know what a Rionah is?" We exchanged confused glances. "There are forces in the universe that most people are unaware of. These forces constantly oppose each other to maintain balance of the universe. A

Rionah is a person bestowed with the ability to control these forces, and you," he said, looking at James, "are the Rionah Luminae."

"What are you getting at?" James barked. "Quit beating around the bush and tell us who you really are!"

"I am Zenox," he replied, "the Rionah Darknae." My skin turned cold as he spoke more and more. "My goal is to crush the power of Luminae, the force of light, and make this my perfect world of darkness. I could sense Luminae in this town, but it wasn't concentrated enough for me to pinpoint."

"You're lying!" James shouted.

"That's not possible," said Gary in disbelief. "Y-you're making it all up!"

"I had to awaken the power of the Rionah Luminae," said Zenox, ignoring Gary and James, "so I hired someone who could use Soulpower to act as a threat. By putting the Rionah Luminae in danger, his power will awaken. All you needed was a little kick start from your Soulpower."

We heard a gasping sound behind us. Dexter had gotten back on his feet. His face was bloodied and bruised.

"You," he choked when he saw Zenox. "You used me."

"Yes," Zenox replied, grinning, "you were nothing more than my tool."

"You lied to me!" Dexter growled. "You told me these kids were going to expose me and put me back in prison."

"That's not true!" said Gary. "Zenox told us you were evil and wanted to use your Soulpower to hurt people!"

"I didn't tell you that," said Zenox. "You came to that conclusion on your own."

He held up his hand, and an ominous sword with a long, black, curved blade appeared, which he grasped tightly. It gave off a dark feeling that could only be described as the polar opposite of good.

"Shadow Blade," James murmured.

"Until the Rionah is at full strength," said Zenox, "killing him won't do me any good, so I needed to awaken his power. You must admit it was quite an ingenious plan. I was growing impatient and unable to control Darknae much more. It was beginning to cause some nasty weather, so I needed to find the Rionah Luminae quickly before these storms killed everyone for me."

"You bastard!" Dexter clutched his fists tightly.

"Would you rather go to prison?" Zenox laughed darkly.

"Be grateful, though. I let you have that car I confiscated from Base 15 years ago. A Zoe car is quite the gift, if you ask me."

Zoe car. I knew what they were…but at the same time I didn't.

"Base 15." Gary looked at Zenox with a disturbed expression. "It was destroyed a few years ago. Was that you?"

"Arrrgh!" Dexter snatched his sword from Gary and charged at Zenox. His fists were sparking with electricity as he swung his blade as hard as he could. Zenox blocked his attack with Shadow Blade and knocked Dexter onto the ground with a blast of dark energy. His moves looked completely effortless.

"My apologies," said Zenox, "but you are now insignificant."

He forcefully stabbed Dexter through the chest with Shadow Blade. Gary and James cringed at the sound of the blade going through flesh and Dexter's dying scream of pain. A blue flame poured from Shadow Blade as it stuck out of his chest and engulfed him. Seconds later, the flames disappeared and he was completely frozen. When Zenox ripped his sword from Dexter's chest, he shattered into thousands of pieces and evaporated into black smoke.

"He killed him," James croaked. "He killed him."

"How could you do that?" said Gary, clenching his fists.

"Everyone needs to have fun sometime," said Zenox. I was beginning to despise his grin. "You should try it sometime."

"*Shut up!*" James roared. "I've heard enough from you!"

He fired a long beam of light at a car from over fifty yards away and picked it up, much like a fish hooked on a fishing line, and flung it at Zenox. Zenox caught the car as if catching a baseball, then flung it back at James, who easily dodged it.

"I've waited too long for this!" said Zenox amusingly. "I will destroy Luminae. Now awaken and die."

He shot a beam of dark blue energy out of his sword, which James deflected into a small building. The walls exploded and the entire building collapsed.

Gary lunged at Zenox with flaming fists, but Zenox swung around and knocked him straight into the ground with a powerful blast of invisible energy. James fired another ball of energy at him, but Zenox hit it midair with his own energy blast, causing them both to blow up.

I tried to run away, but Zenox spun around and grabbed me

with his mind and held me up. It felt as if a huge hand had me by the throat. Before I could even think about what just happened, James hit Zenox with a bright blast of blinding light, freeing me. As soon as I hit the ground, I ran for cover behind a parked car on the other side of the street. Gary and James looked as if they were struggling, but Zenox made his fighting look easy. Just how powerful was Darknae?

Zenox caught Gary off guard and struck him with his sword. Instead of cutting through him, it let out an explosion of ice cold energy and sent Gary reeling into the air. He hit the ground and bounced. Zenox jumped over thirty feet into the air with a dark cloud of ominous energy billowing behind him. Gary narrowly avoided a downward stab into the ground, but a miniature earthquake erupted from Shadow Blade that ripped up the ground, sending Gary and James flying into the air.

"This is rather fun," said Zenox happily. "I'm enjoying this." He fired a beam of dark energy that hit James, sending him bouncing off the ground into the street. "Awaken your powers."

Gary attempted a sneak attack from behind, but Zenox simply spun around and backhanded him with immense force. I watched as Gary soared across the street and through the window of an electronics store. Immediately after going through the glass, there was huge fiery explosion as Gary burst through the wall, causing the entire building to collapse on one side. He staggered back into the street and collapsed. I could see he was bloody and beat up.

Once again, that furious rage surged through me. But instead of disappearing instantly like it did before, it exploded and filled me. When it went away, I looked at Zenox as he fended off James. My heart was so full of pain. Then I looked over at Gary again, and an excruciating pain burst inside me. I doubled over in pain, and a mixture of fury and despair swirled inside me. Almost as soon as it began, it disappeared. I looked back at Zenox who was taunting Gary and James.

Without thinking, I ran across the street and ripped a streetlight out of the ground and charged at Zenox. Wielding it like a baseball bat, I struck Zenox as hard as I could. He flew back and flipped off the ground. His expression was confusion, but quickly turned to amusement. He grabbed the other end of the street light and swung me straight up. While I was helplessly falling back down Zenox fired a ball of dark energy up at me. I attempted to knock it back with my bare hands, but it exploded on impact.

"Krystal!" Gary shouted as he watched me fall facedown onto the road.

I tasted blood as I stood back up. My hands felt like they had been blown off from trying to deflect Zenox's attack, but they were just fine, aside from being a little bloody.

"We're not doing so good!" James hollered. He tried some unsuccessful melee attacks on Zenox, but suffered a powerful dark energy attack to the chest. James soared down the road and slammed into a pickup truck, totaling it and flipping it over twice.

I charged Zenox again, but was hit by an energy blast. He grabbed me by the leg and swung me across the park onto the other side of the pond. I quickly stood back up just to see another dark energy ball flying at me from across the pond. The water underneath the energy ball was freezing as it got closer to me.

Holding out my hands, I wished I could just stop the attack. To my surprise, the energy ball actually slowed down as if I was emitting some invisible energy that was trying to push it back. My body began to get tired as I attempted to hold the attack back. After a while, I couldn't resist it anymore, and the dark energy ball hit me. A painful, icy cold explosion knocked me on my back. I was covered in extremely cold, blue fire that froze everything it touched. Rage surged through me for just an instant, and the fire and ice was blown off me.

I cheered inside my head, but was caught off guard when Zenox came straight down out of the sky on top of me. I jumped out of the way, but Zenox performed a series of punches and kicks on me, then was going to finish it by chopping me into cubes with his sword. Shadow Blade hit me on the shoulder, exploding and blowing me back again with another icy blast.

"You're lucky," said Zenox darkly, fending off James and tossing him into Gary like a bowling ball with a single fluent movement. His smile broadened. "You three have enough power to withstand the power of Shadow Blade. Instead of cutting you in half, it only explodes with emissions of Darknae energy."

I looked over at my shoulder, which had a layer of ice on it. I quickly brushed it off, avoided Zenox's sword, and counterattacked by punching him in the face. He stumbled back, smiled darkly, then grabbed me with his mind, lifted me straight into the air, and slammed me into the paved path that went through the park. My body created a small crater when I hit, and was unable to move for a while. Blood filled my mouth as the sound of Gary and James being knocked around filled my ears. Explosions echoed around me, and I could barely get up. When I did, the first thing I saw was a city bus come hurling towards me. Just before I was hit by it, Gary stood in front of it and knocked it aside, engulfing it in flames as it flew into the half-frozen pond and crashed through the ice. He ran over and helped me up.

"This is looking bad," he told me. Blood was dripping down his face, and he was completely covered with cuts. James was sent flying through the air towards us and landed on the ground right at our feet. He jumped up, and Zenox approached us. We all charged him, but he blasted us back with a single wave of powerful energy. I flew all the way out of the park and into the street, smashing into a building. James hit a palm tree, knocking it down, and Gary slammed into a car.

"What's this?" he asked with an evilly happy tone. "Am I too much for you? Pitiful. The Rionah Luminae is no good until you're at full power. I'll be back when you're ready. If you don't get stronger soon, I'll just destroy you and everyone you love. Take care, you hear?" He disappeared in a dark cloud of smoke, just as he did in front of my house.

The three of us stood in the middle of the wrecked and shredded streets, across from the park that lied in ruins. Smashed cars were burning everywhere, shattered glass glistened in the streets. Rubble and splintered wood was all over the place, and the three of us stood in the middle of it all, bleeding and hurting on the inside and outside.

CHAPTER EIGHT

Nine months had passed since the incident with Dexter and Zenox. It was the month of April, and the school year was going well. My grades managed to stay above average all year, which was good, considering that I hadn't slept much since that day in the park with Zenox. The moon still haunted me at night. I would stay up every night, waiting for the moon to sing its lullaby again. That's what killed my parents. I will never forget that.

Gary, James, and I had explained our injuries to our parents as being from skateboarding accidents with our other friends. It was hard to believe that we weren't killed after sustaining that kind of damage. Soulpower really was as amazing as Tyler had said. However, I didn't have Soulpower. What happened to me that day at the park? What was that energy that filled me?

Zenox was put on the backburner of our thoughts as the school year went on. The three of us decided it would be best to not worry so much about it. Nothing had come up since then that seemed Darknae-related, so we chose not to think much of it anymore, although Zenox's words still lingered over us. We knew that something would eventually need to be done.

"Krystal, could you answer the next question please?" Mr. Nohrm, the math teacher, was writing problems on the dry-erase board and calling random students to go up and do them. I looked up from my doodles on my paper, then stood up and slowly made my way up to the board.

"Go Krystal!" James whispered from behind me. Since he was terrible at math, he worshiped me like a queen in that class. I wasn't all that great myself, but that's how bad James was doing in that class.

I picked up the marker and started doing the problem. Everyone knew I was the slowest thinker in the class, so I never felt rushed. All those years of no sleep slowed down my thought processes.

"Very good," said Mr. Nohrm after I had finished the problem. "You may sit back down."

I headed back to my desk and sat down as Mr. Nohrm wrote the next problem on the board. James leaned over and patted me on the back.

"I don't know how you do it," he said.

"I don't know how you *can't* do it," said Nick jokingly. "This is easy stuff."

"It's not my fault," said James. "I'm not good at math, just video games."

"Until Krystal came along," said Nick. I turned around and smiled at Nick. He had such a good personality that I smiled at almost everything he said.

"Don't start with that," James groaned. "I'm still not over that."

"Thanks for volunteering, James," said the teacher. "You seem very interested in what I'm teaching, so why don't you do the next problem?"

"What?" James squeaked. "I didn't volunteer!"

The teacher crossed his arms. James groaned and stood up, then drug his feet to the front of the class. He took the marker from Mr. Nohrm, then stared at the problem. A few people snickered as he started writing random numbers on the board. When he wrote down the last number, he put the marker down and gave a stupidly triumphant grin. More people laughed.

"Did you even try?" the teacher asked, raising his eyebrow.

"Yes, I did," James answered. Then his face became serious. "It's wrong, isn't it?"

"Looks like it," Mr. Nohrm replied. The class laughed as James strolled back to his chair, acting as if he gave it his best shot and was cool about it.

The last forty-five minutes of the class breezed by quickly. Finally the bell rang, setting us free to lunch. Lunch was my half hour period to be with all of my friends. I loved being around them all, especially Gary. He seemed to be the only one who understood me and my insecurities. For some reason, I always felt safe around him. James also is a good friend, but a little too immature to give a good sense of security.

James, Nick, and I headed to the cafeteria and took our place in the lunch line. The menu was hanging overhead, and James was studying it.

"Aw, not meatloaf!" he said. "It tastes like rubber here."

"That's what everything in this school tastes like, bro," said Nick. He reached into his pocket, pulled out a comb, and began to slick back his hair. Nick practically combed his hair seven or eight times a day in school, and always wore the most fashionable clothes. The girls usually drooled over him, and I had to admit myself that he was very handsome.

The line moved up. I grabbed a tray from the stack, then started slopping random things onto it. James, who was carefully analyzing everything he put on his tray, looked over my shoulder and shook his head.

"Seriously," he told me, "you can eat anything, and lots of it. I don't know where you put it all! I thought I was an eating machine, but you're a black hole!"

I smiled, then grabbed a fork and looked for a place to sit. The usual spot was open, so I took my seat and started eating. James sat down across from me, then Nick sat down next to him. I looked back at the line to see where Gary was, and he was just picking up his tray. Gary had a longer way to walk to get to the cafeteria, so he usually joined us last. Stephanie came over and sat down on my left. Her boyfriend, Patrick, sat next to her. Stephanie met Patrick at the Christmas dance four months ago, and they became really close after that.

"I can't wait for spring vacation," said James, poking the meatloaf on his tray.

"Me too," Stephanie replied. "A full week to do nothing. Only two days away."

"It'll be my time to practice football," said Patrick. "I have to get ready for next season."

Gary came and sat down on my right. I smiled at him, and he smiled back.

"Say, Krystal," said Stephanie, "You should be a cheerleader next year. I had a lot of fun this year so far, and I think you'd like it."

"I don't know," I told her quietly. "I'm not active."

Stephanie looked a little disappointed. I wasn't the type of person to be a cheerleader. There was too much stuff going on inside my head to get involved in something like that.

When lunch ended, I headed to my locker to get my supplies for my next class. As I was rummaging through my heap of books and folders, someone came up and leaned against the next locker.

"Hey there," said Brandon. "Me and the guys are going to the bowling alley this weekend, and I wanted to see if you'd like to come."

I looked up and down the halls to see if Gary or James were

around. I didn't want them to see me around Brandon. He had started hanging around me a lot, but Gary and James didn't really like that very much. I didn't necessarily dislike Brandon, actually. He didn't seem as mean spirited as he did when he fought with Gary and James.

"I might have plans," I told him.

"Okay," he replied, "just tell me if you make up your mind. Catch ya later." He turned and walked off. I grabbed my things and headed off to biology, the same class that Brandon had that period.

I entered the room and took a seat in a desk at the back of the room. Brandon, who was sharpening his pencil, came over and sat down two desks away from me to my right. When I looked over at him, he gave me a friendly smile, so I smiled back.

When everyone had come in, the teacher passed out our assignment. I received my paper, then flipped open my book to look for the answers. As I was working, a paper airplane soared over and landed at my feet. I reached down and picked it up, then looked around the room to see who threw it. Everyone was working diligently, not talking or doing anything. My biology class was extremely well-behaved, and I never expected a paper airplane to fly in that room.

Curious, I unfolded the airplane, revealing a colored doodle of a grand piano with blood dripping out of the keys. The hair on the back of my neck stood up, and my heart began to beat faster. This was a picture from my haunting dreams. I looked around the room again, studying everyone to see if they were looking back at me. No one was.

I folded up the paper and stuffed it into my pocket, then wondered if I should tell Gary and James, or keep it a secret. Surely they would think I was paranoid, so I decided to keep it to myself. The last thing I wanted was to make them worry about me.

After school that day, I went to the school statue out front where I met Gary, James, Abby, Nick, Stephanie, and Patrick. That was our meeting place everyday before and after school. They were talking about the school dance coming up in a few weeks.

"I'm going to show off my smokin' moves there," said James smoothly.

"What smokin' moves?" Abby asked. "The best move I've seen you do was on roller blades."

"Roller blades?" Stephanie asked curiously.

"You should've seen it!" said Abby amusingly. "One leg

went one way, and the other went the opposite way!"

"Ha ha," said James indignantly. "That was an accident, and it hurt!"

"You may think you're the best," said Nick, "but I'm the smoothest one around."

"So, baby brother," said Abby, wrapping her arms around Gary from behind. She gave him a squeezing hug that turned his face purple. "Are you going to the school dance?"

Gary broke out of Abby's hold and gasped for air. I looked at him, eagerly awaiting his answer.

"I don't know," he said. "I don't have anyone to go with."

"Hmm," said Stephanie thoughtfully, "how about Monica?"

"She's not for him," said Patrick. "Believe me on this one."

"You could go with Angie," Nick suggested. "I'd go with her, but I've already got someone."

"Are you kidding?" said Gary. "She scares me. The last thing she said to me was that her dog was sexy. That's not right, man."

"How about Krystal!" James blurted. If anything could catch my attention, that remark worked like magic.

"Yeah!" said Stephanie. "You two have been friends for a long time!"

"Uh." Gary scratched his head. I could feel myself beginning to turn red.

"Hey, looky there," James teased, "Krystal's blushing!"

Gary looked right at me, and I immediately felt extremely embarrassed. For some reason, I began to smile uncontrollably, blushing like a ripe apple.

"Well," said Gary, scratching his head again. "I don't know if she'd want to. She's not the type to do things like that."

"I think she'll go," said Nick. "Look at her. I think she likes you."

Whether Nick's last comment was serious or a joke, I didn't want to be around Gary at that time any longer. I started to walk back home, trying hard not to make eye contact with anyone.

"Bye," I said, smiling and blushing against my will. I glanced back and saw that Gary was still watching me curiously, so I wheeled around and picked up the pace. Just before I was out of earshot, I thought I heard James whisper something.

"I think she likes you, Gary."

I hurried home, trying not to think about what had just happened. When I walked through the door into our living room, I noticed that Jack and Laura weren't home. Walking through the dining room, a small piece of paper sitting on the table caught my eye. It turned out to be a letter from them, saying that they had something come up at work, and wouldn't be home until late. They also apologized for not telling me, and how they were notified at the last minute.

My heart sank a little. The two of them were hardly ever home. Even when I was first adopted by them nearly four years ago, they had numerous business trips and meetings that were mandatory. I crumpled up the note and threw it away. Once in the kitchen, I took a look inside the fridge to find something to eat. Finding nothing, I opened the freezer. Still nothing.

I went around the kitchen, rummaging through the cabinets. The only thing I found was a box of ice cream cones. Feeling a little discouraged that Laura didn't leave me anything to eat, I ripped open the box and devoured its contents. Food seemed to be the best thing to keep me from being depressed, and I never gained hardly any weight. In fact, my doctor told me that I was perfectly healthy. At least, physically healthy.

After eating half the box of cones, I headed upstairs. The door to my room was wide open, and I tossed my backpack haphazardly onto the pile of clothes, books, papers, and other random accessories strewn across my floor, then thumbed through my organizer to find my English and social studies homework. My desk was piled with random papers and folders, so I pushed everything onto the floor to make room for me to do my homework. My drawing pad was in my drawer, so everything else was unimportant.

Just as I put my pencil to the paper, I remembered the drawing in my pocket. Reaching inside and pulling it out, I was just about to open it when I hesitated. Did I really want to see it again? The picture that depicted one of the images from my dream? I slowly began to open it, but I quickly stopped myself and ripped it apart. The pieces of confetti were put in my trashcan, and I started back on my homework.

My homework was completed in under an hour, and I put it back into my organizer for tomorrow. I looked over at my bed, which I hated. Ever since I started having those dreams I forced myself to stay awake. Dreams about the moon and Darknae were somewhat understandable, but that little girl, angels, operating rooms, and a black horse with wings were all unexplained. On top of that, what was that piano? I knew it played the moon's lullaby, but why?

I went downstairs to the living room and looked out the sliding glass door that led to our pool in the backyard. That dream I had about the little girl with wings on the other side of the pool...just who was she? Why was she in so many of my dreams and visions?

I opened the sliding glass door and stepped into the warm sun, which reflected off the surface of the water. My bare feet burned on the sun-baked cement, but I didn't think anything of the pain. The faint smell of chlorine mixed with the smell of cookouts and springtime. At the pool's edge, I kneeled down and swished my hand around in the water, watching the ripples spread across the surface. Standing back up, I shook my hand dry and headed back inside.

The couch seemed to be calling me, so I plopped down and stretched out. One of the thoughts that went through my head was how a lot of the people at school thought I was weird. I didn't wear any makeup or nail polish, I didn't have any earrings, I dressed like a boy sometimes, I never said a whole lot...the list went on. Personally, it made me feel alone and separate, but at least I had friends. Good friends at that.

The sound of the doorbell rang throughout the house. I jumped up and hurried to answer it, filled with joy and excitement that someone came to visit me. When I opened the door, Gary and James were standing outside.

"Hi," I said.

"Gary's here to ask you something," said James with a satisfied smile. "Aren't you?"

"Uh..." Gary sounded nervous, and I didn't have a clue to why. He was talking into the ground, not even looking at me. "I just wanted to know if...if you want to...you know..."

"No," said James, "she doesn't know."

"If you want to go to the dance with me." Gary started to turn red, just as I felt myself do the same.

"Sure," I said quietly, looking away.

"Okay," Gary replied. He looked up at me.

"Yeah," I said.

"Well...bye."

"Okay…bye."

Gary turned around and started walking away at a very quick pace. James was about to follow him when I stopped him.

"Can I ask you something?"

"Uh, yeah." I pulled him inside and closed the door.

"Does he *like* me?" I asked quietly. "Seriously, I want to know."

"Oh, me and him had this conversation before," James replied, looking a little entertained. "He, uh…no."

I felt a little depressed.

"Did he say so?"

"Actually, he did," said James. "A little while ago, I asked him if he liked you, and he said that he likes you only as a friend. Why?"

"No reason," I said quickly.

"Okay." Then James's face changed from confusion to comprehension. "Oh, I get it. You *do* like him, don't you?"

My face grew really red.

"No," I told him. "I was just curious. You know, that little conversation we had after school today. I just wanted to know, that's all."

James studied my face. "Okay. I know what you're saying." He looked around the room for a little bit, then changed the subject. "Hey, you remember that day, nine months ago, don't you?"

I was caught off guard by this question.

"Yeah," I replied curiously. "Why?"

"I was just wondering about what happened that day," he said thoughtfully. "The whole thing about Darknae. We should do some research on that, shouldn't we?"

Was I hearing correctly? James, of all people, wanted to do research on something.

"I guess so," I said.

The doorbell rang again. I opened it up to find Gary standing there.

"Of course we should," he said, stepping in. "We promised to work on that."

"What the?" James looked shocked and confused. "Where'd you come from? Were you standing outside the door and eavesdropping?"

"Next week," said Gary, "we start looking for answers."

"Oh boy," said James sarcastically. "We're going to spend our spring break just like our summer break. Whoop-de-doo."

"We'll see you tomorrow, Krystal," said Gary. He and James opened the door.

"Gary," I said, stopping him in his tracks. "Do you have anything to tell me?"

He looked perplexed. James looked at Gary eagerly.

"No," said Gary, "why?"

"Nothing," I replied. He and James looked at each other, then left.

As soon as the door closed, I quickly turned and looked through the glass sliding door at the pool. I had the feeling that something was watching me a moment ago. A vision flashed in front of me as I made my way up to my room. Just as I made it to the top of the stairs, the doorbell rang again.

Only this time, it was different.

I made my way back down the stairs, then looked at the front door. The silence was heavier than usual. When the doorbell rang, it sounded empty. Instead of the doorbell sounding like someone was coming by for a visit, it sounded as if someone was stalking me. I was picking up threatening vibes from the door, and I waited for it to ring again, but nothing happened. Slowly, I made my way over to the door. I gripped the doorknob tightly, then flung the door open.

Nothing.

Looking around, I didn't see anyone or anything. I closed the door, then started to go back upstairs when the doorbell rang again.

This time, I knew what that feeling was. It was Darknae, and it was toying with me. I felt the same empty, cold feeling that I experienced the night after the movies. The thought that Zenox was right outside my door with his sinister grin made me shiver. Zenox himself didn't frighten me, but Darknae did. I heard a noise in the living room. When I checked to see what it was, the sliding glass door to the pool was wide open.

My heart beating faster, I hurried over and closed it, taking good care of making sure it was locked. Cool air was beginning to surround me, and it wasn't the air conditioner. I began to shiver from the cold and from fright. Knowing that I probably wasn't safe in the house, I quickly decided to go to Gary's. Just as long as someone was with me, I would feel more comfortable. I hurried over to the door and grabbed the doorknob, just as a knocking sound came from the other side.

I jerked my hand off the doorknob and backed away. At that instant, the dark and threatening vibe disappeared. Hesitantly, I slowly walked up to the door, opened it, then shut it. Everything seemed safe and secure again, but I was still unconvinced that I was out of the forest.

Feeling as if I needed to rest a little, I headed back over to the couch and lied down. My entire body was trembling and I could start to feel sweat on my face. While I wiped it off with my hand, a blurred vision flashed in my mind. I grabbed my head, trying to make sense of why I was seeing visions that weren't clear. Ever since I learned about Soulpower the previous year they became a lot less frequent, but why didn't they go away like the visions Gary and James saw?

I felt safe enough not to go to Gary's. I was too afraid he and James would think I was weak. After my parents died, I trained myself to hide my emotions. At night, I'd cry alone in the dark until my pain was released, but after a while I found it harder and harder to cry until I couldn't anymore.

As I lied on the couch, I looked at the huge scar on my left hand. It was frustrating not knowing how I got such a big scar on my hand, or just a small one on my face.

For the next few hours, I stared up at the ceiling, pondering over all the things that didn't seem to make sense. Darknae, the moon, the piano, the horse, the little girl, operating rooms, my blurred visions…none of it fit together. I was being faced with one mystery after another, all of them were hitting me from different directions at the same time.

Out of nowhere, a piece of paper floated across the room and landed on the floor about six feet away from where I was lying. I stared at it, wondering where it came from, or how it even floated across the room without a breeze. As usual, curiosity overcame my fear. I got off the couch, went over and picked it up. It looked and felt like very old paper. It was covered in a yellowish tint and the edges were worn out and torn. Above all, it was blank. Flipping it over numerous times, I found nothing. I even held it up to the light, but no luck. Deciding that it wasn't dangerous, I took it up to my bedroom and set it on my desk. Then I went back downstairs to the couch, where I continued to think about things until Jack and Laura came home.

"How was your day, Krystal?" Laura asked at the dinner table.

"Fine," I said timidly.

"Nothing interesting happened at all?" Jack asked.

"No," I lied. "Nothing."

"Well," said Laura, "Jack and I have to go on a business trip this coming Monday and we won't be back until Thursday."

I think they waited for me to say something, but I had nothing to say at all.

"It's to Oregon," Jack added, apparently to make me interested. "And this time, we want to know if you'd like to come with us."

I wanted to tell them yes, but then I thought about all of the things going on.

"No," I muttered, poking at my mashed potatoes.

"Why not?" Laura asked, sounding astonished. "You can stay in a hotel. We'll be able to go sightseeing and hiking. We could even rent a kayak or a canoe to take down a river. Wouldn't that be fun?"

"I want to stay here," I said politely. "It sounds like fun, but I have things to do."

"Oh, homework, eh?" said Jack. "Well, I understand. Maybe some other time."

"You'll be okay by yourself?" Laura asked. "It's a four day trip."

"I'll be fine," I assured. "I'm a big girl."

"Well, in that case," said Laura to Jack, "you'd better buy only two plane tickets."

"Yeah, okay." Jack wiped off his mouth with his napkin. "Hey, Krystal, you've never been on a plane before, have you?"

"Not that I remember," I said.

"You'll have to go somewhere with us sometime," he said. "They aren't that bad."

"Hmm, sure," I mumbled. "May I leave the table?"

"Go ahead," said Laura.

I got up and took my dishes to the kitchen where I placed them in the sink. Then I trudged upstairs to my room and landed on my bed. The evening sun was pouring through my window. It was going to set soon, and I was going to have to spend another long and lonely night awake.

CHAPTER NINE

Gary and James found a clear spot in the woods that separated the town from the city, and we used it to train ourselves without anyone knowing. Being able to use more Soulpower in combat increased our speed, both physically and mentally.

"How much longer until we can move things with our minds?" James asked while we were out training. "I'm tired of using my sword all the time."

"I don't know," Gary replied. He created a fireball and pitched it at James, who used his beautiful, glistening sword to bat it up over the trees.

"Holy cow!" James exclaimed. "You can throw those things fast now!"

"Maybe I should go out for baseball," said Gary with a laugh. "I wonder if fireballs are all I can do, and that we each have different abilities."

"I think we might," said James. He thrust out his hand, firing a beam of light at a nearby tree, making it splinter straight up the trunk and fall down in two halves. "You can't do that, but I can't make fireball thingies."

"You don't need Soulpower," said Gary. "You have that Luminae power."

"Hey, Krystal," said James, "what can you do?"

I looked over at James.

"I don't know," I replied. If Gary didn't know what all he could do, how could I? I didn't even use Soulpower. I wanted to tell them that I didn't think my power was the same as Gary's, but I didn't think there was a need to.

"Well, try something," James urged. "Experiment with stuff."

"I can't use energy attacks," I told him. "I think I can only do physical things."

"She has a point," said Gary. "She can run a lot faster, and can lift heavier objects. I can't beat her at arm wrestling, either."

"Ha! That's kind of funny," James chortled. "You mean to say that she's got those scrawny little arms, but she's stronger than both of us? That's...hey, wait. That's not cool, man! She's stronger than us!"

"Only physically," said Gary. "Remember, she can't use long-range attacks like us."

"Does that mean she won't be able to use her mind to move things?" James asked.

Gary turned his eyes towards me.

"I'm not sure," he said finally. "I guess we'll have to train more to—"

A vision flashed in front of me. James looked a little upset. Did he see it too?

"Ugh," he mumbled.

"What's wrong now?" Gary asked impatiently.

"I'm hungry," James replied.

"When are you not hungry?" said Gary, rolling his eyes. "How long have we been out here?"

"A few hours," said James. "It's past lunchtime. Let's call it a day and go back into town."

I felt disappointed. I was the only one seeing these visions now. Tyler had said that until we learned about our souls we'd continue to see visions. Did that mean there was more left for me to learn?

We had gotten new bikes near the end of summer last year to ride around on, which was our best mode of transportation to and from our training spot. Although they were really handy, we still preferred walking through town sometimes, so we only occasionally used our bikes. There was something nostalgic about walking and taking your time to enjoy the world around you.

The three of us hopped on our bikes and rode back into town for lunch. Even though we had our bikes, and our Soulpower allowed us to ride faster for longer periods of time, it still took a while to make it to the Shady Palm Café, especially since we decided it was best to avoid letting people know about our powers. Putting our bikes on the side of the restaurant, we walked up to the entrance, only to find Bernie locking the doors.

"Hey, what're you doing?" James asked. "It's not closing time yet."

"I'm afraid it is," said Bernie sadly. "I'm glad you three came by here just in time before I left."

"Why?" Gary asked. "Are you out of business?"

Bernie looked away and let out a deep, sorrowful sigh.

"W-what?" James sputtered. "But…why?"

I could tell that Gary and James were upset. They'd obviously been going to the Shady Palm Café for years, and they had grown close to Bernie. Their responses were to be expected. Even I felt a little disappointed.

"My aunt got sick a few years ago," Bernie explained dismally, "and when she passed away, I received the house. I've been trying to sell it ever since. There wasn't quite enough money to pay for the house and keep up with my business."

"You were the owner of this restaurant?" Gary asked. "I didn't know that. I thought you just worked here."

"When I had to close the restaurant for a few weeks after the incident last year," Bernie continued, "it really hurt my business. No one would have guessed that the Shady Palm was going downhill with all of the customers we had, but in the end, there just wasn't enough money to pay for the expenses."

"No, you can't close!" James told him.

"Yeah," said Gary. "We'll help you around the restaurant for free! I'm positive we'll be able to get you back in business!"

"Thanks, you two," said Bernie, "but I don't think that will be enough." He gazed through the windows into the empty, dark restaurant. "You did enough already. If you three didn't come here as much as you did, I'd have gone out of business a long time ago."

"Wait," said Gary as Bernie turned and started to walk off, "what are you going to do now?"

"I'll have to find another job somewhere else," he said.

"But…we'll still see you around, won't we?"

Bernie paused to think about it.

"I really don't know," he replied sadly. "You kids look after yourselves."

He turned around and walked over to his car. We stood on the sidewalk and watched as Bernie pulled out of the parking spot and drove down the street.

"Hey, what's going on over here?" Nick happened to be walking by and noticed us standing in front of the closed restaurant. "Is this place closed?"

"Yep," said James dully. "They just went out of business."

"Wow, bummer," Nick replied. "I kind of liked this place."

"Were you going to come here, too?" Gary asked.

"Nah, I was on my way to the supermarket." When he saw me, he said, "Yo, Brandon wanted me to ask you something."

"No, not Brandon," James groaned. "He's not going to give up, is he?"

"He wants you to swing by his house sometime," Nick told me. He took out a comb and messed with his hair, which really didn't need anymore fixing.

"Oh," I said, "okay."

"No, you're not," said James. "What's he want, anyway?"

"Beats me," said Nick. "I asked him the same thing, but he said that he didn't want to say why. I don't know, I just did what he asked, that's all."

"I think we should let her do it," said Gary.

"Are you crazy?" said James.

"We can go along with her," said Gary. "That way we'll know she's safe."

"I don't think you should do that," said Nick. "He wants Krystal alone."

"Doesn't that sound suspicious?" said James. "Think about it, man!"

"Well, if that's the case," said Gary, "then it's probably not a good idea to let the two of them be alone."

"Fine with me," said Nick. "It's none of my business, anyway. I'll catch you guys later."

After Nick had left, Gary and James put their faces against the windows and peered in at the restaurant.

"Man," said James. "I never thought this place would close."

Without warning, a vision flashed in front of me, catching me off guard. However, I wasn't caught off guard by the vision itself, but by what I saw. Instead of appearing as a blur, it was perfectly clear; an old bloodstained grand piano...the same one in the drawing. I looked at Gary and James to see their reactions, but they continued looking through the window. They didn't see it.

Then it happened again. The other two still didn't seem to notice. Again, the vision flashed. Did I see the same piano in my dreams? The vision flashed again. Had I seen it before somewhere? Then again. Then once more.

I grabbed my head as it started to spin. The visions kept coming, playing like a broken movie in front of me. Blood gushed out of the piano, pouring onto the floor. Lightning seemed to come out of the very walls. My skin crawled as the temperature dropped. I could hear voices...angry voices...scared voices. Death, darkness, blood. Death, darkness, blood. Death, darkness, blood, angels, voices, tranquilizers, moon, piano, horse...

Everything had gone away. I was back on the sidewalk with Gary and James.

"Are you hot or something?" Gary asked me. "You're sweating."

"Huh?" I wiped the sweat off my face. "Oh, I'm fine. Yeah, it's just a little hot out here."

"And I'm still hungry," James mumbled. "Where are we going to eat now?"

Gary scratched his head, looked up and down the road, then shrugged.

"I don't know," he said. "I guess we could go get tacos."

"At that Mexican place?" James replied, screwing up his face in disgust. "That place messes with my insides, man."

"It's just around the block," said Gary. "You told me that you've been there a lot with your parents."

"And I had diarrhea a lot with my parents," said James stubbornly. "We can try that Mario's Italian restaurant."

"That's a little expensive, isn't it?" said Gary, wrinkling his forehead. "It's a real restaurant, not a fast food place."

"Well, what else is there?" James grumbled. "I'm hungry, and there's no place to go now."

"I guess all we can do for now is go to the beach," Gary suggested. "They've got hotdogs and nachos."

"Uh, fine," James agreed, sounding a little disappointed. "I really want to go to that Italian place, though..."

"It's too expensive!" said Gary irritably. "We're not going there."

"I have enough money," I told him.

Gary looked puzzled. "You do? Where'd you get it?"

I thought about it for a while. I had received a lot of money a few years back, but never told anyone about it. Did I really want to tell him where I got it? No.

"Birthday money," I lied. "I kept it over the years."

"Oh yeah!" said James happily. "How much do you have?"

I thought about that one too. Did I really want to tell him how much I had? No.

"Sixty dollars," I told him.

"Whoa," James replied in amazement. "That's more than I've ever had all at once."

"Hold on, Krystal," said Gary. "You don't have to do this for us."

"Yes you do," James added quickly.

"It's your birthday money that you've saved over the years," said Gary.

"And she's going to spend it on food for us," said James.

"You should spend it on something you really want."

"Like food."

"James! Shut up!"

"Foooooooooooooooood…"

Gary reached over and smacked James on the back of the head, but James only seemed amused by it.

"Hey man, I'll stop, I'll stop."

"Don't worry about it, Gary," I said sweetly. "You two are my friends. If you want me to spend it on something I want, then I want to spend it on you."

"Yeah, Krystal!" James cheered. "You rock!" He started dancing around on the sidewalk, chanting the word 'food'. A man who was getting a newspaper across the street looked over at us.

"Well, if you say so," said Gary, smiling.

"Let's go back to my place," I said, "so I can get my money."

We jumped on our bikes and took off to my house. When we got there, I told Gary and James to wait outside while I run up to my room. I hurried upstairs to my closet and started rummaging through a bunch of stuff that I never touched in years. Jack and Laura always told me that I was packrat, but everything I was ever given is connected to me by a touch of sentiment. At last, I found the large stainless steel box where the money was, pulled it out, and looked at it. Running my fingers over the words "Property of the United States Government", I tried to remember how I got it, but no luck. Still, it was my secret and no one was to know I had it, and if they found out, I wasn't planning on telling the truth.

A vision flashed in front of me and lasted not even a fraction of a second. Ignoring it, I opened the lid and looked at the thousands of dollars inside. I took out twenty bucks and stuffed it in my pocket, then returned the box to where it was hidden in the back of my closet. I hurried down the stairs and back outside where Gary and James where waiting.

"Did you get it?" James asked eagerly. When I nodded, he said, "All right, let's go! I'm hungry."

Gary looked at me and shook his head. I couldn't help but smile a little.

As we were about to get on our bikes, I felt the money in my pocket and automatically thought about the stainless steel box I held it in. Another vision came across me quicker than a flash of lightning. So many visions lately, and I had no idea what they were about.

"What's wrong?" James asked me. "You look…funny."

"Nothing," I said, smiling. "Let's go to the beach."

I followed Gary and James down the street on our bikes. As we rode through town, I couldn't help but wonder when it'd be a good time to tell the boys about my visions. Whenever it was, it would have to be soon.

"We're here," said Gary, stopping his bike. The salty breeze calmed me as it filled my lungs, and the sounds of the ocean soothed my mind.

"You guys wanna walk?" James asked. "It's better to stroll around here, anyway."

"Yeah, okay," Gary replied.

We put our bikes in one of the bike racks and began walking down the beach's sidewalk. There were quite a few people there despite the fact it wasn't quite summer yet. That was a major difference between Florida and Michigan, I guess.

It was my first time to the concession stands at the beach, and Gary and James showed me around. I was surprised at how big the area was. Gary explained the place was really busy in the summer and we'd have to come back for me to enjoy the true experience.

James stopped in front of one of the stands selling nachos. Using my twenty dollars, I bought us each an order of nachos and small drinks. Then we all took a seat on a bench facing out towards the ocean.

"Thanks, Krystal," said Gary.

"Yeah, thanks!" James cheered. "Food, food, I love food! And I love you too, Krystal, for giving me this to buy the thing I love!"

"No problem," I said, smiling.

The ocean was beautiful. I could sit and stare at the flowing water forever. Something about it brought a powerful sense of serenity to my heart. Some birds flew past overhead. A small breeze rustled the palm trees before rustling my hair.

Like a hole burnt through the middle of a perfect photograph, a vision ripped through my peaceful moment. Feeling my appetite dying with my tranquility, I quietly stood up, walked to a nearby trashcan, then dumped the rest of my nachos and drink in it.

"Not hungry?" Gary asked me as I walked back.

"What's up?" James asked when I didn't answer. "You look funny again."

"The vision," I said slowly, thinking it was time to let them know. When their faces looked more confused, I quickly added, "Just a few seconds ago. Didn't you see it?"

"I didn't see any visions since last year," said James.

"You didn't?" I asked, feeling a little uneasy. I really was the only one who saw them all.

"What was it?" Gary asked concernedly. "Could you make it out?"

"No," I said quietly. "I've seen a lot of visions since then, and I didn't know if you two saw them too."

"Why didn't you tell us?" Gary asked. He pressed his hand on my forehead. "This isn't good. James, we have to go see Tyler."

"Why is this only happening to me?" I asked Gary in a whisper. There was nothing I could do to keep back the hint of fear in my voice.

"I don't know," said Gary, "but Tyler might know something. He seems to know more about these kinds of things than anyone else. Let's go."

The three of us got on our bikes and hurried off to the antique store. When we arrived, Tyler was sorting through a pile of old books. He gave us a big smile when he saw us.

"Oh, hello!" he greeted. "I haven't seen you youngsters in quite some time now!"

"How're you doing?" Gary asked.

"Oh, pretty good," said Tyler. "Just the same ol' thing I've been doing for a while. Keeping up the store, ya know?"

"That's good," said Gary. "We have something we wanna ask you."

"What's the matter?" Tyler asked, immediately putting down the book he was examining. "You look a little desperate."

"You told us about the visions we saw," said Gary, trying to sound as calm as he could, "and said that they're caused when our souls want us to know something about them."

"Go on," Tyler urged, looking both interested and worried.

"Just today, Krystal told us that she's been having visions, but me and James didn't see them. Do you know what that could

112

mean?"

Tyler seemed to be in deep concentration for a short moment.

"They're not as blurred anymore," I said. "They used to be hard to make out, but I can see them really well now."

"All I can bring to conclusion is that her soul is trying to tell her something," said Tyler, rubbing his chin. Gary looked as if he had just been given a very obvious answer that he hadn't thought of. "It's only natural that she would have some vision that you two don't have."

"But why would our souls wait so long to tell us that?" Gary asked. "If we were able to use Soulpower, why did it take so long for our souls to try to tell us?"

"They probably only responded to danger," said Tyler.

"You mean to Darknae?" James asked.

Tyler looked at James with a shocked expression.

"What did you just say?" he asked.

"Uh," said James, scratching his head, "do you think our souls responded to Darknae? What, have you heard of it?"

"How do you kids know about Darknae?" Tyler asked, looking at us suspiciously.

"Well," said Gary, "it's a long story."

"You three should come look at something I found in an old book," said Tyler. "Come on back and I'll show you."

Gary and I followed Tyler to the back of the store. James gave a look of impatience, then followed behind me. Tyler gestured to us to sit down around the table in the backroom. He took a large book that looked worn by a considerable amount of age and rested it on the table. When we were all seated, he opened the book to a previously marked page and turned it around so that the three of us could see. We all leaned forward over the table to get a better look. The pages were yellowed and worn around the edges, and the handwritten words were in a strange language that I didn't understand. Somehow, the paper looked familiar.

"Hey, it's in Spanish," said James. "Wait, that's not Spanish, is it?"

"It's Latin," said Gary, scanning the page with his eyes. "You can read Latin?"

Tyler nodded. "Not very much, just a little. But this book mentions Darknae."

"What's it say?" James asked.

"Most of it is worn out and beat up," said Tyler. "All I could get out of it is that Darknae and Luminae are opposing forces or something like that. Let's see, Luminae commands the White Phoenix, and I think it says Darknae controls something else."

"What about that?" Gary asked, pointing out a phrase scribbled in the margins. "I see the word Darknae written in it."

"Let's see," said Tyler, "it says that when the moon sings, Darknae takes your soul."

I couldn't believe what I had just heard. Gary and James both knew what I thinking. It was the same phrase that I remembered hearing but didn't know from where.

"Where'd you get this book?" I asked.

"It was early last summer," said Tyler. "I got it in an anonymous package one day. This book was in it, and I couldn't refuse an old book like this, so I kept it."

"How old do you think it is?" Gary asked. "It looks pretty old."

"Well, actually," said Tyler, flipping through the pages, "I don't think it's more than ten or twenty years old. It just looks really old because it's beat up."

"Huh, weird." James ran his fingers along the book's edge. "Why would somebody write it in Latin then? Maybe if it was really old, but Latin's a dead language nowadays. And why wouldn't they just type it instead of write it by hand?"

"I don't really know," said Gary.

"Can I see it?" I asked. Tyler nodded and I pulled it closer and started going through the pages. I wasn't sure what I was looking for, or if I'd be able to read it at all. Gary, James, and Tyler were discussing the book while I examined it. As I was flipping through it I came to a page that was torn out. A vision of an old piano flickered in front of me, reminding me of what I had in my pocket.

"Tyler," I said, "you said you had a page missing from that book."

"Right," said Tyler, looking at me closely.

I dug into my pocket and pulled out the blank paper that floated out of nowhere in my living room. I carried it with me ever since I found it in case I had a use for it. As luck would have it, I actually found a use for an old piece of paper.

"I think I have it." I showed him the blank page I was holding.

"There's nothing on it," he said, taking it from me and looking at both sides, "but it looks and feels the same as the rest of the pages. Hold on."

He took the book and placed the page in its place where the torn part was. Just as I had thought, it was the perfect size, and the torn side fit like a puzzle. To our surprise, the page immediately bound itself back into the book, completely patching up the tear as if the page had never been removed.

"Did you see that?" said James excitedly. "That was cool!"

"I'm not sure if I'd describe it the same way," said Gary quietly.

A picture started to form on the page as if a dozen invisible pens were drawing on it. The four of us were now leaning directly over the book, watching as the page's contents came out of nowhere. When the picture was done, the other three were completely awestruck. However, my heart skipped a beat.

"A grand piano?" said Gary quietly after a few seconds of silence. "Krystal, where did you get this paper?"

It took a second or two for me to be able to talk.

"I found it in my living room," I told him. "I was on my couch, and it drifted out of nowhere." I shook my head, trying to get over the uneasy feeling bubbling in my stomach. "When I was in school the other day, a paper airplane came to me…" I trailed off, thinking about the piano sketch on it. "The picture drawn on it had this piano on it, but it had blood all over it."

"Do you still have it?" Tyler asked me.

"No," I said. "I ripped it up."

"But, what's this picture doing here?" Gary asked, looking closer at the picture in the book that we had just watched draw itself. "What's it mean? Kinda creepy, don't ya think?"

"Ya think?" James looked really unsettled.

"I see it in my visions," I added. "The ones only I see."

The three of them looked at me, and I avoided their eyes.

"This is getting really strange," said Gary quietly. "Krystal, who are you?"

I looked directly into Gary's eyes. They were both confused and frightened. I just shook my head and looked back at the picture. Who was I? Not even I knew.

"I don't know," I whispered.

I tried to think about my life over the past years since my parents were killed. Then I realized something. I couldn't remember the six years in between. My parents were killed when I was six…then I moved to Michigan with Jack and Laura when I was twelve. There wasn't a single memory of anything between then. I couldn't believe I never noticed that before. What happened to my memories? Oh well.

My eyes once again became transfixed on the picture of the old grand piano. This particular drawing was sketched very well, and the piano looked nice, clean, and in good condition. The picture that was on the paper airplane was poorly drawn and the piano was damaged, worn, and bloody. Then there was the one in my visions that gushed blood out onto the floor. Somehow, I knew it was the same piano.

"That thing creeps me out," said James, looking back at the book. "I really don't know what's going on here, but I don't like it."

"Let's get going," said Gary. "If anything else comes up, Tyler, let's keep each other informed."

"Right," said Tyler. "Hope you find out what you're looking for. Take care."

I tore my attention from the book and left with Gary and James. We climbed onto our bikes and headed to the park. The three of us parked our bikes in a secluded area by the pond.

"I think we should think this over," said Gary. "It'd be best to recap on everything that's happened to us so far. So, the three of us have this special power, right?"

"Soulpower," I said.

"That's what we started with," said Gary, "but James doesn't need it anymore, because he has the power of Luminae. It's the opposite of Darknae. Both are forces that balance the universe, and that's about all we know about that."

"I'm a Rionah!" said James, sounding important. "The Rionah Luminae."

"We know that a Rionah is someone who can use these forces of the universe," Gary continued. "James is the Rionah Luminae, and Zenox is the Rionah Darknae.

"Zenox's goal is to crush Luminae with the power of Darknae, but he needed to awaken the Luminae powers inside James first. Unless the Rionah Luminae's powers are fully awakened, it won't do any good to kill him."

"Uh, yeah," James replied weakly.

"In order to awaken the Luminae power in James, he needed to be in danger and put under stress, so Zenox used Dexter for that. Dexter could use Soulpower, and Zenox knew that only someone with the same power as us could threaten us. Zenox set us up to believe we were enemies so we'd fight and awaken Luminae. Also, since he didn't know exactly who the Rionah Luminae was, he targeted the entire town and eventually narrowed it down to us.

"As for the bad weather we had last summer, Zenox said it was the power of Darknae going out of control because it needed to oppose Luminae.

"Now, about our visions. We saw them because our souls were trying to warn us of the oncoming threat. At the time, we thought the threat was Dexter, but learned it was really Zenox and Darknae. After learning what the threat was, the visions went away for me and James, but not Krystal. That's probably because her soul is still trying to tell her something else."

"But why aren't our souls telling us anything?" James asked.

"They probably only have something to do with Krystal," said Gary.

"Okay," said James, "what about that car Zenox gave Dexter? That black one."

"It was a Zoe car," I said. "I know it from somewhere, but I don't remember anything about it."

"Zenox said he took it from Base 15 a few years prior," said Gary. "It just so happens that Base 15 was destroyed around that time. Since we don't really know anymore about it, let's set that aside for now."

I never knew how good Gary was at putting things together like that. He sounded like some kind of detective. But something was still bothering me. Tyler could sense Soulpower, but didn't sense it in me. Also, my power was different from the boys' powers. Just what exactly was my power anyway? And why could I sense Darknae? My parents were killed by Darknae. Did something rub off on me?

A terrible feeling sank into my stomach. I looked at James, and I knew he felt the same thing.

"What is it?" Gary asked concernedly.

"Darknae," said James quietly.

Without a second thought, we all jumped onto our bikes and pedaled as fast as we could through the streets. Everything was a blur as we zoomed past so fast that I could hardly hear anything else over the wind in my ears. I had no clue exactly where I was going, but let my instinct guide me.

In what seemed like no time at all, we found ourselves in front of James's house. Without slowing down the least bit, we jumped off our bikes and ran full speed to the front door. Our bikes were going so fast that Gary's burst apart when it came in contact with a tree, which made a loud splintering noise. James flung the door open and ran into his house ahead of me and Gary. The air was icy cold. We ran into the kitchen and stopped instantly in the doorway.

My mouth dried up and my insides turned upside down. Gary let out a small gasp and took a step back. James stood frozen in place. The beautiful sword Flare Blade that he had acquired nine months ago had appeared in his hand once again. His lips quivered as he croaked his only word.

"M-Mom?"

James's mother lay on the kitchen floor in a pool of her own blood, dead. Her body was slashed open, and blood trickled down the side of the counter. A taped-together shredded piece of paper lay at our feet. I had seen that paper before. The doodled piano was as bloody as the kitchen.

CHAPTER TEN

I sat next to Gary on the curb in front of James's house. The police were investigating the house as the paramedics carried out the black body bag. James's dad had come home from the store about half an hour ago. He was holding James tightly in his arms and being interviewed by an officer. The news crew had just arrived and was setting up cameras. A couple of reporters from the newspaper were taking pictures while the others scribbled on a notepad. People had left their homes and gathered around to see what was going on. A car pulled up and screeched to a halt. Gary's parents and sister all burst out and ran over to us.

"We heard what happened," said Gary's mom worriedly, wrapping her arms around him. Gary's dad hugged him after his mom let go, and Abby's surprised eyes darted around the scene.

"Do you know how it happened?" Abby asked me quickly.

"No," I replied. We looked over at James who pointed us out unenthusiastically to a group of news reporters, then buried his face in his dad's chest. The reporters hurried over to us, crowding me and Gary with microphones, cameras, recorders, and questions.

"What happened here?"

"What do you have to say about this?"

"Do you have any comments for us?"

I glanced over at Gary, who glanced back.

"We found her in the kitchen," Gary replied flatly.

"What were you doing in the house?"

"Is there anything else?"

"How long have you known her?"

"Look," said Gary gruffly, "it's been a long day." As soon as he left, the media's attention zeroed in on me.

"I..." My voice died and my face turned red. I hated a great deal of this kind of attention. Without answering a single question, I turned and followed Gary back to his parents. Looking over to see where James was, he was going back into the house with his dad and some policemen. Even though he didn't look in our direction, it was clear that he was crying. Gary hurried over to him, but was stopped by the crime scene investigators. He walked back to his parents.

"Mom? Dad?"

"What is it?" his dad asked.

"Krystal's parents are gone on a business trip for the week," said Gary. "If it's okay, can she stay with us until they come back? That way she doesn't have to be alone."

I looked at Gary, who looked back at me with a heart-warming smile. What he had asked his parents was the very best thing I heard in a long time, and I felt a strong sense of care from him.

"Well, I don't see why not," his mom replied, trying her best to smile. "Would you like to, Krystal?"

"Y-yes," I said almost immediately. I noticed that Abby was smiling at her brother, but it was a kind smile, not a teasing one. She was obviously glad that Gary had offered to do something so generous, and so was I.

"Well, get in," said Gary's dad, opening the back door of the car for me. I climbed in and sat between Gary and Abby.

"Can I pick up some stuff at my house?" I asked as we made our way back to Gary's house.

"Sure thing," said Gary's dad.

"It'll be like a sleepover," Abby told me. "You're like my little sister for the week!"

I smiled at her. I was an only child and sometimes got really lonely. Thinking of Abby as my sister was a very nice thought.

After we reached my house I hurried inside up to my room, found a large grocery bag, and piled random clean clothes into it. I ran back outside, put the key to the house under the welcome mat, then locked the door. Ever since Gary showed me where he put his key, I started doing the same thing.

The sun was beginning to reach the horizon when we made it to Gary's house. When I walked in the door, I could smell 3omcthing cooking.

"This is the first time you've been here in a while, isn't it?" said Gary.

"Yeah," I said. The last time I was in Gary's house was last year when I first met him and James. "It's nice."

"Well, it usually isn't," said Abby. "Mom was in one of her cleaning moods yesterday and made the whole house spotless. Hey, Gary, why don't you get Krystal situated before dinner."

"Okay," he said, taking my bag. "We have a guest room upstairs for our grandparents when they visit during the holidays. Follow me."

I went with Gary up to the second floor and down the hallway. He led me into the last room, where he put my bag next to the bed.

"We have extra blankets in the closet over there," he told me.

"Thanks," I said sweetly, giving him the same smile I usually give him. He seemed to blush a little.

"I'll be downstairs," he told me, turning to leave. "If you need anything, just say so."

"Wait," I said just before he left.

"What is it?"

"Do you think James will be okay?"

Gary didn't answer right away, but seemed to think about it first.

"Of course," he said, but his face and tone said otherwise. "He's with his dad. We should probably go check on him tomorrow."

"Yeah." I looked away, not wanting Gary to see my sorrow.

"Look," he said warmly, putting his hands on my shoulders, "why don't you just take a shower and relax. Try not to think too much about it. Dinner should be ready in about forty-five minutes. I'll get you a towel."

He left the room for a few seconds, then came back and handed me a towel. I smiled again, and he smiled back just before he turned and walked out. Grabbing some clothes out of my bag, I followed him into the hall and watched him go down the stairs before going into the bathroom.

After my shower I made my way downstairs and into the kitchen. Abby, who was helping her mom in the kitchen, noticed me come in.

"Just a few more minutes," she said, taking something out of the oven.

"Why don't you go sit at the table, sweetie," Gary's mom told me while she mashed a big bowl of potatoes. "Dinner should be ready shortly."

I walked over to the table and took a seat. Gary had just walked into the room and sat in the chair next to mine. Although he drummed his fingers on the table, never looking in my direction, I knew he was paying full attention to me.

Gary's dad walked into the room and took a sniff of the air.

"Smells good," he said. When he looked over at me and

Gary sitting next to each other at the table, a grin spread across his face. He came over and took a seat across from us. "So, how long have you two been friends?"

"Since she moved here last summer," Gary answered.

"Oh, so for a while now," his dad replied interestedly. "Krystal, is it? Where'd you move from?"

"Michigan," I said automatically. Gary glanced at me, knowing that I said Jack and Laura were from Michigan. I was only adopted by them.

"All the way from Michigan, then," said Gary's dad.

"How do you like it here in Florida?" Gary's mom asked, bringing the steaming bowl of mashed potatoes to the table.

"It's good," I told her.

"You've never been much of talker," said Abby, setting a roast on the table. "I never would have guessed you'd be one of Gary's friends. All of his other ones flap their mouths constantly."

"Like yours don't," Gary snapped. "I won't forget that birthday party. They wouldn't shut up."

"That's because they all thought you were so adorable," Abby replied in a baby-talk voice, rustling his hair. When I giggled, he turned red and sank a little into his chair.

"I think we should say grace," Gary's mom announced. "After all, a tragedy had just occurred and we have a guest." She smiled at me. "Why don't you say it, Gary?"

Gary seemed a little surprised at this request. He immediately sat up and clasped his hands together, then the rest of us did the same. After he cleared his throat, he said grace (and did so as if he'd done it many times before), and we started helping ourselves to the food.

It was the first time I'd ever been invited to a dinner at someone else's house. Only Gary wasn't surprised when I mounded food onto my plate. Abby looked over and raised her one eyebrow as she remembered that day at the Shady Palm Café.

"She'll eat it all," said Gary amusedly. "I don't know where she puts it all." I felt myself become a little embarrassed when the rest of his family chuckled.

"A good eater," said Gary's dad, "that's what I like. Gary here's supposed to be eating twice as much as us at his age, but he doesn't."

Gary gave me an embarrassed smile, and I returned to him a small smile of my own. I thought it was cute when he was embarrassed. His cheeks turned a pinkish color and he looked away. Abby was smiling over at me. After about ten minutes, she rustled his hair again.

"Isn't my little brother adorable, Krystal?" she asked.

"Gary, you're looking really red," his mom teased. She, too, looked over at me and smiled. His dad looked over at the two of us and chuckled again. Gary couldn't seem to stop smiling; his face was burning with embarrassment. Without saying a word, he shoveled down half the food on his plate, got up, took his plates over to the sink, then hurried out of the room.

"May I be excused?" I asked. Gary's mom nodded her head, and I stood up, placed my dishes in the sink, then hurried upstairs.

"I think I should take a shower now," he said as I walked into his room. He hurried past me out of the room, and I thought he still looked a little red. I walked over and lied down on his bed, gazing up at the ceiling.

"Hey." Abby had appeared in the doorway a few minutes later.

"Hi," I said, sitting up.

"You know," she said, sitting on the bed next to me, "I don't know if he'd want me to say this, but I'm his older sister and it's my job." She glanced over at the door to see if anyone was around. "He likes you."

"I know," I told her. "We're friends. James is too."

Abby looked a little confused at first.

"No, you don't get it," she said. "I mean, *like* you, as in a crush."

A funny feeling welled up in my stomach, but it was a good funny feeling.

"He does?" I asked, looking at Abby eagerly.

"I'm only guessing," she replied. "Just the way he looks and acts around you. He never gets embarrassed like that, and I think it was because you were around." When I didn't say anything, she said, "Oh, what do I know? It's probably just my imagination. But you know, it was really nice of him to invite you over tonight. As his older sister, I never thought I'd be saying this, but I was proud of him when he asked if you could stay with us. I shouldn't have been so surprised, because I always thought of him as a big sweetie. Anyway, I hope you enjoy staying with us." She got up and left the room, leaving me to think about what she had just said for a little while before Gary came back in.

"You're still in here?" he asked. "I thought you'd have gone somewhere else by now."

"Gary," I said.

"Hmm?" He tossed his old clothes into his laundry basket.

"What do you think of me?" I couldn't believe I was asking him, but I had to say something after what Abby had just told me.

"Well," he said, sitting on the bed next to me in the exact same spot Abby was, "uh, I think you're one of my best friends. Why?"

"I don't know," I said. "It's just that when you asked me to spend the night here so I wouldn't have to be alone after what just happened...that was just really nice."

"You're one of my friends," Gary replied. "I'd have asked James, but I figured he wanted to be with his dad."

"But, I don't think you understand," I said. "I was really touched. You're one of the best people I've ever met." He didn't say anything, but looked at me. After a short silence, I asked, "So what do you think of me?" I was eager to get something out of him, but wasn't quite sure what.

"Like I said," he told me, "you're one of my best friends."

"Anything else?"

"You're...nice, and fun to be around," he said, looking confused.

"Anything else?"

He looked a little uncomfortable now, and he spoke slowly, as if he was trying to be careful about what he said.

"I like being around you. You seem to be...I don't know..."

"C'mon," I told him, dropping my voice. "What do you *really* think about me?"

There was a longer, more definite pause. I looked directly into his eyes, and he looked directly into mine. I could feel his heart beginning to beat a little faster, and for some reason, mine did the same.

"I...think you're pretty," he told me finally, "and...I guess I kind of have...feelings for you..."

"Feelings?" I asked, leaning closer.

"Good feelings," he said. "Deep..."

"Can I ask you one last thing?"

"...Yeah."

"Well, I've never had a boyfriend, so…"

"You don't have to ask…"

I didn't get to finish what I was going to say. Before I knew what had happened, we were no more than a couple of inches away from each other, closing the gap every few seconds…

"Whoa! Uh, oops!"

Abby had once again appeared in the doorway, and she immediately turned and hurried away just as quickly as we had forced away from each other like similar poles of two magnets. I looked over at Gary, who looked over at me. We had been barely half of an inch away from each other.

"Um, maybe we should go to bed now," said Gary, standing up. He was obviously amazed at what had just happened.

"Yeah, okay," I agreed, getting up and going over to the door. Just before I walked out, I stopped. "Did we just do something…bad?"

"I don't know," Gary replied. "Did it seem bad?"

"N-no," I said, feeling a little skeptical.

"Don't worry about it," he said. "We didn't even…just try to get some…well."

"It's okay," I told him. "I feel like I can sleep soundly for once in over two years."

I left the room without either of us saying good-night. When I collapsed onto the bed in the guest room, I closed my eyes and rolled over on my stomach, gripping the pillow tightly in my arms and smiling.

CHAPTER ELEVEN

The long hallway that I stood in reminded me of a hospital. I was the only one there. Everything felt empty and completely lifeless, including myself. The cold air was penetrating the thin hospital robe I wore, and my bare feet pressed against the freezing floor. All the doors were open, exposing rooms shrouded in complete darkness. It was too dark to see inside, but I didn't want to see. There were frightening things in those rooms.

I slowly made my way down the hall. A strange silence pushed against my ears when I stopped. My eyes were transfixed on the large steel door at the end of the hallway. I wasn't allowed to go in, but I wanted to.

After glancing behind me into the pure loneliness, I moved closer to the door, which seemed to be calling to me. When I reached the door, I stood in place and stared at it. There was a strange energy radiating from the other side that wanted me to proceed. Without a second thought, I pressed my hand on the scanning pad next to the door. Almost instantly, the door creaked open partway with a loud and echoing moan.

My heart was pounding, and sweat poured down my face. I knew I was entering a forbidden place. But I had to. As I stepped into the dark room, I could feel something deep inside me beginning to churn; my soul was being ripped at by some unseen force that was calling to me. It felt as if an invisible hand was pulling me in by my soul.

Broken shelves and machinery littered the room. Hundreds of feet of wiring laced the ceiling, hanging down like mechanical veins. Books were torn, beaten, and scattered among the debris of the destroyed laboratory. Shattered test tubes glistened in the strange, blue light radiating from the only machine that remained in tact.

In the middle of the room stood a giant glass tube filled with a foggy liquid. The tube was clearly an incubator of some sort, emitting a strange, blue glow. I pushed through the mangled machinery to get a closer look at what was growing inside, then pressed my nose against the glass. Right then, the fog in the tube cleared to reveal what was being bred inside of it. My very blood turned cold at the sight of the little girl staring back at me...and she looked just like me.

I flung myself out of the bed onto the floor. My heart was beating so fast I thought that I was going to go into cardiac arrest if it didn't explode first. There was a horrible piercing in my head, and my very soul felt frozen solid. Random thoughts and memories raged through my mind like a tornado of subliminal messages as I rolled on the floor.

"*Why do you look like me*?!" I screamed at the top of my lungs. It hurt so bad to scream that I couldn't even cry.

People scrambled into the room, but I couldn't make sense of anything that was going on. They were trying to grab me, and I subconsciously beat them back. I heard voices of people, and I felt blood dripping from my face. Burning needles seemed to pierce every inch of my body as distorted visions obscured my vision. Blood exploded from the piano, the moon's lullaby rang in my ears and choked me; needles everywhere, burning me and stabbing me and pumping me full of tranquilizers. I began to drown in blood; the sky was streaked with crimson as an endless field of fire swirled and lightning split through the darkness. Night Stallion was summoned and devoured the tortured souls as the hollow-eyed angel emerged out of oblivion and created eternal emptiness…

A gush of icy cold water splashed in my face, and I found myself lying on the floor, looking up at Gary's family. Gary's dad was standing over me with a bucket that he had just used to pour water all over me. Trembling violently, I reached over and wrapped my arms tightly around Gary, who was kneeling down next to me. My heart was pounding, and I was gasping for air as if I had done strenuous exercises.

"Don't worry," he told me gently, "it's going to be okay."

"Pills," I whimpered. "I need my pills." I had been so excited to go to Gary's house that I forgot to grab the most important thing.

"We have to get her pills," Gary told the others. "Where are they, Krystal?"

"Home," I choked. "M-medicine…cabinet…bathroom."

"I'll go, Irene," said Gary's dad promptly to his wife. He quickly wheeled around and hurried out of the room.

"Where's Mommy and Daddy?" I asked shakily, looking hopefully into Gary's eyes. He didn't say anything, but looked at his mom and sister.

"We should try to put her back in the bed," said Gary's

mom. "On three. One…two…*three*!"

As soon as they lifted me into the air, I flailed my arms and legs viciously. They weren't going to inject me with any more drugs if I could help it.

"No!" I shouted. "No more tranquilizers!" In surprise, the three of them dropped me on the floor with a thud. Tears started streaming down my face as I assumed the fetal position. "I don't want any more tranquilizers!"

"We're not giving you tranquilizers," said Abby patiently. "We're going to put you in the bed."

"*Liars*!" I yelled. "I hate it when people lie to me! *Why does everyone always have to lie to me*? I'll kill you all!" They attempted to subdue me, and I fought them back. It lasted several minutes until Gary got a good hold on me.

"Krystal!" said Gary sharply, grabbing my shoulders and pinning me to the floor. "Get a grip, it's going to be *all right*."

His voice seemed to reach down and touch the pit of my heart. Everything in my head cleared up, and I realized exactly what I was doing. Gary's dad swiftly entered the room with my pills and a glass of water. As soon as he gave them to me, I washed them all down with every last drop in the glass.

"Better?" Gary asked quietly.

Without saying a word, I once again wrapped myself tightly around Gary. He gestured for the others to leave the room.

"You're so nice to me," I whispered. He put his arms around me and hugged me closely. I felt like I wanted to cry, but no amount of pain in the world could make me cry anymore. All of my crying had been spent years ago.

"It's okay now," he told me softly, "I'm here. It'll be okay."

I hugged him tighter. He was the best person I had met since my parents were killed. Right then, I realized exactly what I was feeling. It was the same exact feeling I experienced when my real parents hugged me. "Gary…"

"What is it?"

"I love you."

CHAPTER TWELVE

The following day was a dreary and rainy one. When I woke up, Gary was lying on the floor next to the bed. He had dragged his blanket and pillow into the guest room to spend the night with me. I rolled over and gazed at him while he slept. There was a relaxed, calm look about him when he was sleeping. Quietly, as not to wake him, I reached out and ran my fingers through his dark hair. It felt as soft and smooth as fine silk.

"Hmm…" His eyes opened, and he yawned and stretched.

"Good morning," I told him, smiling.

He smiled back. "Good morning." Then he stood up and stretched again.

"I like this bed," I said. "It's nice."

"Yeah," said Gary, "probably a lot softer than this floor." I giggled as he walked over to the window and peered out. "Ugh, what a crappy day it's starting out as. At least we don't have to go to school today. Or all week for that matter. It's spring break now."

I pulled the blankets off me and turned so that I was sitting on the edge of the bed.

"Do you think James is okay?" I asked him.

Gary thought it over for a moment.

"I don't know. We should try and visit him after breakfast."

"You mean lunch?" said a voice in the door. We looked over to find Abby standing there with a slight smile on her face. "You overslept again, baby brother. Looks like Krystal is a sound sleeper just like you. I would say you two would make the perfect…hee hee…"

"What?" Gary demanded.

"You know what I'm talking about," Abby teased. When she looked at Gary's confused expression and my blank one, she added, "Oh, come on, Gary! You can't say that Krystal's…" She trailed off with an amused look on her face, as if she was forcing Gary to urge her to go on.

"Spit it out!"

"You can't say that Krystal's not your…*girlfriend*." She looked highly satisfied by Gary's extremely red face, which I thought made him look very adorable. Then Abby turned and skipped away.

"I guess she's right," he said admittedly, looking over at me. I could feel myself blush a little. "But, I feel a little guilty. James's mom was just killed, and now the two of us…I mean, right after what had just happened to James."

"I know," I said quietly. "I do feel a little bad."

"We're still going to go visit him," said Gary, "but we can't make this too obvious, or he might get a little upset."

"Right," I said. "I'll get ready."

Gary left the room while I quickly put on some clean clothes. I looked in the mirror on the dresser at my hair, flattening it down with my hands. When I walked down to the kitchen, Gary was just putting his shoes on.

"Tell him that we're sorry, too," his mom told us as we went out the door. The sun was barely peeking through the clouds overhead, and it smelled like it had just rained. Just before we rounded the corner, I reached over and grabbed Gary's hand without thinking. He looked over at me, then put his arm around me as we continued to walk to James's house.

"Oh, wait," he said, quickly putting his arm back to his side. "We can't let James see us doing that kind of stuff. At least not yet."

"Okay," I said.

The walk was a somewhat dull and gray one, but Gary seemed to brighten up everything. Just the fact that he was walking next to me was enough to make me feel warm inside.

James's dad was outside on the sidewalk leading to the front door to their house, talking with a neighbor and pointing at the window that looked into the kitchen. He was so busy explaining what had happened that he didn't even notice us walk up.

"Excuse me," said Gary. "Is James here?"

"Ah, yes," said James's dad dully, "he's in the house. I appreciate you two stopping by to visit, and I'm sure he'll be very happy. Just go right in."

"Right, thanks," said Gary, making his way up to the door with me. He opened the door and stepped slowly inside. "James?" he called.

I followed him in and closed the door behind me. James was sitting on the couch in the living room, staring at the television that was off. He looked slowly up at us; his face looked like it had aged twenty years.

"Hey," he said flatly.

"Hi," said Gary, walking into the room. "We came to see how you were doing."

"Fine," he replied in the same tone.

"So," Gary continued, noticing that a conversation wasn't going to come easily, "I thought that maybe we could go do something today." James didn't answer, but just stared at the floor. "We could go get a bite to eat at the Shady Pa—" He stopped dead in his sentence as he remembered that the Shady Palm Café had just closed the day before.

"I don't want to go anywhere," said James, sounding a little angry. Gary opened his mouth, but closed it as words failed him. "I don't want to do anything, except train. I want to get stronger." He clenched his fists.

"Well, okay," Gary responded. "We can go right—"

"I want to kill him," James growled. "I swear that I'll kill him for what he did." He looked up with a face expressing pure hatred. I never saw James look that way before, and taking by the way Gary reacted, neither had he. "*I'll kill him!*"

James's last words had exploded out of him so suddenly that Gary and I both jumped and automatically got close to each other. Without thinking, I wrapped my arms around Gary for comfort. Apparently, James had noticed. He stared at the both of us with disbelief.

"What's this about?" he asked coldly, wrinkling his forehead at us. "I sense something between you two."

"What do you mean?" said Gary quickly, trying to cover us up.

"Don't give me that garbage," James growled, standing up. "I'm not stupid, okay? I see exactly what's going on here." His eyes moved back and forth between us.

"James," said Gary calmly, "let's just talk about this."

"Talk about it?" said James, his voice hinting hysterical anger welling up inside of him. "We don't need to talk about anything." He got right in Gary's face, who stood his ground. It was then that I realized how much taller James was than Gary. "I don't need an explanation to understand the situation. While me and my dad are here, living in grief over my dead mom, you two are off on your own, not caring about anything in the world except your relationship!"

"That's not true!" Gary snapped. "If you would just let me—"

"Let you what?" James barked, advancing even closer to Gary, who took a step back. "Explain? You two were probably flirting and making out! What's to explain!"

"The truth, that's what!" Gary yelled. "Would you just listen to me?"

"*I'm not listening to your lies!*" James thundered. A wave of energy burst out of him, making the lights flicker and pictures rattle. "Just get out of here! I don't want to see you two around here! Then you two can go back and make love to each other if you hadn't already!"

"What's going on in here?" James's dad overheard the shouting and ran into the house. There was a quick burst of cold, dark energy and he collapsed unconscious to the floor. The tension in the room hit a peak when Zenox stepped over him into the room.

"*I'm going to rip out your heart!*" James bellowed. Flare Blade appeared in his hand, and he flung himself at Zenox, who knocked James to the side with a simple flick of the wrist. He hit the wall and bounced onto the floor. Gary jumped back in surprise, and I inched away from the action.

"Don't overdo yourself," Zenox chortled, wearing his usual satanic grin.

"What have you done to my dad!" James demanded.

"Calm yourself," said Zenox in a sinister voice, "I didn't do anything to harm your father. Darknae does not kill when it is unnecessary."

"What are you saying?" James growled through his teeth. "Are you saying that you killed my mom for a reason?"

"Yes," Zenox replied. A sense of uneasiness was pulsating through the room. It was the same feeling I had felt when I was alone in my house.

"What reason could that possibly be?" James roared. "Answer me, dammit!"

"Yes, I had a reason," said Zenox. "I needed to give you some motivation to get stronger so that you can fight me."

"Why are you so intent on fighting us?" Gary demanded, holding up his fist as it became engulfed in his Soulpower flames.

"I don't intend on fighting you," Zenox told him. "I don't need you or that girl anymore, now that I know which one of you is the Rionah. You are still too weak, James, so train hard," he looked at James's dad lying on the floor, "or else you'll have to be put up for adoption and live with a new family...like Krystal." He turned and headed for the door.

My heart skipped a beat. "How did you know—"

"I remember you, Krystal," said Zenox. "We've met before." He started walking away before I could ask him anything else.

"You're not going anywhere!" James roared at Zenox, cutting me off. He practically sailed across the room at Zenox, holding his sword up high.

Zenox turned back around, pulled Shadow Blade out of nowhere, and used it to deal a powerful blow that sent James hurtling through the window into the front yard.

"James!" Gary shouted.

We flew out the front door. A burning tree had fallen across the road, making a loud noise. James was standing in the middle of the road, throwing a furious fit while screaming profanity in all directions.

"He's gone!" he thundered when he saw us hurry over to him. "I would've had him! Get back out here, Zenox! I'll kill you!"

"What were you thinking?" Gary yelled at him. "You know very well that you weren't ready to face him! All three of us put together wouldn't have done any good! Look at you, you're hurt." James's side was cut badly from Zenox's sword. Blood was oozing down his leg, and his shirt was completely stained on one side.

"Ugh...oh man..." It was as if James was fully unaware of his wound until Gary had pointed it out. He fell to the ground, holding his bleeding side.

"Krystal, stay here," said Gary, "I'll call the hospital." He hurried back into the house, leaving me with James. I looked over at a group of people standing on the side of the street, looking completely shocked that something had happened two days in a row. Somebody was on his cell phone, calling the fire department about the huge tree that was flaming in the middle of the road. I hurried over to them.

"Could somebody bring me a towel?" I asked them politely. A woman ran back into her house to find one as I kneeled down beside James. "It's going to be all right."

"Krystal," said James painfully, "I was stupid. I'm sorry."

"Don't worry," I said. "I forgive you, and I'm sure Gary will."

The woman came running back with a large towel as Gary ran out of James's house.

"The ambulance is on its way," she told us.

I wrapped the towel tightly around James's body to hold back the bleeding. The cut was a lot deeper than I thought. The fire truck had just arrived, and the firemen were rushing to hook the hose up to a nearby hydrant. The sirens of the police cars came wailing down the street, followed by the ambulance shortly after, accompanied by the news crew again.

"We'll take it from here," a paramedic told me and Gary, hoisting James onto a stretcher. A camera was practically in his face as he was lifted into the ambulance.

"It appears that yet another incident has occurred at the same house from yesterday's murder," said one of the news reporters from yesterday. The same cameraman was filming us as the reporter held the microphone up to us yet again. "Can you tell us exactly what happened here?"

Gary and I looked at each other, knowing that neither of us wanted to tell the real story of Zenox.

"We, uh...really don't know," Gary replied. "We were on our way over to visit our friend, and...the tree was burning." He looked back at me with an expression of uncertainty, knowing that what he had just said was really cheesy.

"I find it truly amazing that this is the second day in a row something astonishing happened," the reporter continued. "What do you think about that?"

"It sucks," I said quietly. Gary gave me a surprised look. Even I was shocked at what I had just said.

"There you have it," the reporter told the camera. Gary grabbed my shirt sleeve and pulled me off to the side of the road away from the action.

"We have to go follow James," he said just so I could hear. "It would be a bad idea to leave him by himself. We'll need our bikes."

"Okay," I said. The two of us started running down the street. Gary took James's bike from the garage and followed me as I ran back home to get mine. We took off in the direction of the town as fast as we dared without looking inhumanly fast. About halfway through, we saw the flashing lights up ahead.

"There's the ambulance!" Gary called. "We'll follow it to the city. Don't get too close behind it, or they might notice us."

I slowed down to match the ambulance's speed and fol-lowed it about a hundred yards back with Gary. It pulled onto the road that led through the woods to the city, then sped up a little once the driver realized that it was a straight shot with no traffic.

When the ambulance finally made it to the city, we decided to take an alternate route to the hospital. Since I didn't know the city at all, I had to follow Gary. There was a lot more traffic, making it harder for us to go as fast as we wanted. For the first time since I learned of my power, my legs began to get tired, and sweat dripped down my face. It was a long ride for being on a bicycle and keeping up with an ambulance, and I soon realized that even these powers had limits.

Before long, we made it to the hospital. The ambulance had just entered the parking lot and was going to the emergency section. We found a bike rack on the side of the building and parked our bikes, watching the ambulance disappear around the other side of the hospital.

"Let's go," said Gary. We ran after the ambulance to let the paramedics know that we were with James. They had just taken him in through the door when we reached them.

"Hold on there," said one of the paramedics. "You can't come back here."

"We're with him," Gary told him.

"Oh, come with me and we'll sort things out."

As the paramedic escorted us away, I turned to glance back at James as he was being taken out of the ambulance to the emergency room.

I stayed with Gary in the waiting room for nearly an hour. There were a few other people sitting in the other chairs, but it was somewhat quiet. All of the tables had a flower of some kind on them, and most were stacked with magazines.

Gary sat hunched forward, resting his elbows on his knees and propping his head up with his hands. He stared silently at the floor, not looking up. I thumbed brainlessly through a few magazines. I felt strange to be in the hospital. I never liked being in one because they made me uncomfortable. What really bothered me, though, was that I should have felt really bad for James, but I didn't. I looked around the room, thinking that there was something wrong with me. My emotions always seemed a little bit dulled, but why? Was I always like that? I looked at the scar on the palm of my left hand again. Where did these scars come from?

"Gary and Krystal?" A nurse had walked into the room with a clipboard. Gary immediately looked over at her. "Your friend is in room 321. He might be a little out of it from the medication."

"Thank you," said Gary, standing up. As we were walking out of the door, the nurse stopped us.

"It's quite remarkable," she said, "that your friend healed as fast as he did. By the looks of it, he might be able to go home in a couple of days."

I looked at Gary, then followed him to the elevator. When we stepped inside, something was eating at the back of my mind. I could feel Darknae nearby.

"Gary," I said.

"Yeah?" he replied quietly, hitting the button to the floor.

"You don't think…" I paused for a moment. Gary looked at the door. "The reason why he's healing fast…"

"Zenox," said Gary, looking down, then at me. "He's healing James quickly so that we can resume training soon."

"…Yeah."

"What I don't get," said Gary, "is how Zenox can do that. He has the power of Darknae, right? I didn't know that Darknae has the power to heal." The elevator came to a halt, then the door opened. The two of us stepped out and started walking down the hall.

"If that's true," I said, "does that mean Luminae has the power to destroy?"

"Only if it needs to," said Zenox. We whirled around to find ourselves face-to-face with the Rionah Darknae. Gary made a quiet throat noise, and my heart beat faster.

"Gary…," I whispered, keeping my eyes on Zenox. "It's him."

"Darknae heals only what it needs to," said Zenox. "Luminae destroys only what it needs to. I need James, so I'm healing him to keep him alive."

"What were you doing?" Gary growled. "Were you following us?"

Zenox's face cracked into his dark grin. "I believe you were the one following James, as was I."

I saw Gary's face screw up with anger. He wanted to get back at Zenox but couldn't do a single thing.

"There is no need for you two to come here," said Zenox. "I'm not going to do anything to anyone. I simply have no reason to harm anyone right now. James doesn't need either of you in the long run. He's the only one who can do anything against me."

"We're his support!" Gary snapped. "I believe we're doing a lot just by sticking beside him! Of course you wouldn't know that, since you wouldn't know the meaning of friendship and trust anyway! Darknae is completely inhuman!"

"I believe you stand corrected," said Zenox calm. His lack of any emotion was the most annoying thing about him. However, he didn't have a soul. Then I was hit with a chilling thought: Zenox had no soul, so he was emotionless. I had dulled emotions, and no one could find anything physically or medically wrong with me. All of those connections I could feel with Darknae…

"What do you mean?" Gary demanded, sounding a little curious through his anger.

"Everyone has Darknae in them," Zenox explained. "In fact, Darknae and Luminae were created in the human soul. Since that's the case, you'd be surprised how humanlike the force of Darknae is." He turned and looked directly into my eyes, turning my blood cold. "Isn't that right, Krystal?"

I gasped as something inside my mind clicked with my soul.

"I don't know," I said quietly.

"Your power," said Zenox. He looked somewhat curious for once. "What is it?"

"What is…my power?" I stared at Zenox as if hoping for him to answer for me.

"Just ignore him, Krystal!" said Gary.

"You don't know?" he said. He stared at me a little longer, then the vision of the angel flickered again.

I really wished I could have just ignored him, but what did he mean? Before I could say anything, Zenox turned around and walked away. When we watched him round the corner it was obvious that he had disappeared. Zenox was able to recognize Soulpower, Darknae, and Luminae, so why didn't he know what my power was? If it wasn't one of those three, then what was it?

"Let's go," Gary mumbled, walking down the hall to room 321.

"But…okay," I said.

"Don't listen to him," said Gary. "He'll just confuse you if you do."

We followed the hall down to where James was. The door was wide open so we went right in. James was sitting on the first bed by the door.

"Hey," he greeted as we came in and sat down next to each other.

"We heard you're healing really fast," said Gary. "You know why, don't you?"

"Yeah," said James flatly. "Zenox, right?"

"That's it," said Gary.

James raised up his shirt to reveal a big bandage wrapped around him.

"I guess I'll be able to go home tomorrow," he said, lowering his shirt. "Even though I'll probably be healed all the way by tonight, the hospital would like to keep me overnight. You know, just to make sure I'll be all right...even though I will be..." He looked over at the plant sitting on the bedside table. "About what I said to you earlier, I'm really sorry about that. I didn't mean—"

"Don't worry," said Gary. "We understand."

"So," said James, trying to sound a little more enthusiastic, "you two are going out now, right?"

Gary and I looked at each other.

"Yeah," said Gary, putting his arm around me and pulling me closer.

James looked over at us and smiled.

"You two make a good couple," he said.

"Do you think so?" Gary asked.

"Well, yeah, dude," James replied. "Just look at you. You've been friends for almost a year now."

"I guess so," said Gary, looking happily at me. I smiled back, feeling a little embarrassed. At the same time, I felt a little relieved. Unlike Zenox, I still had emotions.

"You shouldn't stay for too long," said James. "How'd you get here, anyway?"

"Bikes," said Gary.

"Ha! Figures."

"Do you have your sword?" Gary asked him.

"Yep," said James, "It appears whenever I want it to."

"Well," said Gary, standing up, "I think we should get going now."

"I'll be back tomorrow," said James. "We can train then."

"Gotcha," Gary replied. "See ya."

"See ya."

"Bye," I said as I left the room with Gary. We walked down

the hallway, and I reached for Gary's hand. That's when I got a weird feeling. I stopped walking and looked around.

"What is it?" Gary asked.

"I don't know," I said quietly. I looked up and down the hallway. "Follow me."

I hurried down the hallway to the elevators, going down to the first floor. Having no clue to where I was going, I made my way swiftly around the floor, Gary following closely behind me. I rounded a corner quickly, running into a custodian as he was pushing his cart, almost knocking him over.

"Sorry," I said quickly. Taking one glance at his face, I froze. The custodian froze when he saw my face as well. He was a middle-aged man with scraggly, graying hair. His face was slightly wrinkled, but firm.

"Excuse me," he said slowly, grabbing onto his cart. We continued to stare at each other for a little bit as he began to continue on his way down the hall. I watched him until he went into one of the rooms a way down, closing the door behind him.

"Do you know him?" Gary asked me.

I broke my attention from the door and looked back at Gary.

"I'm not sure."

Chapter Thirteen

That Friday, four days after we visited James in the hospital, the three of us had just finished training in our usual spot out in the woods. James had fully healed the same night he was taken there by the ambulance, and just as predicted, the nurses wanted to keep him overnight just to be safe. We had trained vigorously each day, and our strength had clearly improved greatly.

"What should we do now?" Gary asked us after we had made it back to Gary's house.

"I don't know," said James. "Let's just go home and call it a day. I'm tired."

"Sure," Gary replied. "We'll see you tomorrow, then."

We waited until James had rode away before Gary put his arm around me.

"I'll be fine," I told him gently. Gary was worried about me now that Jack and Laura had come back and I was staying at home again.

"Yeah, okay," he said. "I'll see you tomorrow."

"Bye," I said, kicking off. My entire body felt drained of energy, making it hard to ride my bike straight. Intense training was definitely taking its toll on the three of us. I got to my house and placed my bike on the side of the garage, not caring to put it away since I was going to get it out first thing in the morning.

"Hi, dear," said Laura as I came into the house. She was watering the plants in the living room. "You look really worn out. I hope you're not overexerting yourself."

"I'm fine," I said wearily. I stumbled up the stairs to my room, dragging my legs, which felt like cement. As soon as I got to my bed, I collapsed onto it. James was really cracking down on our training, and quite frankly, it was wearing me out.

My eyelids were starting to get heavy, and I jerked myself off the bed onto the floor to keep myself from falling asleep. When I hit the floor, it was apparent that I needed to get some good sleep, but I didn't want to have those dreams again. I couldn't afford to make Gary and James worried about me. They wouldn't want me to train for a while, but I wanted to train as much as possible. I had to improve my power...whatever it was. Either Zenox was toying with me like Gary had said, or I wielded something different that not even Darknae recognized.

"Are you okay?" Jack appeared at my door, looking concerned. "I heard a thump and came to see what it was. Did you fall down?"

"Yeah," I replied airily.

"Here, let me help you up." Jack lifted me and sat me down on the bed. "Oh man, you don't look so good. Looks like all those years of insomnia are catching up to you now."

"I'm fine," I assured, attempting to smile, even though it was painful.

"Try lying down," he said, pushing me down flat on the bed. "Maybe if you—" I didn't hear his last words, because I almost immediately fell asleep.

When I woke up, I looked over at my window. I was asleep for several hours. At least I lucked out and didn't have another dream. The sun had gone down, and it was almost pitch black outside. The only light coming was from the full moon shining through.

A strange lurching feeling erupted in the pit of my stomach. I flung myself out of bed and ran up to the window, pressing my face against the glass. The full moon was out. Hurrying over to the calendar, I looked for when the next full moon was, then my heart skipped a beat. It wasn't due for a few more weeks. What was it doing out now?

I burst out of my room and tore down the stairs. Jack and Laura were asleep, and all the lights in the house were out. I ran through the living room to the sliding glass door that led out into the pool area, yanked it open, then shot out. The moon's silver glow was glistening and reflecting off the surface of the water, which appeared black. None of the torches were lit, nor were the lights on. Only the moon shone down, casting its cold light upon the world. Silence pressed against my ears; not a single cricket was chirping. My breathing was the only sound that I heard.

"Please don't sing," I whispered nervously to the moon, "please don't sing."

The air began to get cooler, then I started feeling light-headed again. When I fell to the icy ground, everything went dark. The water from the pool erupted violently, shattering the entire backyard, ripping up the ground. I was engulfed in a freezing whirlpool that glowed with the light from the moon. My heart became cold, and I was embraced by the darkness. I was too frozen to feel endangered. The moon protected me. Darknae filled my eyes and opened the window to the event that would affect the course of history. Luminae was ready, and Darknae had found James.

No lights shone, except for the moon, watching down on everything. The moon watched James as he stood up, looking around. Thunder rumbled in the distance, rolling over the field of flowers that James found himself surrounded by.

He gazed around at the huge, stone-paved opening in the middle of the garden. A beautiful water fountain was in the center of the area, which broke the silence with the gentle sound of trickling water. Giant stone pillars were erected around the outside of the area, which cast long shadows across the stone ground.

Flare Blade was growing warm in James's hand as it teemed with Luminae. Thunder rumbled again as James became aware of the approaching danger. Clouds filled the sky, blocking the moonlight, turning everything pitch black. Lightning shot out of the clouds, splitting through the dark and striking the flowers, making them immediately burst into flames. The fire spread incredibly fast, engulfing the entire field in no time. There was a massive roar coming from the flames that surrounded James, who gripped his shimmering sword tightly. He turned around to find Zenox, stepping slowly out of the raging fire into the clearing, carrying Shadow Blade. Zenox's eyes had been turned into black spheres; his pupils had become a cloud of glowing red smoke that swirled in each eye. James felt the power of Luminae surge through his body from Flare Blade as he readied himself.

The two of them leapt at each other at the same time. An incredible amount of lightning exploded out of the sky and ripped into the flames as Flare Blade collided with Shadow Blade. James and Zenox engaged in a dramatic duel of light and darkness, slashing at each other with blinding speed. Every time the two swords collided, beams of energy blasted out in all directions, tearing up portions of the ground.

The water in the fountain turned to fire and erupted out into the sky. Lightning lashed at the spewing flames as it spilled over the side of the fountain and flowed across the ground. Ashes of burning flowers billowed out of the field, swirling around as they created tornadoes that shredded across the endless field of fire. The flames were being sucked up into the sky, turning the clouds into a raging inferno until the ground and the sky were like two suns that were lashing at each other with solar flares.

James and Zenox continued to battle, ripping the very ground beneath them. Lightning was striking so frequently that it often obscured the entire burning sky. Flowing bands of Darknae spewed out of Zenox towards James, who pushed it back with radiant beams of glowing Luminae. Fire and lightning was everywhere, and the deafening roar of burning flowers and bellowing thunder shook everything. Zenox pounced at James, who blocked the attack.

Before another bolt of lightning had the opportunity to strike the ground, James counterattacked. He swung Flare Blade, slashing Zenox straight across the chest.

The lightning ceased immediately; the fountain exploded into a million pieces; the clouds disappeared, revealing the moon; the fire turned to ice, and became an endless field of glistening bluish silver glowing in the moon's light.

I felt myself hit the ground a few feet away from James. Zenox stumbled to the ground. Shadow Blade fell out of his hand and clanked on the ground. All was calm.

Zenox looked up at James, clutching his chest as it gushed blood that quickly evaporated into a black smoke that swirled around him on the ground. His eyes had returned to normal. Surprisingly, he didn't look very disappointed.

He was losing his power.

"Any last words?" said James sharply.

Zenox looked over at me.

"You," he gasped, "do you know why you are here?" I shook my head. "It's because you are connected to Darknae. It's your power. What is…your…power?"

"My…power?" I placed my hand on my chest. A coldness was sitting in my heart.

The ominous grin spread across Zenox's face for the last time as he died and collapsed. The black cloud swirled and engulfed him, then was sucked up into the sky by the moon. All of the ice shattered with a brain-racking rumble, and James and I landed next to the pool in my backyard. Instead of being a wasteland created when I was absorbed into the vision, the backyard was completely untouched. We stood up, feeling extremely good, but unable to show any of it.

"It's over," said James quietly. I looked over at him. "I

finally got back at Zenox for killing my mom."

"What do we do now?" I asked.

"I don't know," James replied, looking over the surface of the water. He looked back, and a big smile spread from ear to ear. "We have a big party between the three of us. You know, with lots of food."

I smiled brightly. "Sounds like a great idea. Let's tell Gary."

Chapter Fourteen

After Zenox was defeated I felt as if a giant tumor had been removed from inside me. With the lack of Darknae, the weather had greatly improved. The sun shone a lot more, warming each day. Gary and James both seemed a lot more cheerful. Even I had to admit that I felt a million times better. There wasn't really anything eating away at the back of my mind.

Spring break was over now and it was finally time for the dance, meaning that the school's gymnasium was going to be filled with students. When I came home from school that day I knew that I'd have to get ready if I wanted to go with Gary. As soon as I walked in the house, I hurried up to my room to find something to wear. My closet was full of casual clothes, and nothing looked the least bit formal. Eventually, I picked out something that didn't look too tacky.

Later that day, I took a shower and brushed my teeth, trying to get as clean as possible. When I got dressed, I looked in the mirror to see if anything needed fixed, and thought that I should tie my hair back. After doing so, I looked in the mirror one last time to make sure that I did it right.

"What's the rush?" Laura asked me when I came into the living room. "That dance isn't for a few more hours, isn't it?"

"I want to be ready," I said.

"Well, there's nothing wrong with that." Suddenly, she got very concerned. "Are you sure you want to do this? You've never done anything like it before."

"I'm fine," I told her. Then I gave her an assuring smile. "Don't worry about it."

"You tied your hair back?" Jack had just come into the living room with a cup of coffee. "I've never seen you do that. It looks good."

"Yeah, it does," said Laura, looking at me. "I can see your ears for once."

The next few hours slowly trudged by. I was a little excited, but also nervous. This was my first time doing something after school, and I didn't know if everything would go all right.

I killed time by drawing in my sketchbook and listening to the stereo in my room. Of course, I listened to heavy metal because it soothed me. People at my school in Michigan told me that it was weird, that I'm an idiot, and not very girl-like. When they would tell me that, it made me feel even more lonely and different from everyone else. But I didn't dare show it.

"Krystal, are you ready to leave?" Laura finally called. I shut off the radio, put my sketchbook away, and went downstairs. "Jack, I'll be back soon. I'm taking Krystal to her school now."

"Okay, have fun," Jack called from the living room.

I followed Laura outside to the car. When I got in, I peeked in the rearview mirror one last time to make sure I was presentable. It was the first time I was really concerned about my looks. The drive to the school was a long and quiet one, and I kept trying to imagine what it would be like at the dance.

We arrived at the school, and after I got out of the car, I stared at the entrance. Other people were showing up at the same time, and I followed the crowd into the building. A big sign written in marker was sitting on an easel in the hallway that said to go to the gymnasium for the dance. As soon as I was done reading the sign, I heard a familiar voice to the side of me.

"I hope they have food. I'm starving."

"Hi, James," I greeted.

James stopped walking with Nick and gave me a puzzled face.

"Krystal? Is that you?"

"Yeah," I said sweetly.

"Hey, I didn't recognize you with your hair tied back," he said, looking up and down. "Wow, you look…really good. I can see your ears now."

"You look good too," I replied, even though he was dressed in the same clothes he wore to school that day. His hair was just wetted down and combed. "Is Gary here yet?"

"We didn't see him," said Nick. "He could already be in the gym."

"Let's go," said James enthusiastically. "My fans await."

I walked with Nick and James to the gym where the rest of the students had already gathered. The music was playing loudly, and the concessions were giving out pizza and drinks.

"I don't see him anywhere," said James, looking around. "He's probably not here yet…Oh yeah, pizza!" He took off through the crowd of dancing students in a straight line for the concessions. I continued to look for Gary with Nick.

"Looking for someone?" We wheeled around to see Gary coming into the gym.

"Yo, we didn't know if you were here yet," said Nick. "What's up, bro?"

"Nothing much." He turned his attention on me. "Hey."

"Hi," I replied, giving him a hug.

"I like your hair," he complemented. "It, uh…brings out your…ears."

I giggled quietly. "Thanks."

"There you are, Beth." Nick greeted a short, redhead girl who was wearing a blue ribbon in her hair. "Beth, meet my pals, Gary and Krystal."

"Hello," said Gary.

"Hi," I said.

"Me and Beth, we're gonna be chillin', so catch ya later."

"All right," said Gary. "See ya."

Nick and Beth joined the crowd of dancing students as James came over to us. He was holding a paper plate with nearly half a pizza stacked on top of it.

"Is that all for you?" Gary asked, eyeing his plate with slight disgust.

"Yep," James replied happily through a mouthful of pizza. "They have more."

"Do you need something to help wash it down?" said Gary. "A glass of cooking oil to lube your throat?"

"No, I'm fine," said James, completely missing what Gary meant.

"Hey, Krystal, you want some pizza?" Gary offered. "I can get some for you."

"Yeah, sure," I said. "It doesn't matter what kind."

Gary made his way over to the pizza, leaving me with James who continued to stuff his mouth. Miraculously, he managed not to get anything on his shirt or face. When Gary came back, he handed me a plate with two slices of pizza on it.

"Thanks," I told him, smiling. I picked up a slice, then started to practically inhale it.

"You two are animals," said Gary amusingly. "It's like watching a pizza-eating contest."

"Ha, I could easily win one of those," said James, slurping down the rest of a slice. "There'd be no contest as soon as I enter, because I'm that good. Hey, look who just showed up."

147

We focused our attention at the main entrance of the gymnasium to find Brandon walking in. He was wearing a button-up shirt that looked as if it were about to rip from his bulging muscles.

"Oh, this is just great," Gary groaned. "What's he doing here? I didn't know he had a girlfriend."

"I don't think he does," said James, licking his fingers. "He's probably here to find one. That'll be the day."

After I finished my pizza, I walked over to the trash to throw my plate away. However, Brandon was standing next to it.

"How are you?" he asked nicely.

"Fine," I said.

"I like what you did to your hair," he said, smiling. "I never knew you had ears."

I giggled softly.

"Yup, I sure do."

"So, you going out with him?" He nodded in Gary's direction.

"Oh, yeah,"

"That's what I thought." He sounded really disappointed.

I glanced over at Gary and James, who were looking over in our direction.

"Do you have a date tonight?" I asked.

"No," he said dully.

"Uh…" I wasn't sure what to say. Brandon, for reasons unknown to me, always acted so nice and polite when he talked to me.

"So," he said, "I guess I'll let you get back to what you were doing."

I looked directly into his eyes, which were full of hope and desperation. Just I was about to open my mouth, I was interrupted.

"What are you doing?" James asked rudely. "Brandon, leave her alone."

"Hey, I was talking to her!" Brandon's kind and gentle tone disappeared like a camera flash.

"Well, now you're not," said James, taking my arm. "Come on, you don't need to be talking with this moron."

"What did you say?" Brandon growled, getting right up in James's face. "I have a right to talk with whoever I want to!"

"Except for her," said James, pulling me away. "If you hadn't noticed, she's taken, so find your own!"

"Whoa, now hold on!" Gary had come over after he saw that Brandon and James were clashing. "Let's just keep our cool here!"

"Shut up!" Brandon snapped. He turned back to me. "I guess I'm not wanted here, so I'll talk to you later, Christine."

"Her name's Krystal!" James barked. "Get it right!" He pulled harder on my arm until he pulled me a few feet back. I watched as Brandon stomped away and left the gymnasium. I actually felt really bad for him. He wasn't doing anything wrong, and I really didn't mind talking to him.

"What'd you have to go and do that for?" Gary asked James irritably. "He wasn't doing anything wrong."

"He was talking to Krystal," James huffed. "Anything that kid says is trouble, Krystal, so just forget about anything he told you."

A few moments later, I was caught off guard by another blurred vision. I looked at James and Gary, examining their expressions. It was obvious that they didn't see it. Those visions were the only things that kept me from feeling completely fine. They kept coming back even after defeating Zenox.

"There's Stephanie and Patrick," said Gary, pointing at them across the room. They were standing over by the snack bar that was set up next to the pizzas.

"So what?" James mumbled.

"What's wrong?" Gary asked. "You're not still mad about Brandon, are you?"

"Well, he's an ass!" James replied hastily. "He thinks he can come around here, making trouble and acting so tough!"

"He wasn't doing that," said Gary. "I know he can be a real pain sometimes, but he wasn't doing anything wrong just a few moments ago. Actually, *you're* the one who started making trouble this time, not him."

James looked insulted, then ashamed.

"Crap, I hate it when you're right."

"Alright, guys," the DJ announced into his microphone. "Are you all having a good time, or what?"

There was a loud roar from the mass of students in the gym.

"Okay, listen up," he announced, "I'm about to slow things down a bit with one of my personal favorites."

The lighting became smoother as the next song began its slow rhythm. The mass of students slowed down into a synchronized, flowing movement.

"Oh yeah," said James, "time for me to put on my smooth moves." He hurried off into the crowd to find someone to dance with, leaving me with Gary.

"So," he said, scratching his head. "Do you…want to dance?"

Instead of answering, I gave him a smile, then wrapped my arms around his neck as he put his hands on my hips. The music took us in, and we fell into the synchronized, flowing movement that surrounded us.

It was a lot easier than I expected. All I had to do was concentrate on the music, and my body did the rest. No matter how hard I tried to look away, Gary's eyes were pulling mine into them. In just a few seconds, everything that I ever worried about was washed away, and I felt a warm feeling beginning to fill me. It was a feeling that I hadn't felt since I was six years old…when my parents were alive…when they tucked me into my bed on that cold winter night…

Everything that I had forgotten snapped back so quickly, I fell out of the synchronized motion. Before Gary could react, I immediately corrected it, and sank back into the synchronized, flowing motion that washed my troubles away.

When the dance was over Gary and I met up with James, Nick, Stephanie, and their dates by the school statue. I listened to them all talking about the night. James had slow-danced with five different girls and was very proud of it.

"I could've beaten you," said Nick, "but Beth was all I needed. Having an actual girlfriend beats you automatically!"

"Oh yeah?" said James cockily. "I don't think so, man. I'm the smoothest here! Isn't that right, honey?" A girl that was walking past looked at James and gave him a flirty smile.

"Who was that?" Gary asked, looking at her as she walked away.

"Not sure," James replied, "but she was hot."

After most of the people had left, Gary and I remained by the school statue. Before long, it was just us. Gary was waiting for Abby to come pick him up in their parents' car, and Laura hadn't shown up yet.

"Well," he said, "I had fun tonight."

"Me too," I said.

"So, uh…yeah." He looked back up at the sky. The moon

didn't threaten me anymore, so I didn't worry about its silvery light as it lit up his face.

"Hey," I said, putting my arms around him.

"Hmm?"

"I love you."

"I love you, too," he said.

We stared into each other's eyes for a while. I felt him pull me closer to him, and soon we weren't even an inch apart. What happened next was inevitable, and it was the greatest feeling in the world. We separated, then I noticed Abby standing next to us. She had a kind smile on her face as she looked at us. Gary looked completely lost for words.

"Ready to go, little brother?" she said softly.

Gary nodded, then looked at me.

"See ya tomorrow."

"Bye."

Abby smiled at me. "Bye, Krystal."

"Bye, Abby."

I watched them walk to the car and drive away. When Laura showed up to take me home shortly after, I didn't even pay attention to anything she said to me. That night was a great night, and I slept better than I ever had.

Those good feelings lasted all weekend and into Monday. I was at my locker after lunch, getting my biology stuff, when Brandon came up to me again.

"Hey," he greeted, "what's up?"

"Not much," I said.

"Nothing at all!" James came up out of nowhere with Gary right behind him.

"Just go away!" Brandon snapped at James. "Otherwise I'll rip you apart!"

"Brandon," said Gary firmly, "I don't mind you talking to her, but just remember she's my girlfriend."

Brandon looked down at the ground. He didn't say anything at all. Gary began to look a little sympathetic.

"You liked her, didn't you?" he asked.

I looked at Brandon, waiting eagerly for his reply. At first, he didn't answer.

"It's my father," he said quietly. His voice was completely different from what I ever remember coming from him.

"What about your dad?" James asked, sounding a little

curious.

"He's a real jerk," Brandon replied, not looking up. "He's afraid that people will think bad about him if his son can't even get a girlfriend."

"Really?" said Gary, sounding astonished.

Brandon slammed his fist against the locker. A few students turned to see what was going on, then hurried on their way to class.

"He always treated me like his inferior instead of his son! Ever since Mom died in that car accident when I was four!" He looked up at us, clearly fighting back tears. "That's why I wanted Krystal to hang out with me. I wanted to pretend that she was my girlfriend, and then my dad would lighten up a little. I chose Krystal, because she seemed like such a nice girl...and she was attractive." He paused, and a weird feeling bubbled up inside me. "Over time, I eventually started to have feelings towards her." Avoiding our eyes, he took off to his next class, and I quickly followed after him.

We entered the classroom just as the bell rang. I took my seat, looking over at Brandon. He was staring down at his desk. The weird feeling inside me began to take the form of sympathy. It wasn't his fault that he was a bully. His dad treated him badly, and he naturally became mean.

After about twenty minutes, we received our assignment for the day. I took out a sheet of paper and began answering the chapter review questions out of the textbook. Every few seconds, I kept glancing back at Brandon. He wasn't doing the assignment, but dragged his pencil lazily across some notebook paper. Perhaps it wouldn't do any harm if I just went to his house a few times...

My thinking was interrupted by a bone-chilling occurrence. A paper airplane had just landed on my desk.

I scanned the room quickly to see if I could find out who threw it, but like the first time, everyone was doing their work. Holding the airplane, I debated whether I should unfold it or not. Deciding that I couldn't be hurt by a piece of paper, I unfolded it.

The blood in my veins turned cold. It was another doodle, obviously created by the same artist. This time, it was a drawing of the moon in the sky with musical notes coming out of it. Two people, a male and a female, were lying on the ground underneath it. A red crayon was scribbled over the two dead stick figures to represent blood.

I hastily folded up the paper and stuffed it in my pocket like the drawing of the bleeding piano. Trying to force all negative thoughts out of my head, I picked up my pencil and continued working. Then the vision flashed.

Dropping my pencil, I clutched my head. The vision flashed again, and it felt like my head was being pierced. Again, the vision flashed, and again, my head throbbed. Over and over, the vision flickered quickly in front of me. Each time it did, my head hurt more and more, until I thought my brain was going to explode.

"*No!*" I yelled, falling to the floor, still clutching my head. My body began to tremble uncontrollably. The visions stopped, but my head was still hurting incredibly. I could hear people shuffling around, but couldn't put anything together.

Moments later, paramedics came into the room and picked me up. I was screaming on the inside for them to put me down, but my body was unable to do anything except tremble and groan.

I remember being carried through the school on a stretcher. As I was taken out of the building, communication with my body started to come back.

"Leave...me...alone," was all I could get out. My tongue was lolling around in my mouth, and it was hard for me to speak.

"It'll be okay," I heard a paramedic say.

There was the sound of doors slamming, then sirens. People were around me, but I didn't know how many there were, let alone what they were doing. There was a light shining in my eyes, and I closed them.

"Mommy," I managed to say. Voices were around me. "Daddy...make the angel go away. She's not a real angel..."

I'm not sure how much time had passed, but next thing I knew, I was in a hospital being taken down a hall. People were still around me, and my head stopped hurting. However, I felt like someone had given me ether and adrenaline. My heart was pounding furiously, but I was extremely tired. Sweat covered my face.

More bright lights shone in my eyes. The people around me were standing over me, talking. Sounds of metal and plastic echoed in my head. Everything was blurred, and I felt dizzy, nauseated, and suffocated. Something was over my mouth, then I could breathe a little better. I felt a prick in my arm...

Everything came into focus. I looked around, and noticed that I was in the hospital. The sun was setting, casting a red-orange glow across the room. Voices were coming from the hallway, and I was able to identify them.

"Is there anything we can do?" Jack asked concernedly.

"Luckily," said the doctor, "there is." I recognized him right away. It was Dr. Grant, the doctor I met before moving to Florida. We visited him when I came with Jack and Laura to look at the new house. They wanted to get familiar with my new doctor before hand. "We'll put her on this last medication. However, if this doesn't work, we will have no choice but to put her in a correctional facility."

"Understood," I heard Laura say.

"I'm sorry," Dr. Grant apologized. "I wish there was a better way. It appears that she suffers from post-traumatic disorder, supposedly from the death of her parents. She may need special care to cope with it, rather than fill her up with medication."

I heard footsteps coming up to my bed. Jack and Laura both stood next to me, and Dr. Grant waited against the wall.

"Krystal." Laura reached over and took hold of my hand. "How are you feeling?"

"Good," I whispered. There was barely enough energy in me to keep me alive.

"The doctor has prescribed more medication," said Laura, holding my hand tighter. "Everything should be okay."

More footsteps came into the room. Gary and James appeared on the other side of my bed.

"We came as soon as school was over," said Gary. "Abby said I can use her bike since mine got annihilated."

"You two are really good friends," Jack told them. "Thanks for coming."

"Hey, no problem," James replied. "She *is* one of my best friends, after all."

"Krystal and Gary are really close," said a voice from the door. To my surprise, Abby had just come in.

"They are?" Laura sounded rather curious.

"Yep," said Abby, coming up from behind Gary and rustling his hair. "Looks like Krystal found a boyfriend. Right, baby brother?"

"Uh…" Gary looked kind of embarrassed.

"Well, isn't that sweet?" said Laura, smiling at me.

Jack chuckled. "Looks like Krystal's finally growing up."

"Excuse me," said Dr. Grant, "did you say that she has a

boyfriend?"

"That'd be me," Gary replied quietly.

"This is good news!" said Dr. Grant happily. "At least she has the ability to have affection for someone. How long have you two known each other?"

"Since last year," said Gary.

"Ah, okay," said Dr. Grant. "Looks like you've been a good friend to her after all this time."

"What about me?" said James irritably. "I'm her best friend!"

"No," Abby butted in, "Gary is."

"Gary's her boyfriend!" James argued. "That would make me her best friend."

"Someone's boyfriend *is* their best friend," said Abby, sounding annoyed.

"You're a fine friend for Krystal," said Jack, breaking up the argument. "She's lucky to have you as a friend, Joey."

"It's James," James corrected, beaming. "I agree. She's lucky to have me for a friend. Anyone who has me for a friend is lucky. In fact—"

"I think it's time for Krystal to rest," said Dr. Grant, stopping James from telling everyone how amazing he is. "She could probably go home tomorrow. It might be a good idea to keep her out of school for a while."

"Right," said Laura. "We'll be here to pick you up tomorrow, maybe around noon." She leaned over and kissed my cheek.

"Take care," said Jack, running his hand through my hair.

"We'll stop by your house after school," said James.

"See you tomorrow," said Gary. He gave me hug, and I forced my arms up around him.

"I'll drop by, too," said Abby.

"Bye, sweetie," said Laura. "We'll have to remember you're in room 321."

It was the same room James was in. That was weird. Must have been a coincidence.

Dr. Grant turned and walked out, and everyone else followed. Gary was the last one to leave, and before he did, he turned around and gave me a smile. My heart warmed up when I saw his smile, and it was much easier for me to give him one back.

After everyone was gone, I relaxed and stared up at the ceiling. Every bad thought was driven out of my head by thoughts of Gary. He made me feel so happy. Happier than I had felt in years. I had a strong sense of security whenever he was around me. A good feeling built up inside me. I had fallen in love with him.

I felt so good that evening. When the nurse came in with dinner, I ate everything I was given, submerged in a dreamy sensation. I watched the sun set behind the trees until night came.

That night, I had gone to the bathroom. When I came back out, I didn't notice anything peculiar. I was completely lost in thoughts about Gary. It wasn't until I decided to peer out the window at the city that I noticed what was wrong.

The full moon was shining. With this observation, I snapped back to the real world. My room was filled with a silvery glow. I stared at the moon, transfixed by it. Why did I have to get the bed by the window? A female voice was heard, and I rubbed my ears to try and make it go away. My imagination always played tricks on me, and it was starting to get annoying. I rubbed my ears again. Then I thought my heart was going to stop.

The moon was singing.

Everything seemed to freeze. A horrible sense of shear terror filled every inch of me until my very soul was trembling. The beautiful song drifted in through the window and filled the room. It was the moon's lullaby. It was the same lullaby I had heard on that cold winter night. It was the same lullaby I had heard when my parents were killed by Darknae.

"This can't be happening," I whispered to myself. "*This isn't happening!*"

I reached over and grabbed a chair, then smashed the window with it. Before I could make any second thoughts, I leapt out of the window and fell straight down three stories. I instantly stood up when I hit the ground, frantically looking around for something that could help me. To my fortune, a bicycle was chained to the bike rack. I hurried over, yanked the bike away from the rack, snapping the chain that was tied to it.

The beautiful lullaby was growing louder as I kicked off so hard that both tires jumped off the ground. Then I pedaled. I pedaled so hard that I thought my legs were going to break. I raced through the city, powered by an incredible amount of adrenaline and Soulpower…or whatever my power was. Weaving in and out of traffic was extremely tricky, especially since I was moving at blinding speeds.

At last, I made it out of the city and onto the long stretch of road that went back into the town. As soon as I realized that it was a straight shot, I pedaled as fast as I could possibly go. Nothing was holding me back; I was giving it all I had. The wind howled in my ears, but it still was not enough to block out the moon's lullaby. Silvery light shone down on me, and the moon appeared larger and brighter than normal as it beamed through the trees. I had to find Gary and James. I just had to.

Something was following me. I glanced behind me quickly, but couldn't see anything. I forced myself to try and go faster, but I didn't know if I could go faster than what I was doing. I glanced back again, only to find nothing.

The moon was still singing loudly. Tears of pure fright streamed horizontally across my face from the wind. My lungs felt like they were going to burst. I looked behind me once more, and I could see a shadowy figure charging down the road a few yards behind me. Whatever it was, it was chasing me, and it was determined to catch me.

If there was any possible way for me to go faster, I found it. I pedaled furiously, trying to escape my pursuer. The moon sang its beautiful lullaby. As soon as there was an opening in the trees, the moonlight struck my shadowy pursuer, giving it full strength. Looking back, I saw an eruption of blue flames from the figure. Of all the things that I had seen recently, what I saw just then was breathtakingly frightening.

In the clear moonlight came a horse galloping after me, but it was different from any horse alive. It had pure black fur and long, glistening fangs. Huge, feathery wings protruded from its back, giving it the look of a demonic Pegasus. Massive talons stuck out from its hooves, tearing into the pavement as it ran. Its mane wasn't fur, but flowing blue flames that streamed behind it down the back of its head and back. The glowing red eyes were burning like fire in its head. But that wasn't what disturbed me the most.

I had seen this horse in my dreams. It was there when my parents were killed. I remembered it. That horse killed my parents.

I finally made it to the town, and the horse was practically breathing down my neck. I had absolutely no idea where I was going, or what I was going to do when I got there. My only instinct was to run as far as I could go.

The sound of huge wings lifting off was heard behind me. When I turned around to look, the demonic horse had taken flight and disappeared. The moon stopped singing, and I slowed down to look around. Unfortunately, I didn't know that I had slowed down in the middle of a high-speed intersection. A blast of a horn caught my attention, and I turned to see a tanker barreling right at me. I had just enough time to realize what was going to happen.

SMASH!

The truck hit me at over fifty miles an hour, ripping apart the bicycle and sending me reeling through the air. Twenty feet away, the back of my head slammed into the rear bumper of a car parked on the side of the road. Pain surged through me as I crumpled to the hard asphalt.

In its attempt to avoid me, the tanker slammed on the brakes, slid out of control, rolled over, then collided into a gas station. Sparks that were shooting everywhere ignited the gas pumps, and a massive, ground-shaking explosion incinerated the entire gas station. As everyone ran from the explosion, no one seemed to notice me on the ground, bleeding from my ears. I could only watch as cars crashed into one another in the chaos. Glass and metal shards flew everywhere, and the moon watched everything from high above.

I tried to crawl out of the way of the action, but couldn't move very well. Looking into the flames from the gas station, I saw something moving around. Then the winged horse leapt out of the flames. It slowly walked over to me, stepping over the broken glass and metal, which sparkled on the ground from the fire and moon. There was nobody around to see it but me.

"Go away," I choked. Smoke began to clog my throat. The horse continued walking over to me. Its long fangs reflected the fire. The black fur shined in the silvery moonlight. As it came closer, I noticed that its glowing eyes were the exact same as Zenox's when he fought James; dark spheres with red clouds that swirled.

"Go away!" I cried, rolling over. Every part of my body seemed to ache as I dragged myself onto the sidewalk. I collapsed as my arms started to give out. My vision was going out. I was suffering from brain damage. Blood oozed out of my ears and down to my neck. When I looked back, the horse was standing no more than four feet away, watching me struggle to get away from it.

"Please," I begged, "go away. Go away…" I tasted my blood as it dripped from my mouth and nose.

I started moving backwards. The demonic horse used its sharp teeth to grab me by the leg. I fought with all my strength (which wasn't much) as it dragged me off the road. I couldn't hear anything but the roaring fire and the moon singing.

When I was off the road I felt a strong nudge. The horse rolled me onto my back. Then I gazed directly into its eyes. It seemed to be stimulating my soul. Visions flickered in front of me, then they fell into place, playing like a movie.

CHAPTER FIFTEEN

Police were investigating the house around six-thirty in the morning. Freshly fallen snow covered the ground, eliminating any possible footprints that would be useful to the investigators. FBI agents had gone into the bedroom where the incident took place that night while everyone slept. News reporters collected photographs and information, trying to get the best possible story. Neighbors were gathered around, shaking their heads at the fact that such a terrible thing happened on Christmas. In the midst of everything, the six-year-old Krystal sat in the warmth of a police cruiser and wept over the loss of her parents. Two cops were standing right outside the car, and Krystal was overhearing their conversation through her sobs.

"What are we going to do about the girl?" one officer asked another.

"She'll have to be taken to an orphanage," the other replied. "It makes me absolutely sick. How could someone do something like this, especially on Christmas?"

"We'll have to catch this criminal," said the first officer.

At that time, a black minivan pulled up and parked along-side the road.

"Who are *these* guys?" one of the officers asked.

Krystal watched as two men wearing casual clothing stepped out of the van. One of them was a middle-aged man with scraggly, graying hair, who looked around with a wrinkled and firm face. The other was much younger, with blonde hair and glasses, and he carried a large envelope tucked under his arm.

"Hello officers," said the older man to the two cops standing next to the police car in which Krystal sat, wiping her eyes. "Merry Christmas to you both."

"Can we help you?" the first cop asked.

"Yes," said the younger man, "it concerns the girl."

"If we could speak to you over here in privacy," said the older man, "we'd appreciate it."

The two cops followed the men to the other side of the black minivan, out of Krystal's range of hearing. She peered out through the windshield to see what was going on. The younger man opened the large envelope and removed a stack of papers, then showed them to the officers. They skimmed through the papers, glanced back at the rest of the police and FBI agents around the house, then shook their heads and handed the papers back to the younger man.

Even though Krystal couldn't hear what they were saying, it was obvious that the two men were trying to talk the cops into something. The cops kept glancing back at the others, then glancing over at Krystal. After a few more minutes, the men apparently talked the police into what they wanted, because they shook hands. The two police men hurried back to the others.

The older man got into the driver's side of the van, and the younger man with glasses came over to the police cruiser where Krystal sat. He gave her a friendly smile as he asked her to come out. At first, Krystal was a little scared, but she then opened the door and slowly got out of the car. Looking over, the two cops were distracting everyone's attention so they wouldn't see what was happening.

"Hi there!" the man told Krystal. He was extremely friendly. "My name's Charlie. Is your name Krystal?"

"Yeah," Krystal sniffed. "What happened to Mommy and Daddy?"

"They're not here anymore," Charlie replied dully. "You'll have to be living with me now."

"I w-want my M-Mommy and Daddy," Krystal sobbed.

"We'll have to hurry," said Charlie, picking Krystal up and carrying her over to the minivan. He opened the backdoor and set her in the back seat, making sure that she was buckled in tightly.

"Hi!" said the older man after Charlie had closed the door. "I'm Thomas, and you must be Krystal." Krystal didn't respond, but just sniffed. "We're going on a long trip, so try and get some sleep."

"It'll all be better soon," Charlie assured as he got in the passenger's side and buckled up. "You're going to a new home now."

The van started to move, and Krystal gazed out the window at her home that she would be leaving. Tears streamed down her face, and when the van rounded the corner, she began to cry. Charlie and Thomas exchanged looks of pity at the sound of Krystal's sorrow, and said nothing. They obviously understood what kind of immense pain the girl was suffering.

Nearly an hour later, Krystal calmed down and stared out

the window. The sky was covered with gray, and everything was blanketed with snow. An awful feeling was lingering in her heart; a feeling of emptiness and hopelessness. She had felt a spine-chilling sensation the night of her parents death. The moon was out that night, and she had heard its beautiful lullaby.

"We're almost to the airport, Krystal," said Thomas.

"Hear that?" said Charlie excitedly. "You get to ride an airplane, Krystal! Won't that be fun? We'll be way up in the air, like the birds!"

Krystal looked up at Charlie, then nodded weakly.

At the airport, Thomas drove around the parking lot, looking around for something. When he found it, he immediately drove over and parked the van and climbed out. Charlie got out of the minivan, then helped Krystal out.

"Thank you," Thomas told another man. He was dressed in a suit that matched the color of the black minivan. Thomas handed him the envelope. The man took out a lighter and burned it, bid Thomas and Charlie farewell, then got in the van and hastily drove away.

"This way, Krystal," said Charlie, taking Krystal's hand. They followed Thomas into the airport, which was full of the holiday crowd. Krystal gripped Charlie's hand tightly as the three of them had to weave through the people to their terminal. When they reached the waiting area, Krystal took a seat next to Charlie.

"We have half an hour," said Thomas, "then our flight takes off. I'll go check on Alexandria to see if she's ready to go."

"We'll just stay here then," said Charlie. Thomas hurried off, peeking at his watch. "Would you like a candy bar, Krystal?" Charlie asked, reaching into his pocket.

Krystal shook her head, but when she was presented with the candy bar, she snatched it away and devoured it.

"Take as many as you like," said Charlie, pulling out a handful. Krystal took them all, then ate them quickly one by one. She never was much of an eater, but she quickly realized that eating took away from the pain she felt over the loss of her parents. A mental note was taken that she would have to eat more often to get over her pain.

After eating the last candy bar, Krystal sat quietly next to Charlie, looking around the waiting area at all of the other people. She would sometimes look out the window at the planes that were taxiing, boarding, taking off, and landing. Charlie remained quiet, and whenever Krystal would look up at him, he would smile down at her. Before long, Krystal started to feel a little comfortable with him.

Nearly thirty minutes had passed when Krystal looked over at another little girl who had sat down across the room. The girl's parents sat down next to her, and Krystal began to whimper when she saw it.

"There now," said Charlie gently, picking her up and putting her on his lap, "it'll be okay soon. Don't worry."

"Mommy...Daddy..."

Krystal wrapped her arms around Charlie's neck. She began to calm back down as Thomas returned with a lady with long, brown hair.

"Ben said that the plane's ready," said the lady. Charlie stood up, holding Krystal. "We'd better hurry, otherwise the airport will notice us. This is a top secret flight that we must never attempt again."

"Thank you, Alexandria," said Charlie earnestly, "but I already know the policies, so you don't have to tell me any of this."

"Let's go," Thomas urged. They hurried through the airport, pushing through the crowd. Krystal looked around, innocent and oblivious to everything that was going on. Hurrying down a hallway through a restricted area, Thomas glanced at his watch again, and they sped up the pace. At the end of the hall, another man in a black suit opened an emergency fire exit that led outside to the runway. He was probably a little younger than Thomas. The man closed the door behind him, and all of them hurried over to a small jet waiting around the corner.

"Quickly," said the man in the suit, looking nervously around as he ushered the others up the stairs to the jet. After everyone had entered the plane, he rushed up the stairs and closed the door behind him. Charlie placed Krystal in a seat next to a window, then quickly sat down next to her. When they were situated, a tall black man came out of the cockpit.

"Is everyone ready to go?" he asked.

"Aye, Captain Ben," the man in the suit replied.

"Thanks, Jeff," Ben told the man in the suit. "We'll be taking off now, everyone."

Krystal peered out of the window. It was her first time on an airplane, but she was anything but excited. Ben and Jeff went back into the cockpit and positioned themselves for takeoff. The plane started to move, and Alexandria let out a small groan.

"What a long flight for such a small plane," she muttered.

"The smaller the plane," said Thomas, "the better we are. Also, this is a special design, so it's somewhat faster than a normal plane."

"Hmm, I guess you're right," Alexandria replied dully, "but it's still small."

Ben steered the plane around until he was on the runway. Charlie reached into his pocket and took out a candy bar, which he unwrapped. Krystal was looking at him eagerly, and when Charlie saw her, he chuckled.

"I have to eat, too," he said. He broke it in half and handed a share to Krystal, who munched it down. "We'll get you a real meal once we get there."

"Uh oh," said Jeff from the cockpit. "That's not good."

"Damn right!" Ben replied. Everyone (besides Krystal, who was still eating her candy bar) leaned out into the aisle to see out the windshield. A large passenger jet was coming in for landing on the runway they were using and was coming down straight at the little plane. "Hold on, everyone!"

Ben turned the airplane to the side and accelerated. Krystal felt herself being pressed against the back of the chair as the plane started to speed up, and then a voice sounded over the captain's radio.

"Air control to idiot! Do you read?"

"I hear ya!" Ben barked, trying to force the plane up out of the way of the oncoming passenger jet. "What d'ya want?"

"What are you doing?" the radio yelled. "You're heading right for that jet!"

"Tell me something I don't know!" said Ben, struggling with the controls.

"You are an unauthorized aircraft," said the radio. "Do not take off! I repeat, do not take off!"

"Oh, shove it!" Ben pulled back on the controls as hard as he could. The other plane noticed the smaller one, and swerved to the side just before landing. The little jet lifted off the second the passenger jet touched down, and the two barely missed each other.

"Let's try to avoid anymore incursions, shall we?" said Jeff to Ben.

"It's not like I did it intentionally," Ben replied.

"Air control to unauthorized aircraft! Prepare for landing

immediately!"

"Like that'll happen," said Jeff, wiping off his face. "They'll never find us. We have the secret accessory."

"I didn't want to use it," said Ben. "It takes up a lot of power, but I guess we don't have a choice." He reached over and flipped a toggle on the wall. A few seconds later, there was a strange flash and a shake. Then the plane leveled out. Krystal grabbed the arms of her chair tightly.

"This should keep us covered," said Thomas.

"Of course it should," Alexandria replied. "It was my design."

"It was *my* idea, though," said Thomas. "If it wasn't for me, you never would have installed the invisibility device."

"That's *cloaking* device," Alexandria corrected. "It's much more sophisticated."

A few minutes passed, and Ben reached back over and turned off the cloaking device. There was another flash and a shake, and Krystal once again gripped the arms of her chair.

The rest of the ride was boring. No one said a whole lot, and when they did, it wasn't very interesting to Krystal. She continued to stare out the window at the ground thousands of feet below her. Her main thoughts were about where she was going, and why these people went through so much just to get her.

"Charlie," she said timidly.

"What is it, dear?" he replied.

"Where are we going?"

Charlie chuckled again. "I thought you'd ask that. We're going to a laboratory for scientists. A lot of people there want to know about you, so we're taking you to them. You'll live there from now on."

He looked down at Krystal, then realized that what they were doing was somewhat inhuman. They were forcing a little girl to live in a laboratory just for the sole purpose of scientific research. She was intended to be a human guinea pig for life. Charlie leaned back in his chair, letting out a sigh. Krystal looked at him, then slowly looked back out the window, crying silently.

A few hours later, Ben started to bring the airplane down. When Krystal gazed out of the plane, she saw a huge desert that stretched as far as she could see. She gripped the seat tightly once more as Ben aimed for the landing strip. The plane touched down, and the tires chirped as they came into contact with the ground.

"We're here," Ben announced once the plane came to a halt.

"Follow me," said Charlie as he unbuckled Krystal. Jeff opened the door and led everyone down the stairs. Even though it was Christmas, the desert was still warm during the day. Krystal took off her coat as soon as she made it to the bottom of the stairs. Jeffrey went back into the plane and closed the door, then Ben taxied the plane into a hangar.

The place they were at looked like a military base. The entire area was closed in by huge fences. Beyond the fence was nothing but desert. Krystal had to shield her eyes from the sun as it beat down on her.

"We'd better get inside," said Alexandria. "Charlie, you take Krystal. Thomas and I will go to the lab and we'll start first thing tomorrow. For now, we'll let the child rest and try to get settled in." She looked down at Krystal, who was still shielding her eyes from the sun. "Terrible, isn't it?"

"What is?" asked Thomas.

"What we're doing," Charlie replied. "She's just a child."

"I know," said Thomas grimly, "but research is research. We're doing it for the pursuit of knowledge about this thing, right?"

"Darknae," said Alexandria thoughtfully. "A mysterious force, no doubt. Well, let's get going now."

"Come with me, Krystal," Charlie told Krystal. She followed him with the others into one of the nearby buildings. The inside looked like a typical office building as she went with Charlie to the back where the elevators were. He pushed the down button, and the four of them stepped in the elevator. They rode the elevator down until it stopped at Level 5.

"We'll begin tomorrow, then?" said Alexandria as she and Thomas stepped out.

"Right after breakfast," Charlie replied.

The door closed, and Krystal rode the elevator down with Charlie to Level 10. Krystal looked up at the number of levels, and noticed that the lowest level was 15.

Charlie walked out of the elevator and down the hall, which looked like a hallway in a hotel. Krystal tagged along, sticking close to Charlie.

"Here we go," he said, stopping at a door. "Room 321. This is your room from now on." He took out a keycard and swiped the slot next to the door. There was a click, and Charlie opened the door. Krystal walked in and looked around. The room was more or less a studio. There was a bed, a television, a small refrigerator, a microwave, a dresser with a mirror, and a full bathroom. In the corner of the room was a small stack of presents wrapped in colorful paper.

"These are from everyone who you'll meet tomorrow," said Charlie when Krystal made her way over to the presents. "It's not much, but it's a little Christmas cheer. I'll be in the room right across the hallway if you need me. Just come right in if you want something, okay?"

He turned and walked out, then slowly began to close the door, watching Krystal sit down in front of the stack of presents.

"Merry Christmas, Krystal."

"Merry Christmas, Charlie."

The next day, Krystal woke up, glanced around the room, then realized in a state of panic that she was no longer in her old bedroom. Since the room was underground there were no windows, and the only source of light came from a nightlight shining from the bathroom.

"*Mommy*! *Daddy*!" Krystal sprang from her bed. The walls seemed to close in on her, and she began to feel suffocated. She cried out for her parents, but they did not come to her.

The sound of scuffling came from outside her door. Charlie burst into the room and flicked on the lights, looking shocked and concerned. He was wearing pajamas, a sure sign that he had just woken up.

"What's wrong?" he asked, hurrying across the room and scooping the sobbing girl into his arms.

"I w-want my m-mommy and daddy!" Krystal choked through tears.

"Don't worry," said Charlie soothingly. "I've got you. You're safe now."

Thomas came running down the hall and into the room, shortly followed by Alexandria. Both of them were also in their pajamas.

"I heard something," said Thomas. "Is everything all right?"

"It's fine now," Charlie replied, hugging Krystal tighter. "She just panicked a little, that's all."

"This was to be expected," said Alexandria. She yawned and stretched. "Ugh, what time is it?"

"About seven-thirty," said Thomas, glancing at the clock on the wall. "Not bad timing, too. Considering we usually get up at eight in the morning day after day, I say the kid's going to get along well here."

"She's a lot like us," said Alexandria as Charlie set Krystal on the bed. "We live and work here, twenty-four hours a day."

"That's what we agreed to when we volunteered for this field of research," Thomas told her. "Not like those guys in the extraterrestrial sector who can go home every day."

"I guess we'd better get ready," said Charlie, glancing at the time. "The meeting was arranged to be held at noon."

Krystal was standing in front of a large conference room next to Charlie, Thomas, and Alexandria. About fifteen people who looked like scientists were sitting around a table, looking eagerly up at them. Alexandria stepped up behind a podium, speaking to the group.

"We're gathered here today," she said formally, "to discuss the direction of Project Darknae. As you know, for the past seven years, we've been working to improve our knowledge about the force of Darknae. We have been studying it to see exactly what it is, what it does, and why it exists."

"Since the beginning of Project Darknae," Charlie announced, "I have been in charge of recording everything about our progress. Everything is written here in this book." He held up a book that looked nearly a hundred years old. "All of the records have been written in Latin to help ensure that if it fell into the wrong hands, it would be difficult to decipher. Also, the book has been infused with Luminae, giving it a resistance to damage."

"Our progress," said Thomas, "has been rather slow recently. Not much more could be learned about Darknae. However, we believe that we will be able to once again continue Project Darknae. We have brought to Base 15 a subject who has been exposed to Darknae and its terrible effects. Everyone, please welcome Krystal." The entire room applauded as Krystal shyly wrapped her arms around Charlie's waist.

"Krystal's parents were taken by Darknae," said Charlie, and the room immediately became noiseless. "More specifically, by the moon. Research has shown us that the power of Darknae is too incredible for its own good. When existing by itself, Darknae is forced into a physical form. The form that is taken resembles a horse that is similar to Pegasus, but demonic in appearance. This phenomenon has been given the name Night Stallion."

"Darknae," said Alexandria, "does not like being in the form of Night Stallion. When in a physical form, it possesses extraordinary power and combat abilities, but has to follow the laws of physics, and since it's a physical being, it can be killed. Its ability to be anywhere and everywhere at one time is taken away. This is why it will look for a host body to possess that we call the Rionah Darknae. The Rionah Darknae is used to channel the power of Darknae through a weapon called Shadow Blade."

"When Darknae is in control of its Rionah," said Thomas, "it will seek to find the Rionah Luminae. Naturally, the goal of Darknae is to destroy Luminae. To achieve this, it must kill the Rionah Luminae. After the Rionah Luminae is dead, Luminae will be forced to take a physical form as well. Luminae will take the form of a large bird we call White Phoenix, and will be vulnerable to death and eternal defeat."

"This is where the moon comes in," said Charlie, pulling Krystal closer to him. "The moon is a tool of Darknae. When Night Stallion needs a Rionah Darknae, it needs to feed upon a certain type of soul. If a soul contains the right balance of Luminae and Darknae, Night Stallion will dissipate as Darknae inhabits the host body and use it as the Rionah Darknae."

"The moon sings a lullaby," said Alexandria, "which it uses to put people into a trance-like state as it stimulates the soul. Once in this state, Night Stallion is able to extract the person's soul and eat it. This is exactly what's happening at this very moment. As we speak, Darknae is in the form of Night Stallion, roaming the country for the right soul. If it finds a new host body, a violent storm similar to a hurricane will strike the area as a result of the shifting of Darknae energy."

"The moon's lullaby," said Charlie, "is an extremely dangerous weapon. We have named the lullaby Darknae Sonata, after Project Darknae. Very few have ever heard it and survived. One of them is standing right here."

Krystal could feel the eyes of every person in the room burning into her. She felt very uncomfortable, holding onto Charlie even tighter.

"Luminae is different, though," said Thomas, breaking everyone's attention away from Krystal. "Luminae has no tool it uses. Unlike Darknae, Luminae does not destroy or harm the soul in any way. Also, Luminae does not choose random people in an attempt to find a new Rionah, because it already knows who the Rionah Luminae is. It will simply wait until the Rionah's soul has matured enough to handle its power, then bestow that person with the ability to control Luminae. The Rionah Luminae is not possessed like the Rionah Darknae, and he or she will retain all free will and personality."

"Right now," said Charlie, "Luminae is the dominating force. We live off its power. Luminae and Darknae struggle against each other for eternity, striving to become the dominant force. The supreme goal of both forces is to create a perfect world for themselves."

"We will be doing research on Krystal," said Alexandria, "hoping that her exposure to Darknae, Night Stallion, and Darknae Sonata will be of use to Project Darknae. We ask that you welcome Krystal, for she is now one of us. That is all."

There was an applause from the group of people in the room. Krystal looked around, still clutching Charlie tightly. She had no clue as to what was just explained, but it sounded scary.

The twelve-year-old Krystal sat in a fancy dining area that looked like a nice restaurant. Everyone who was in the conference room was there, singing happy birthday as Charlie set a cake in front of Krystal with twelve burning candles.

"Make a wish, Kristy!" Charlie told her. Krystal took a deep breath, then blew out all of the candles at once. Everyone clapped cheerfully as Krystal smiled broadly.

"Alright, everyone," Alexandria said loudly, "everyone grab a plate and get some cake and ice cream!"

Charlie served a large piece of cake to Krystal as Thomas came over with a tub of ice cream. He scooped out a big serving and heaped it on Krystal's plate. The others were all waiting in line with their plates and forks, and Charlie and Thomas served them all one by one.

Before everyone had settled down and began eating, Krystal had eaten everything and was going back for seconds. When she finished, Alexandria and a few other people carried

Krystal's presents to her. Krystal saw them and let out a small squeal of joy.

"Oh, this is great!" she said happily. The entire room watched as she picked up the one on top. "This one's from Lenny!" she announced, tearing open the wrapper and revealing a sketchpad and a box of crayons. "I love it!" she said. "Thanks, Lenny! You know how much I love to make pictures!"

"No problem," said an elderly man sitting near the back.

The next present Krystal unwrapped was a calendar. As she flipped through the pages, her eyes scanned the pictures of the nice sports cars.

"It's a sports car calendar!" she said excitedly. "I love fast cars! Do you think I'll be able to drive one of the Zoe cars someday?"

"Those are SP weapons we made," Charlie told her. "They aren't for joyriding, but I'll see what I can do."

After going through the entire pile, Krystal finally made it to the last one. She picked it up and put it on the table, reading the label.

"This is from you guys," she said, grinning at Charlie, Thomas, and Alexandria.

"Hope you like it," Charlie told her with a smile.

Krystal ripped it open quickly. Inside, she found something that she never expected, but was altogether happy to get.

"I hope you like it," said Thomas. "A video game system."

"You mean like in the arcade?" Krystal asked, getting excited.

"Even better," said Thomas. "You can play it on your TV, and you get hundreds of different games, not just the same one. Our arcade here at Base 15 is small, but I know how much you and Charlie liked to go there."

"Wow, guys, thanks!" Krystal got up and gave Charlie, Thomas, and Alexandria a hug. "I'll be the best video game player ever!"

"Nothing but the best for our dear Kristy," said Alexandria, rustling Krystal's hair.

Krystal was sitting in the lounge, drawing a picture on her sketchpad. Alexandria was trying to find out the notations for the Darknae Sonata on the grand piano as Charlie was putting an entry in his book. Thomas walked over to him, looked over his shoulder, then chuckled.

"What're you drawing the piano for?" he asked.

"I feel like it," Charlie answered. "Kristy's drawing it too."

"Really?" Thomas went over to Krystal and looked at her crayon doodle of the piano. "Say, that's pretty good. How come you have so much blood all over it?"

"Because of the song," Krystal replied. "The song that Alexandria's trying to figure out is bad, right? Doesn't it kill people?"

"Hmm, true," said Thomas, walking back over to Alexandria.

"Yeah, I think I'll put blood on mine too," said Charlie. "I like that idea. Thanks, Kristy."

"You guys are so violent," said Alexandria. She played around with the piano some more. "I think I have it. Kristy, do you mind if I ask you if this is the song?"

"Go ahead," said Krystal dismally. She hated to hear the song again, with all of its terrible memories tied to it. Alexandria began to play a beautiful song, and chills shot down Krystal's spine. The hair on her neck stood straight up. "Stop," she said shortly.

Alexandria instantly stopped playing and looked over at Krystal.

"Is that the song?"

"That's it," Krystal replied dully.

"Are you okay?" Charlie asked, looking up from his book.

"Yeah," she said, flipping the page of her sketchpad. Then she began to draw a picture of the moon as it sang. There was silence as Charlie continued to record in his book, Alexandria wrote the music for Darknae Sonata down on paper, Thomas flipped through the newspaper, and Krystal finished her drawing with two dead people under the moon.

"You know," said Thomas, putting down his newspaper, "I was thinking—"

"Don't start with that," Alexandria interrupted quickly.

"We should just go ahead with it," said Thomas. "I don't see why not."

"The risks are too great," said Alexandria sternly. "Even though I see how it could be extremely beneficial, it could be extremely dangerous at the same time."

"But you don't know that," Thomas argued. Krystal looked

up, knowing that this conversation was about to lead to her. She'd heard it before.

"Extracting part of someone's soul is inhuman," Charlie told him. "Even if it's just a small part."

"But we need to study it more closely," said Thomas. "The emptiness that Kristy feels from the loss of her parents may be a key to how the Darknae works. If we take out the hole created in Kristy's soul and study it, then—"

"*I said no!*" Alexandria barked. "It may be just an emptiness, but it's still part of her soul. Removing it could cause Kristy permanent damage! As far as we know, it could even kill her, so don't even think about doing such a thing!" Alexandria snatched up her things and stormed out of the room, muttering curses to herself.

"You know," said Charlie after Alexandria had left, "she's right, Thomas. There's no telling what that could do. We don't even know if it'll work."

"Hmm," Thomas replied unenthusiastically, raising his eyebrows. He picked up his newspaper and resumed reading.

Shortly after, Alexandria came running back into the room, looking excited.

"Guys, come quick!" she said breathlessly. "They just caught something out in the desert!"

"What is it?" Thomas asked, standing up with Charlie.

"I don't know," Alexandria replied. "They said it's nearly dead from the heat, and they're bringing it back. C'mon, hurry!"

She whirled around as Charlie and Thomas hurried after her. Krystal put down her sketchpad and crayons and ran with them. They raced through the sector until Alexandria led them to a long, white hallway that resembled a hospital. At the end was a large, steel door that was tightly closed. Krystal was strictly forbidden to enter that room, and for a split second, thought that was the room they were heading to. However, they followed Alexandria into another room halfway down the hall, and Krystal's eyes flickered curiously toward the restricted room at the end of the hall as she followed them in. When they saw what Alexandria was excited about, all of them froze in shock.

"We finally got it in the containment chamber," Lenny said to them. "It didn't put up much of a fuss, since it was nearly dead, but we were inflicted with a weird and chilly pain every time we touched it."

"What is that?" Thomas asked, awestruck at the creature

floating inside the large, glass tube. "No, it can't be…"

It was a horse, no bigger than a pony. The fur was completely black, and two large wings protruded from its back and pressed against the glass. Massive talons extended from its hooves, and long fangs stuck out of its mouth, in which an air tube was inserted. Its eyes were closed, and, just as described, it looked nearly dead.

"Our equipment picked up a saturated concentration of pure Darknae from it," a female scientist said from behind her computer desk.

"We believe," said Lenny, "that we have captured Night Stallion."

"Incredible," Charlie whispered, staring at the demonic horse through the glass.

"Do you know what this means?" said Alexandria excitedly. "We have the Darknae in our custody! Now we can study it to the fullest! Sorry, Thomas, but there's no need for your asinine experiment with Krystal's soul anymore."

"Perhaps," Thomas replied coolly, squinting his eyes at Alexandria.

"So," said Krystal with a shudder, "is this what killed my parents?"

Everyone in the room turned and looked at her. They didn't seem to realize that she was even in there with them.

"That's correct," said Charlie quietly.

Krystal didn't say a word, but instead walked slowly up to the glass chamber that imprisoned Night Stallion. The cold, frightening energy that radiated from it swept through her. She stopped a few inches away, gazing at the creature that killed her parents six years ago on that cold, lonely winter night on Christmas Eve…

Krystal was in the dining area eating breakfast with Charlie, and Alexandria was having the same argument with Thomas.

"I don't think it's Darknae," Thomas tried to explain. "Whatever energy radiated from the emptiness in her soul, it definitely isn't anything that I've—"

"If it's not Darknae," Alexandria growled, "then it's not our concern."

"This is a new field of study!" Thomas told her impatiently.

"We have to find out exactly what it is, otherwise it'll go unheard of!"

"Let it go unheard of!" Alexandria slammed her fork on the table, and it bounced and clinked against the plates. "Come on, Charlie! We have to help study Night Stallion's brain waves." She stood up so quickly that she knocked over her chair. Without picking it up, she marched out of the dining area. Charlie got up, pushed in his chair, and took off after her.

"Why is she so mad?" Krystal asked Thomas.

"She doesn't understand my research," he replied. He looked around the room, then lowered his voice almost to a whisper. "Say, why don't we just go ahead and do it anyway? We don't have to tell her."

"But won't she get mad?" Krystal asked.

"Not unless she finds out." Thomas wiped off his mouth, then stood up. "Just think, you'll be doing us all a big favor."

"Really?" Krystal loved being a big help. "Okay, let's go!"

She went with Thomas down the long hallways. Along the way, she beamed with the thought of helping out with something so important. Maybe Alexandria would finally realize that they were doing something good. They made it to the long hallway that they were in the week before, passing by the room that contained Night Stallion. The door was shut, and the words "Project Darknae" were on the door.

"Here we are," said Thomas, stopping in front of the steel door at the end of the hallway.

"I'm not allowed in there," Krystal told him.

"Not without permission," he said, taking out a keycard. He swiped it through the pad next to the door. Unlike the other doors, this door hissed loudly as it cracked open, shooting out steam. Looking around, Thomas stepped inside, pulling Krystal in with him. He turned on the lights, then closed the door behind him.

The room looked a lot like an operation room at the hospital. There was an operation table in the middle of the room, and a number of large and high-tech machines were all over the place. Wires were strung across the ceiling and along the floor and walls. Next to the operation table was a giant glass chamber identical to the one Night Stallion was being held in.

"Go and lie down on the table, Kristy," said Thomas. "I'll get everything ready for the experiment."

Krystal eagerly climbed up onto the table and stretched out

on it. Thomas began running the machinery and computers, filling the room with a dull, low humming sound. After a few minutes of setting up the equipment, he moved behind a control panel and began to operate what looked like a large laser that hung down directly over Krystal, who watched it slowly aim directly at her chest. Looking over, she noticed that a big tube was connected from the laser to the top of the glass chamber.

"There we go," said Thomas. "This laser is called a Heart-fire Cannon. Heartfire is an energy type used to do surgery on souls. It can distort time and space, and it can cause serious damage to someone's soul if it's not controlled. I'm going to extract the empty hole in your soul created from the death of your parents. It'll travel from the cannon through a tube and go into the containment chamber where I'll be able to study it more closely."

"Why is it called Heartfire?" Krystal asked.

"It's just a name," said Thomas. "Don't worry, it's not as bad as it sounds. Are you ready?"

"Ready," said Krystal, who was so used to experiments that she didn't feel the least bit nervous.

Thomas activated the laser, which shot a bright beam of red light directly into Krystal's chest. Her entire body began to glow like the sun as an ice cold sensation poured over her, but there wasn't any pain. The lights in the room dimmed as a tremendous amount of power was fed into the laser.

After a few seconds, there was a loud sucking noise as a bright glowing orb of white light came out of Krystal's chest and traveled up the red beam of light coming from the laser. The beam stopped when the sample of Krystal's soul entered the laser and came out through the tube. Thomas watched, transfixed on the glowing orb as it came out of the other end of the tube and entered the containment chamber. The water inside instantly fogged over and began to glow brightly.

Thomas turned off all of the equipment and slowly made his way across the room to the glass chamber. A victorious smile spread across his face as he examined the glowing fog inside.

"I did it!" he whispered excitedly. "Kristy, look! It worked...Kristy?"

Krystal had sat up, and was staring straight ahead of her, wearing a completely blank and emotionless expression. At the sound of her name, she slowly turned her head to look at Thomas.

"Kristy? Are you feeling all right?"

Krystal slid off the table onto her feet, then straightened herself up.

"I'm fine," she said timidly. "I'll be in my room." Her face was completely blank.

"Are you okay?" Thomas asked her. He felt as if he had just made a grave mistake. Maybe he should have listened to Alexandria.

Krystal walked over to the door, opened it up, and without even looking back, stepped out. Thomas glanced at the glowing glass containment chamber, then hurried out of the room, making sure to turn off all the lights.

"Kristy, are you sure you're okay?" He stopped her a little ways down the hallway.

"I'm fine," she repeated quietly, giving Thomas a weak smile.

"Look into my eyes," Thomas told her. He looked directly into Krystal's beautiful blue eyes, then realized with absolute horror that something had gone terribly wrong. It seemed as if she was looking straight through him instead of at him. He took a couple of steps back, observing Krystal's behavior. She stared at him with no emotion on her face, then gave another meager smile, turned around, then walked away.

"Oh God," Thomas whispered to himself, putting his hands over his face. "What the hell have I done?"

He stared down at the floor, thinking about how Alexandria had argued with him, saying that his experiment would be dangerous. Thomas felt extremely guilty; his experiment had succeeded, but with the consequences he was warned about. He looked back up to see Krystal standing a few feet away, staring at him. The expression on her face made the hair on his neck stand on end. If looks could kill, he'd have been killed on the spot. She had an extremely bloodthirsty look in her eyes and a deathly chilling grin.

"Kristy?" Thomas asked nervously. He took a few steps back.

"I want to kill you," Krystal replied in a playful voice.

"Don't say things like that." Thomas backed away some more.

"I want to kill you," Krystal repeated in the same childish voice. "I want to rip open your chest and eat your beating heart."

Thomas backed up against the steel door leading into the

restricted room. Krystal didn't move, but continued to give him the same murderous smile. Without warning, she clapped her hands over her ears and began whining.

"Make the moon stop singing," she whimpered. "It won't stop singing!" Krystal staggered around the hall, still covering her ears. She started screaming, then fell to the floor in a fit of convulsions. Doors flew open as scientists rushed into the hall to see what was happening. Charlie and Alexandria were amongst them.

"Take her to the medical sector immediately!" Charlie ordered. He and a few others hurried over and picked her up, but she flailed her arms and legs, making it difficult to get a good hold on her.

After much struggling, Krystal was hauled quickly to the facility's emergency room. The doctors and nurses had to slam her body onto the operating table to tie her arms and legs down.

"Get away from me!" Krystal yelled. "*Don't touch me!*"

"Bring the tranquilizers!" the head doctor ordered. A nurse rushed over to the shelves and retrieved a tranquilizer needle. They had to hold her arm down to inject it into her blood. A few more moments passed, and the tranquilizer had no effect.

"We need more!" the doctor shouted over Krystal's screaming. The nursed fetched him another dose of tranquilizers. They attempted to inject her again, but she fought them back harder. She slammed her left hand down on the tray of surgical tools, slicing a deep gash into her palm.

"*No more tranquilizers! Please, no more!*"

Eventually, the medical team was able to subdue her and pump her full of enough tranquilizers to calm her down. Just as the doctors wiped off their foreheads, a loud explosion was heard echoing down the halls. A few of them took off to investigate, while the others stayed to watch over Krystal. Moments later, one of the doctors returned, extremely frightened and pale as a ghost.

"It's the specimen from Project Darknae!" he sputtered. "It broke loose!"

Before anyone could react, there was a flash of blue fire, then Night Stallion came up from behind the doctor and dug its huge talons into his back. The doctor let out a yell of pain as Night Stallion slammed him into a wall and ripped his back open, spurting blood everywhere. The horse leapt into the medical room and growled, exposing its sharp teeth, making all of the doctors and nurses cower in the corner.

Night Stallion saw Krystal laying on the table. She was full of tranquilizers and wasn't moving much, leaving her completely defenseless as the demonic horse advanced closer to her. Charlie and Alexandria both charged at it, determined to protect Krystal with their lives.

The horse went berserk, slashing both of them at once. They collapsed, badly injured, and Night Stallion began to attack the other doctors and nurses. Krystal, however, remained on the table, looking at the horse with almost no expression. She had one of the cutting tools, using it to mindlessly cut herself just above her right eyebrow.

Out of nowhere, Thomas burst into the room and snatched Krystal, then ran out of the room. He slung her over his shoulder, then tore down the halls to the elevator. Explosions were heard from other parts of the facility as Night Stallion rampaged around, destroying everything it came into contact with.

Thomas got to the elevators, but knew that taking them would be a bad idea. If Night Stallion continued ripping the building apart, it could damage the electrical system and they'd be stuck in the elevator shaft. Instead, he flew up the stairs one flight at a time, powered by adrenaline. More explosions and screaming could be heard behind him as he raced for the top floor.

The emergency alarm went off, adding to the tension building up inside Thomas. His lungs felt like they were going to explode if he kept running up the stairs, but he didn't dare slow down. The last thing he wanted was Krystal to die.

At long last, they reached the top floor. Thomas burst out of the emergency exit onto the runway. Turning around, he saw others had already made it out of the building. Wasting no more time, Thomas hurried over to the airplane hangar. Once inside, he set Krystal down and looked her straight in the face.

"I'll have to get you out of here," he choked. "You'll be taken to a place somewhere in the Midwest, far away from this place." His hands fumbled through his pockets, then he pulled out a device that resembled a pair of binoculars. "I'll have to erase your memory of this place, for your own sake. When you get a new place to live, I'll follow you and watch over you. We'll have two of our top-model robots take care of you." An explosion from outside interrupted him. "I have a degree in the medical field, so I'll be working at a hospital close to you. I'll make sure you somehow find

Charlie's book to help inform you of all of this when the time comes. The Luminae will make sure you'll find it. I'm also taking my experiment with us. I'm so sorry for all of this." He held the memory eraser in front of Krystal's eyes. "Good-bye, Kristy."

There was a bright flash of light.

The vision faded out and disappeared, leaving me bleeding on the sidewalk, staring into the glowing red eyes of Night Stallion just before everything went black.

CHAPTER SIXTEEN

I woke up screaming. I was back in the emergency room in the hospital I broke out of, fending off the horde of doctors trying to tie me down to the table. Lights were shining in my eyes, and my head throbbed painfully. I could feel hands forcing me down, and I struggled to escape.

"We need some tranquilizers and sleep gas over here now!" I heard one of them say.

Harder and harder I tried to break free, but the blow to my head severely weakened me. A mask was put over my face, giving me the impression that I was being suffocated. I began to panic, sucking in the gas in large volumes. A calmness swelled through me, and I slowly fell back onto the table. Everything began to get out of focus as they tried to put me to sleep completely.

"Is she asleep yet?" one of the doctors asked.

"There's nothing we can do," another one replied. "This is as close as we can get. Nothing we give her is knocking her out."

"I guess we'll just have to do the operation with her awake," someone said. "Lord have mercy on this poor girl…"

Their voices echoed around me as they began to drill into my skull to release the pressure. I could feel everything they were doing, and I tried to scream and cry out in pain, but I couldn't. There was the sound of clinking metal and cutting of skin and bone. I was trapped between consciousness and sleep, unable to make out what was going on, but feeling the agonizing pain of brain surgery.

Years seemed to pass as they continued with their procedure. I was feeling the worst pain I had ever felt, and I prayed and begged that I would go into shock so I wouldn't have to feel it anymore. Everything I heard was muffled and echoed, and everything I saw was blurred and obscured by the overhead lights. Deep down inside, I was crying and screaming like a tortured child, which is exactly what I was at the moment.

Then came the stitching. I felt the needle being inserted every time. I felt the needle exiting every time. I felt every millimeter of thread pulled through. My heart was crying, and I wanted to do the same, but I couldn't.

I lay awake, drugged up the eyeballs in tranquilizers, as people took me to a room. I heard their voices, saw their faces, and felt their touch, but didn't make sense of anything. It was like a web of nightmares intertwined with each other, each trying to cancel each other out and fill my mind with only their own memories.

The people eventually left the room, leaving me by myself in absolute pain. Whatever medication they gave me started to wear off, and I gained control of my body again. The curtains were opened, and the moon was gone. Light from the city came into my room, casting long shadows on the walls and floor. Night Stallion had shown me my past. I could remember those six years of my childhood. Thomas had erased them, and Darknae restored them.

I sat up, grabbed my bandaged head, and began to scream. I had to cover my mouth with my pillow to muffle the sound. Tears streamed down my face and soaked into my pillow. I wanted to cry, but couldn't.

After the pain had subsided a little, I lied down, facing the ceiling, feeling downright miserable. Certainly they were going to take me to the insane asylum now. That would mean that I would never see Gary and James again. At the thought of that, I rolled over, stuffed my face into the pillow, and forced myself to cry. I wanted to bawl my eyes out. Crying was the best way to release excess pain when it wants to overflow. The best I could do was leak tears. I wanted to cry so badly, but couldn't.

I stopped immediately. There was a dead silence as a dark and terrible feeling built up inside of me. Something bad was about to happen. Hurrying over to the window, I gazed out onto the streets below. The feeling was building up stronger deep down in my soul, and I knew that I had to go find Gary and James.

"Forget it," I mumbled, wiping the tears from my face. I trudged back to the bed and flopped down on it. There was nothing I could do. I was in the hospital with a hole in my head and damage to my brain. My legs felt like jelly and my arms felt like someone had tied weights to them. If Gary and James wanted me with them, then they'd come and get me themselves.

The shadows stretched around the room as silence pressed against my ears. I couldn't sleep, but felt exhausted and washed out. The feeling of inevitable danger began to eat away at my insides. A fine layer of sweat covered my face as I trembled in fright. There was no other feeling like it. It was screaming at me that something purely apocalyptic was going to happen. But there was nothing I could do.

Time seemed to stand still. My heart was beating loudly

and faster every minute. The sweat began to drip down my face. I tried to make the dark feeling go away, but it insisted that I had to do something. The room started to spin as the walls drew closer. I wanted to die. A violent tempest of roaring emotions and controversy swirled inside my mind and soul as the room flipped upside down. Everything started to spin as my stomach contracted viciously...

"Krystal!"

I leaned over the side of the bed and threw up. James turned on the lights as Gary rushed over to me.

"Krystal!" He grabbed me by the shoulders and looked at me. "Oh, what happened?" He wrapped his arms around me, soaking up my sweat in his shirt. "It's going to be fine now. I'm here, don't worry."

I trembled in his arms as he wiped the sweat off my face.

"We came to get you," said James, standing next to the bed. "Some freaky stuff's going on and we thought we'd better get you. I can feel something really bad, so I had to get Gary. Then we came here to get you."

"What'd you do to your head?" Gary asked, looking at the bandaging.

"What room is this?" I asked weakly.

"Uh, 321," James answered, "the same room I was in."

My head started to spin again. Gary hugged me closer.

"What happened?" he asked. "Tell me, babe."

"I broke out." The words seemed to turn into mashed potatoes in my mouth. "The moon...you have to stop Night Stallion..."

"Stop what?" Gary looked into my eyes as if he was trying to read me.

"Night Stallion," I repeated painfully. My chest hurt with every word. "Go now. Don't let it hurt anyone..."

"What's she talking about?" James asked.

"She hit her head," said Gary. "I don't think she knows what she's saying."

"No," I choked. "Please...listen to me. You have to stop Night Stallion."

"Maybe we should keep her here." Gary leaned me back on the bed.

"You're kidding," said James in disbelief. "After all the trouble we went through to get here, you say to leave her here? It's two in the morning!"

"She's really messed up," Gary told him. "Whatever's going on, I think we'll be able to handle it by ourselves."

"You can't!" I spit out, sitting up abruptly. After seeing the two of them, I realized that I had to go with them. They stood no chance against Night Stallion.

"Why not?" said Gary.

"Night Stallion's too strong!" The strange power in my soul was beginning to take control from my concern for their safety. Any physical damage I had was being cancelled out.

"Krystal," said Gary firmly, "Night Stallion is probably something that doesn't exist. We'll be fine."

"I'm going with you," I said. "You'll need me."

"Let's just take her," said James. "It looks like her Soulpower is taking care of things."

"It's not Soulpower," I muttered.

Gary looked at James, then looked at me.

"Okay," said Gary reluctantly. "I really don't want to move you, but it looks like you've made your choice."

"Thanks." I said, forcing a smile. "Let's go."

The three of us hurried out of the room and down the hall. I had no idea to where I was in the building, so I followed the other two. We took the elevator down to the basement level, since the first floor was closed off. Once we were in the basement, we rushed to the underground parking area, then out onto the street. Without thinking, I glanced up at the night sky. The moon wasn't out.

"In case you're wondering, Krystal," said Gary, "the reason why we didn't bring our bikes with us is because we wore them out. Go figure, huh?"

"Well," said James, scratching his head. "What now?"

"We should stick to the alleyways," said Gary. "That way we don't draw attention to ourselves. Let's avoid being conspicuous."

There was a nearby alley that we sneaked into. Making sure no one was around, we got behind a dumpster to discuss our next move. James's brilliant sword glowed a golden yellow in the dark alley.

"First," said Gary, "we have to find out what the threat is."

"It can't be worst than Darknae," James joked. "But we defeated that, so I have no idea what we're up against."

"Darknae," I told him. "Night Stallion is—"

"What did I say about that?" For the first time, Gary sounded annoyed towards me. "It's just a figment of your imagination."

"It's not!" I argued. "This is what—"

"Whoa!" James interrupted. "I've locked onto a location, but it feels…no, never mind. It can't be."

"Well," said Gary, "let's go!"

The two of them took off. I hesitated for a bit, then followed. We darted into the open and across the streets. Cars honked as they nearly hit us. James ran into another alley that was blocked off by a tall fence, which he nimbly leapt over. Gary followed him, and I did the same.

"Soulpower is amazing, isn't it?" said James once we were on the other side.

We ran back onto the streets and down the sidewalk. A few pedestrians scrambled to get out of our way as we charged past them.

"Doesn't this city ever sleep?" James asked while we were running.

I ran with Gary and James for over a mile into the heart of the city. James stopped at a crosswalk and looked around. Gary and I stopped right next to him.

"You know," said James, "don't you think we're conspicuous just by sneaking around like this?"

"Just be swift and silent," said Gary. "How you doing, Krystal?"

"Fine," I said. Whatever power I had inside me was doing a good job of hiding my physical injuries. It had the same properties as Soulpower described by Tyler, but Zenox said it wasn't Soulpower. I was getting really sick of being confused.

We continued through the alleys some more. I never realized how dirty a city is until you hang around the alleys. The dumpsters were all overflowing with any garbage that wasn't strewn all over.

"It's around here somewhere," James whispered.

"Better be on your guard," said Gary. I felt myself tensing up.

"I feel that it's nearby," said James quietly. People in cars were looking out their windows at us.

"Let's hope so," Gary replied. "Some people are looking at us curiously."

"That's not cool," said James, still looking around. "They might call the cops."

"If they do," Gary told him, "that'll be the least of our worries."

"But it'd still suck," said James. "The last thing we need is the cops...hey, do you hear something?"

"Huh?" Gary tried to listen over the sound of traffic for what James was talking about. "It sounds like...," He stopped, and the two of them looked at me slowly with fear in their eyes.

"The moon," I whispered shakily.

The three of us looked directly up at the bright full moon. The beautiful Darknae Sonata flowed down and engulfed us. Icy fear filled my heart, and I had to tear my eyes away from the hypnotic orb in the sky.

An old woman who was in her car got out. She slowly straightened up, staring at the moon. Other people in their cars watched in horror as the moon's lullaby put her into a trance and pulled her into the open.

"Don't listen to it!" I yelled at her. Gary and James also tried to yell at her, but to no avail. The moon had completely taken her over. James tried to hurry over to her, and Gary grabbed his arm to stop him.

To my deathly fright, the sound of wings could be heard over the lullaby. The three of us, along with many others around, watched a black figure no bigger than a pony swoop out of the sky and land on the road, tearing into the pavement with its sharp talons.

"Huh?" Gary gasped.

"Wh-what's that?" James asked in terror.

"Night Stallion," I whispered. The both of them looked at me, and I looked back at them.

Night Stallion approached the possessed woman. A smoky strand of silver light flickered down out of the sky and pierced her through the back, pushing out a ghost-like replica of herself. No doubt it was her soul.

Her soul struggled to break free from the strand of moonlight that entangled her. Night Stallion immediately pounced on it and messily devoured it with its sharp teeth. The lullaby stopped, and there was a strange ripping sound as the soul was torn to shreds and eaten by the demonic horse. James jumped back, Gary stumbled over his feet, and I took a few large steps back. The moon turned crimson, then blood oozed around its edges and slowly poured across the sky. It looked like a raspberry flattened under a piece of glass. The old woman's dead body crumpled to the hard pavement.

"*No!*" I shouted desperately, realizing this is exactly what happened to my parents. My entire body was filled with an agonizing chill.

Night Stallion apparently realized that there was an audience. To take care of that, it reared back onto its hind legs. The mane of blue fire on its back flared up as a white crystalline energy ball took shape inside its mouth.

"Everybody run!" Gary shouted. "It's going to let out an attack!"

Too late. The crystalline energy ball exploded in a massive icy eruption of blue flames, engulfing the entire intersection. Cars were lifted into the air and pushed back, along with everything and everyone else, including Gary, James, and myself. The pavement was shredded up, street lamps were ripped clean out of the ground. Windows exploded and froze over as a wave of freezing cold blasted everything, covering the intersection with a layer of ice. Everyone who was a normal individual was instantly killed.

I hit the ground several yards back. Staggering to my feet, I turned to see a cloud of snow dispersing in the intersection. The blue fire spread quickly over everything, covering it with ice instead of burning it. I quickly brushed the ice off me, glancing nervously around for Gary and James.

"*What was that?*" I heard James yell. He was standing behind me, looking into the sky. "Man, it killed all those people!"

"It's gone," said Gary breathlessly, shaking the ice out of his hair.

"No it's not!" James shouted, whirling around.

Night Stallion flew down, landing about fifteen feet away. Its two glassy eyes with the swirling cloud of red glow stared down the yellow line at us. My heart beat faster as I clenched my fists.

"What is that thing?" James demanded. "Come on, Krystal, you know this more than us! Why does that thing have the same energy Zenox had?"

"It's Night Stallion," I replied hastily. "It's Darknae in a physical form."

"What?" James looked over at me.

"We can talk later!" said Gary. "Here it comes!"

Night Stallion folded its wings back and charged us. It was

so fast that we had little time to react. When it pounced at us, we all attacked at once, but it blocked us with its huge talons and knocked us back.

James fired a beam of Luminae out of Flare Blade, hitting Night Stallion and forcing it back violently against a building. Unfazed, Night Stallion quickly retaliated with lightning-quick speed, head butting James in the chest and sending him flying through the air a few yards. Gary threw a quick fireball at it from behind, but Night Stallion spun around and reflected it. Gary barely dodged it as it soared back and hit an SUV, which exploded and flipped through midair, crashing through a display window.

I was about to attack simultaneously with James, but Night Stallion used its mind to lift an oncoming city bus and hurl it at us. James ducked underneath it and I jumped over, just to find Night Stallion slam its front legs into the ground to create an eruption of fire that exploded out from the road under us.

I was sent nearly fifty feet in the air, and Night Stallion flew up at me with its teeth bared. Putting my hands together, I created a strong pulse of invisible energy that hit it directly in the face. Night Stallion tumbled a little through the air and slashed me across the leg with its talons. I let out a gasp of pain as gravity pulled me back down to the ground. Gary ran over to catch me, but Night Stallion quickly swatted James out of the air, turning him into a projectile which struck Gary at amazing speeds with a sickening crunch. The street was dented with a small crater as I hit the ground facedown after freefalling fifty feet.

Night Stallion dove after the two of them, and Gary managed to roll onto his back and emit a stream of fire that pushed against Night Stallion. James saw what was happening, and quickly aimed his sword and fired a ray of Luminae. The beam struck Night Stallion, rendering it immobile. It fell through the air, and James jumped up and roundhouse kicked it in the side. Night Stallion soared straight across the street and through the window of a jewelry store. The alarm went off as soon as the glass was broken.

"This thing is tough!" James spat, wiping the blood from his mouth. Gary's nose was bloodied, and my leg was covered in blood from the cut.

"We can't give up now," said Gary, holding his finger to his nose to see how badly it was bleeding.

There was a flash of light from the jewelry store, and no more than a second later, the entire store exploded. Night Stallion was in the center of the blast, creating a whirlwind of debris around it. A small tornado took form, then shredded down the streets. Cars, signs, trees, and even people were lifted up and battered against the buildings. Gas tanks exploded, sending ash and smoke into the air. Power lines were torn up and transformers blew, sending sparks everywhere.

Shielding ourselves from the destruction, we didn't see Night Stallion come stampeding at us from the dust and smoke. It pounced on James, knocking him back while attempting to tear him to bits with its talons and fangs.

Gary leapt on its back, but was bucked off. As soon as he fell on the ground, the demonic horse flipped backward onto him. Gary let out a muffled shout, and I ran over, grabbed Night Stallion by one of its wings, and threw it down another street. It bounced off the pavement once and regained balance.

James chased after it as Gary created another fireball. The horse leapt on top of a pickup truck that tried to drive away, picked it up with its talons, and lifted into the air as the driver bailed out. The horse saw the driver try to escape, so it swooped down and bit him nearly in half with a single chomp that emitted a gush of blood, still holding onto the truck. Right before James caught up with it, Night Stallion flew overhead and tried to drop the truck on him. James narrowly avoided it by jumping aside.

Gary threw his fireball, but Night Stallion used its icy fire breath to freeze the attack and turn it into a harmless snowball, which puffed as it hit the horse in the face. The horse swooped after Gary, but James jumped up from behind and struck it in the back with his sword. A wave of warm light erupted from Flare Blade. Night Stallion was struck with surprise and rendered paralyzed by the attack.

James yanked his sword out of the horse's back to stab it again, but Night Stallion regained its strength too soon. The flaming blue mane on its back flared up, blasting James back and onto the road.

I was about to run in and attack again, but I sensed a huge concentration of Darknae build up. Gary and James noticed it too, and all three of us watched in horror as a massive quake of dark energy exploded from Night Stallion. It was much more powerful than the icy attack used moments ago in the intersection. The road was completely ripped down to the sewage line running beneath it. Entire cars and sides of buildings evaporated from the sheer concussion of the explosion. I became buried underneath a huge pile of rubble and debris.

Blasting my way free with my mysterious invisible energy, I saw Night Stallion look up at the moon. It was being called to another victim. Before I could move, the horse took off down the street with James in hot pursuit.

Gary and I quickly ran after James as he leapt onto the busy overpass and into oncoming traffic. Night Stallion was weaving through the onslaught of oncoming vehicles and into a tunnel. I struggled to keep up with Gary, using his flaming energy to guide me.

Up ahead, a van collided head-on with Night Stallion, but the demonic horse simply knocked it aside as if it was made out of cardboard. The van slammed into the wall, and other vehicles slid out of control, smashing into one another and piling up into a large, smoldering wreck. James had barely managed to get ahead of it before it all happened, but Gary and I had to dodge through the chaos.

Once we made it out of the other side of the tunnel, Night Stallion jumped off the overpass into the huge city park. James caught up with it, engaging it close-range combat in midair as they fell to the ground. Gary and I caught up with them, and the three of us teamed up on the horse.

Night Stallion was extremely fast. It mainly used its claws to fend us off, but occasionally would emit powerful dark energy attacks, icy fire, and lightning. Even with it being three against one, Night Stallion was far more powerful than us, and we were at a clear disadvantage.

A forceful strike to my chest from a lightning attack knocked me back. I slammed into a tree and was immediately hit with another energy attack. There was a huge explosion, and I thought my body was going to rip open. I fell to the ground like a lifeless doll, limp and unable to move for a few moments. Struggling, I looked up to see Gary and James being beat up by Night Stallion. They had left the park and taken the brawl back to the crowded streets.

Then that surge of uncontrollable rage welled up inside me again. My head throbbed, my chest ached. I ran up to Night Stallion, pulled back my left hand, focused my energy, then thrust forward. A violent gust of wind exploded out of my hand with the force of a dozen hurricanes. It blasted down the street, tearing up the pavement and ripping the sides off the buildings. Night Stallion was caught in the attack, but so were Gary and James.

"Whoa!" James yelled as he was pushed off his feet.

Night Stallion dug its talons deep into the pavement to avoid being blown away, but caught the gust of extreme wind in its wings and was forced back. Gary tumbled across the ground, then lifted off into the air.

Everything happened in about ten seconds. After it had happened, I fell to my knees. I didn't know where that attack came from, but it sure was handy, not to mention tiring. I looked at my left hand, and noticed that my scar on my palm had ripped open. That was when I thought about how I got that scar. Looking into the night sky, the moon was still there, bleeding across the stars.

The entire street was covered with rubble. The only sign of movement was from Gary and James as they stood up and dusted themselves off.

"Why'd you go and do that?" James asked angrily as he walked over to me.

"Behind you!" I shouted, pointing at Night Stallion as it busted from underneath a pile of debris.

Gary and James both attacked it at once. The demonic horse used its massive talons like swords as it used acrobatic maneuvers that seemed impossible for a creature with four legs and big wings. The two boys were also pulling off some amazing moves of their own. They jumped off walls and flipped through the air as if gravity didn't exist.

However, I continued to sit on my knees and watch, holding my bleeding hand and massaging my wounded leg, which was worse than I had thought. My head started to hurt again. Whatever power I had was beginning to wear off. Deciding that the two of them could handle Night Stallion on their own, I fell back and stared up at the bleeding moon. Is that what it looked like on the night my parents died?

Then the blood in the sky dissolved, and the moon returned to its natural silver color. Over the harsh sounds of Gary and James fighting Night Stallion, I heard something much more soothing. A woman's voice was singing a beautiful lullaby.

My blood froze. Forcing myself back to reality, I sat up with a jolt, looking back up at the moon. It was singing its lullaby again. The others must have heard it too, because they stopped fighting and looked into the sky. Night Stallion did also.

"Oh no," said Gary, looking up at the moon.

Night Stallion recognized its cue, spreading its wings and taking flight again. I jumped to my feet and hurried over to Gary and James as they watched the horse soar away.

"It's going after another victim!" Gary shouted. "We have to follow it!"

The three of us raced down the streets after Night Stallion. Darknae Sonata poured over the city, and I knew that someone was being put into its trance just to have their soul gruesomely eaten by the demonic horse.

Night Stallion flew higher, soaring over and between the buildings. The moon sang louder, as if trying to taunt us. We ran through the streets as fast as we could, leaping over any traffic that got in our way. Night Stallion was extremely fast during flight, pulling slowly away from us as we struggled to keep up.

The horse noticed that we were in pursuit, so it quickly whirled around in the air and fired a black ball of energy at us. It was somewhat easy to dodge, but the explosion it created on impact with a nearby building was earth shattering.

The entire skyscraper erupted into flames in mere seconds, then exploded like a fireworks factory. A huge cloud similar to a volcanic explosion swept through the streets, incinerating hundreds of people and covering us with hot ash. Massive pieces of cement weighing anywhere from one to ten tons rained upon the city, destroying surrounding buildings. Parts of buildings fell to the ground, smashing the streets and caving in the sewers and subways.

An earthquake pulsed through the city from the energy explosion, ripping up anything that wasn't completely destroyed by the falling buildings. The sound was enough to drown out an atomic explosion.

I couldn't see anything through the dust. Everything inside was telling me I was going to die, but I kept running. The sound of enormous chunks of buildings and metal shook the ruptured ground as they landed around me. Fortunately, we were running so fast to begin with, that we eventually broke out of the smoke and away from danger. We stopped to turn and look at what had just happened. It felt like my heart was going to stop.

"Look at that!" James yelled, pointing at the devastation.

"Dear God," said Gary in awe, "please have mercy."

An area of about eight or nine city blocks was completely devastated. The surrounding area looked like it was covered with snow from the ash and dust. Smoke completely blocked out the sky, but the moon could still be faintly heard over the rumble that echoed across the entire city. People had rushed out of their apartments and cars to stand and stare at the destruction.

"No way…" James was lost for words. Nothing could have prepared him for what had happened. "All those people…"

"They couldn't do anything," said Gary sadly, looking at the ground, trying to blink the sight away. Then he stomped his foot furiously, screaming, "*They all died!*"

"We have to find that thing!" James growled, grabbing Gary's shoulder. "We're going to stop all this."

Without looking back, we ran through the rest of the city, trying to find Night Stallion. The moon was still singing, meaning that Night Stallion hadn't killed its target yet. A feeling of guilt boiled up inside me. Was it our fault that so many people died?

"There!" Gary shouted. We arrived just in time to see another innocent soul destroyed by Darknae.

"*No!*" James bellowed. "We're too late!"

The moon stopped singing, then turned red again, symbolizing another death. The victim this time was just a little boy. Its mother was screaming from what just happened. Apparently, she was driving down the street when Night Stallion ripped the car door open and pulled the child out.

Just as before, Night Stallion reared back onto its hind legs to charge up the icy explosion and kill all witnesses. James wasn't about to let that happen.

"That's why it never makes it to the news!" he roared angrily. "It kills anyone who sees it!"

"Wait, hold on!" Gary yelled. James charged at Night Stallion, but Gary couldn't stop him this time. "James! No!"

James raised Flarc Blade up high to slash the horse into pieces, but was too late. Night Stallion unleashed its icy explosion attack again, blasting James back and killing everyone else. Icy, blue flames raged from the horse, freezing everything within a fifty foot radius.

Gary and I rushed over to James. He was lying on the ground, encased in ice. Gary used his Soulpower flames to melt it all off. Once free, James shivered and shook the remaining ice off him, looking enraged.

"What were you thinking?" Gary hissed. "You could've died!"

Ignoring Gary, James stood up, aimed his sword at Night Stallion, then let out a furious yell. There was an explosion of energy at the tip of Flare Blade, and a brilliant golden yellow beam of light erupted out of the sword. Night Stallion was completely unprepared for the attack and was struck directly in the body by the beam. It was lifted off the ground and forced back against a wall.

Once James realized that Night Stallion wasn't going anywhere, he held the beam of light in place. Warm energy radiated from Night Stallion as it writhed and snarled in pain. The wall it was being pushed up against began to crack, but James held the beam and continued to torture Night Stallion.

"You've got it!" Gary shouted. "Keep at it, you can do it!"

The wall caved in, sending the demonic horse crashing into a store. James kept firing the beam of Luminae, slowly killing Night Stallion with it. The horse made horrible screams and growls as its very life was draining from its body. James began to show signs of growing tired. His knees and arms were shaking as he forced himself to hold the beam of Luminae on Night Stallion.

"Come on," I whispered, "don't give up, James."

After a few moments, James fell unconscious and collapsed to the ground. I managed to catch him before his head hit the pavement, and Gary fanned his face.

"He used up a lot of energy," said Gary. "We'll let him rest here."

"I guess we have to finish it," I said.

Gary looked over at the hole Night Stallion had been pushed through, then at me. He nodded his head dutifully.

"Let's do this," I replied.

Gary and I walked slowly over to the hole in the wall where Night Stallion had fallen through. When we peeked inside, we saw the horse lying on the floor. Stopping in front of it, Gary and I watched its chest slowly rise and fall as it breathed. Its eyes were shut.

"I can't believe this is a living thing," said Gary quietly. We each picked up a long, sharp piece of metal and raised them into the air. Both of us brought them down as hard as we could to chop into the body of Night Stallion.

There was a pulse of energy from the horse, and our weapons were deflected out of our hands. The two glowing red eyes opened up and stared straight at us. Quickly realizing what was going on, Night Stallion leapt to its feet and bared its huge teeth at us.

Gary and I stumbled back, too afraid to even speak. Night Stallion staggered a bit, then fell back down. Its big feathered wings brushed against my face. Too my surprise, they were extremely soft and silky. Then I felt warmth trickle down my cheek. Raising my hand to it, I noticed that I was bleeding. The feathers were so fine and sharp that they cut my skin, although they felt like silk.

The demonic horse crawled out of the hole and back onto the streets. Gary and I followed it, being careful to be as quiet as possible. Night Stallion took a look at James lying in the middle of the street, and began to make its way over to him.

"We have to do something!" said Gary.

We raced over to Night Stallion to stop it, but it unleashed another pulse of energy that deflected us. However, doing so seemed to weaken Night Stallion further, for it stumbled again. Looking back at us, it spread its wings and took off into the sky. The blood in the sky dissolved again, then the moon disappeared into nothingness.

James let out a painful moan. Gary rushed over to him, but I remained where I was, staring up into the sky.

"Did we win?" James asked, sitting up.

"No," Gary replied dully, "we didn't."

"Man…" James fell back onto the ground. "After all that?"

"Hey, Krystal," Gary called. "Come over here. Let's help James up."

I walked over to Gary and we both lifted James off the ground onto his feet. Gary bent down and picked up Flare Blade and handed it to James.

"I guess we know what we'll be doing from now on," said Gary dutifully.

"Chasing that Night Stallion thing, eh?" said James miserably. He turned and looked at the huge cloud of dust and smoke that still hovered over the destroyed part of the city.

Gary came up to me and wrapped his arms around me.

"Sorry that I ever doubted you," he apologized.

"Don't worry about it," I told him. Then I chuckled a little.

"What's funny?"

"You're usually the one telling *me* not to worry," I replied.

Gary smiled as James staggered over to us.

"Hey, Krystal?" said James. "What the hell was that thing, anyway?"

"Darknae's physical form," I replied. "It uses the moon to find a new Rionah Darknae."

"Oh, lovely," James muttered. "C'mon, let's get outta here."

"Right," said Gary. "But first, we have to talk about this. Night Stallion depends on the moon to find a Rionah Darknae, right?"

"Yeah," said James. "So, what's the plan?"

"We look for Night Stallion during the day," Gary explained, "that way we won't have to worry about saving people while we fight it."

"Sounds like a plan," said James. "I take it that we'll have to start in a few hours then, since the sun's about to come up."

"Looks like it," said Gary. "We should take it easy until then. Krystal, what happened to your hand?"

I hadn't noticed that my hand was still split open, and completely covered with blood. It was the hand with the scar.

"I cut it," I said quickly.

"We'd better clean that up," said Gary. "C'mon." He took my arm and led me into the building that had the hole in the wall.

"I'll just wait right here, then," James called to us.

We found a bathroom, and Gary put my hand under a sink and rinsed it out. The white porcelain turned a bright red as my blood was washed down the drain.

"This is pretty deep," said Gary. "Does it hurt?"

"Yeah," I told him. "A little."

After Gary washed the cut out, he took some paper towels out of the dispenser and wrapped my hand up. He then took off the bandage that was around my head. I had almost completely healed.

"Isn't that where your scar on your hand was?" he asked.

"Yeah," I said. "It opened after I used that big attack."

"You said you cut it," said Gary, looking at me. Then he looked back at my hand. "How'd you get that scar anyway?"

I looked away. "It was a long time ago."

"Tell me," he urged. "What happened?"

"It's kinda personal," I said quietly.

"Oh, alright," said Gary, hugging me, "I understand."

"Remember when I said I had all that money?" I said. "It was a present for my thirteenth birthday. I didn't know who it was from. All the money was in a box that was labeled as being government property."

I figured that it was probably from Thomas. He must have sent it to me after I left the laboratory. He was most likely the person who sent Tyler Charlie's book.

"It's all better now," Gary assured.

"I have some important stuff to tell you," I said. "It's about—"

"What's taking you guys so long?" James busted in through the bathroom door, smiling when he saw us hugging. "Oh, I know what's going on here."

"Krystal said she has something important to tell us," said Gary.

"Let's hear it, then," said James.

I told them about the vision I received from Night Stallion. I told them about the Base 15 laboratories and the experiments they did with me. I explained the book in Tyler's store, the Darknae Sonata, and the reason why James sucked at video games compared to me. I also told them about Thomas's experiment.

"I see," said Gary. "That's why doctors couldn't find anything wrong with your brain and everything. The problem was because—"

"That knucklehead stole that part of your soul!" James cut in. "Even after everyone told him not to! What a moronic piece of—"

"Don't be mad at him," I said. "He really cared about me. I even saw him the time we came to see you in the hospital."

"That was him?" said Gary, rubbing his chin. "I thought he told you that he had a degree in the medical field. He was the janitor that night."

"Because he's a moron!" James announced.

"One thing still bothers me though," said Gary thoughtfully. "He said that he'd bring his experiment with him. It sounds to me like something such as that requires a bunch of energy, and if he's at the hospital, then he might be keeping Krystal's soul in there somewhere. He could get all the energy he needs from the generators."

"I say that we go find it," said James. "Return to Krystal what's rightfully hers."

"But that's what's bothering me," Gary told him. "What exactly is he doing with it?"

"Studying it," I said.

"That's right, but he said that he believes it's giving off an energy that's not Luminae, Darknae, or Soulpower." Gary began to pace back and forth. "He told the others that it would need to be studied in a field of its own."

"Let's hope it's something good," James mumbled. "I'm sick of everything turning out to be against us. Why can't something go our way for once?"

"We'll have to worry about that later," said Gary. "Let's take care of Night Stallion first."

"I'm worried," I said, grabbing Gary's arm.

"About what?" Gary asked.

"What's going to happen to me?" I looked at Gary and James. "I broke out of the hospital. Everyone's going to find out that I'm missing. Where will I go? What will happen when they find me? I don't want them to take me to an insane asylum."

"We'll worry about that stuff later," said Gary, pulling me close. "We have to focus on Night Stallion first, and that's all that's important right now."

"Yeah," said James, "don't worry about it! Me and Gary will figure something out. I'm sure of it! Just leave it to us. We won't let anyone take you to a nuthouse!"

"Thanks," I said, smiling timidly.

"That's what friends do," said James.

"Guys," I said quietly. "That night at Gary's house when I went crazy, I had a dream. I didn't understand it at first, but now I have a better idea. It was about the big container Thomas put the part of my soul in. I saw something in it."

There was a weird and uncomfortable silence. Gary and James both looked at me concernedly, then at each other.

"What was it?" James asked, sounding more curious than concerned.

"I don't know," I replied. "But it was scary."

CHAPTER SEVENTEEN

Since I wasn't supposed to be out of the hospital, Gary told me that I should stay with Tyler in his antique store while they went to school the next day. That would be the last place Jack and Laura would look when they found out that I was missing. We knew that things would get hairy when the hospital learned of my disappearance, but there wasn't much we could do. Night Stallion was out there somewhere, and taking care of it was much more important than letting the world know that a missing girl in a hospital wasn't really missing at all. I didn't need to go back to the hospital anyway. My powers had mostly healed any physical injuries I had sustained.

Jack and Laura. In the vision, Thomas had said that two top-model robots would be taking care of me. The idea that I'd been raised by robots for about three years was mind numbing. They weren't real people at all, but just machines programmed to create simulated love for me. My heart sank when I realized that two people who I thought loved me didn't love me at all, simply because they were fakes.

"We'll be back right after school," said Gary, kissing me on the cheek. "Don't try to think too much about everything going on, okay?"

"Okay," I said.

"I'll take care of her," said Tyler as Gary and James were on their way out.

"One last thing," said Gary halfway out the door. "You might want to fill Tyler in on everything that we know."

"Okay," I reiterated.

"C'mon, dude," James moaned. "We're gonna be late if you keep dawdling."

"We'll be here A.S.A.P. if anything turns up," Gary called as James pulled him out by the arm. "Love you, babe."

"Love you, too," I said with a smile.

"Let's go to the back," said Tyler once the two had left. "You can tell me everything. Would you like something to drink?"

I nodded, and he led me into the backroom. He gestured for me to take a seat at the table, and he went over to the corner where a little refrigerator was and took out a can of soda.

"This is the only one I have," he said, handing me the can. "Is that fine?"

"Yeah," I replied with a smile. Tyler smiled back, then took a seat across the table from me after handing me the drink.

"So," he said, "what do you three know that I should know?"

I told Tyler the same story that I had told Gary and James the night before. Everything from how Night Stallion showed me the vision to the last thing I remembered before my memory was erased. I even told him about how Thomas might have his experiment stored somewhere in the city's hospital.

"Hmm." Tyler looked as if he was putting everything together in his mind. "That is definitely informative. I wonder why this Night Stallion creature showed you that."

"I don't know," I said timidly.

"Maybe," he thought, "your soul automatically was triggered by the sight of seeing it eye-to-eye. If your brain was ridded of the memories, then they still remained in your soul. Night Stallion was such an important event back then, and the very sight of it was enough to activate those memories and restore them to your brain. Or it could've used some Darknae power to help restore your memories."

"When it showed me my lost memories," I said, "I felt and understood Night Stallion's motives. What Darknae wants to do is kill Luminae completely. To do that, it has to kill White Phoenix, Luminae's physical form. It has to kill the Rionah Luminae first. When it kills White Phoenix, Darknae will be able to make this its perfect world."

"Tell me," said Tyler, "about this angel that you saw in your visions."

"It was evil," I said. "It's eyes were pure white. They were as white as snow, and completely lifeless."

"What did this angel look like?"

"I don't know," I told him. "I don't know what its face looked like, or the hair color, or anything. For some reason, I couldn't make it out, but I know it was an angel. It had wings and everything. And I know it was a little girl. A girl I know..."

"I have no idea to what it could be," Tyler replied. "Oh well, I'm sure you'll find out soon enough."

"The angel scares me," I said quietly. "Something tells me that it's bad."

"Why would an angel be bad?" Tyler asked with a chuckle. "I thought they were supposed to be good."

"It's not a real angel," I said, "or I don't think…"

I opened the can and took a sip. The bubbles fizzed in my mouth for a while before I swallowed. My mind was completely full of worry and wonder, despite what Gary told me before he left.

"Well," said Tyler, "I guess there's only one way to find out what it is, and that's to wait and see what happens."

Of all of the things I didn't want to hear, that was probably the worst. I hated waiting for something to happen without knowing exactly what it was or when it was going to happen. I drummed the side of the can with my fingers, then took a huge gulp. The carbonation made my throat burn and eyes water.

"Sorry there isn't much to do here," Tyler apologized. "If there's anything I can get you, just say something."

"Is it okay if I leave the store?" I asked.

"You want to go somewhere, eh?" Tyler thought it over for a bit. "People might wonder why you're out of school. That is, of course, if they knew you were a high school student." He studied my face. "Ah, what the heck. I've seen adults that look your age. Just don't go too far, ya hear?"

"Okay," I said, getting up. "Thanks for being nice to me."

"No big deal," he said. "Try to stay out of trouble, but I don't think that'll be much of a problem for you. My lunch break's at eleven-thirty if you want to be back by then. We can go and get something."

"Alright."

I walked out of the room and left through the front door. It was another sunny day, just right for a walk on the beach. I had to think about the direction of the beach, then started walking there.

Along the way, I happened to come across the Shady Palm Café. It was abandoned and empty now that Bernie had closed the business. I walked up to the window and peered through the glass at the empty, dark restaurant that used to be always teeming with life and customers. Without Bernie, the place had a sad and lonely feeling about it. Gary and James had said that it was their favorite place to hang out.

Stepping back from the glass window, I gazed up at the blue sky. The two boys were at school, and I was out by myself. A shudder of insecurity quickly fluttered through me at the thought that Gary was far away, but I soon got over it.

Then Thomas came to my mind. I wanted to go see him so badly, and he was so close. The hospital wasn't too far away by car, and I had plenty of time to kill before Tyler's lunch break. I could take Tyler's car. He didn't have to know I had it, and I'd bring it right back.

I hurried back to Tyler's antique store and sneaked around to the back where Tyler had his car parked. Glancing around, I checked to see if the door was unlocked. To my relief, the door opened right up. As soon as I got in the driver's seat, I discovered that his keys weren't in the car. Asking him for them was out of the question, and I didn't know how to hot wire a car. Sticking my finger into the ignition, I wondered if I could use my power to start it.

"Start," I said out loud. When nothing happened, I tried again. "Start…car on…ignition activated…" Nothing worked.

Discouraged, I got out of the car and closed the door quietly. I went over to the sidewalk and looked out at the road, watching the cars drive by. So many cars were out, maybe I could just borrow one…

No, that would be stealing. I'd have to think of something else.

A car approached. Thinking fast, I ran out into the streets in the middle of traffic. The car slammed on its brakes, but didn't stop in time. Its tires squealed as the front bumper slammed into me, sending me bouncing up onto the hood. When the car came to a halt, I rolled off the hood and onto the hard pavement, pretending to be hurt

"Are you all right?" said a panicked man's voice over me. "Alice, she's not moving!"

"You about killed this poor girl!" said a woman's voice. "Quick, put her in the car! We'll take her to the hospital! That part of the city isn't closed off."

"I don't think we should move her!" said the man. "Let's call the cops!"

"Hell no!" Alice barked. "I'm still on probation and don't need anymore crap from the cops! We're not calling them!"

"But we'll be late if we go all the way out to the city!" the man argued.

"Hospital," I whispered. "Hurry…"

"Oh, damn," I heard the man say. "Don't worry, I've got you!"

I felt myself being lifted into the air. There was the sound of a car door opening, then I was hoisted into the backseat of a luxury car. I heard two people hastily get into the car and buckle up. In no time, I was on my way to the hospital.

"Are you hurt badly?" said Alice's voice from up front.

"I think," I said faintly. My act was actually working.

"Hurry up, Kenny!" said Alice in a dreadful tone. I heard the engine crank up as the car gave a lurch forward.

"Ow…" I moaned quietly, trying to add to the scene. "My legs…"

"It's going to be all right," said Ken. "Hang in there."

In a few minutes, I could hear heavy traffic sounds, indicating that we had reached the city. Ken wove between other vehicles, trying to get to the hospital. Moments later, the car stopped. Ken and Alice tore off their seatbelts and rushed to get me out of the car. As soon as the door opened, I sprang out and took off running full speed the instant my feet hit the ground.

"Thanks for the ride, guys!" I said quickly.

I didn't have time to hear what they said, because I ran as fast as I could along the building and through the front doors. Once inside, I immediately started walking at a brisk pace to reduce attention. They had likely noticed I was missing by that time and had people looking everywhere for me, so I had to be as stealthy as possible. Thomas's room was probably in the area that I bumped into him the night I was with Gary.

Making my way around the first floor hallways, I tried to remember where it was that I saw Thomas. I was going so fast that night, and I wasn't paying attention to where I was going. This time, the little feeling deep inside me that I could follow wasn't there. At least, not at first.

The feeling filled up my body again, pointing in the right direction. I wheeled around and hurried in the other direction, following the feeling inside me. A few nurses cursed at me as I rudely ran past them. I was getting closer…I could feel it.

I stopped in front of a door with a sign that had the words 'Custodian's Closet' on it. Looking to see if anyone was around, I reached out and touched the doorknob.

A vision exploded in my head, sending a throbbing pain through my skull and making my ears ring. I stumbled back, taken by absolute shock. The vision was terribly distorted and lasted for a tiny fraction of a second. In other words, I had no clue to what it was. I wanted to touch the doorknob again, but the ringing in my ears told me otherwise. Backing away slowly, I stared at the door, wanting nothing more than to see what was on the other side.

I looked up and down the halls again, then back at the door. What I wanted to know so badly was right on the other side. Approaching the door again, I debated whether to try and open it again, or walk away. If I touched the doorknob, something worse might happen. If I walked away, I might never find out what was on the other side. Acting without conscious thought, my hand flew at the doorknob again.

My head gave another throb as the vision flickered in front of me. I snapped my hand back, feeling dizzy. My fingers were tingling and my toes went numb. Forcing myself to stay on my feet, I leaned with my back against the wall. Slowly, I regained equilibrium and stood up straight. The ringing in my ears subsided as the feeling in my toes and fingers came back.

"Hey you!"

The sound of an angry voice made me jump. I turned around, standing face-to-face with a middle-aged man with scraggly, graying hair. His firm, wrinkled face quickly went from anger to shock.

"What are you doing here?" he asked quickly. Then he put his angry face back on. "This is the custodian's room! What were you doing trying to get in?"

I didn't answer, but continued to stare at the man. When he noticed that I was staring at him, he started to look a bit uncomfortable.

"Why are you looking at me like that?" he asked.

"Who am I?" I asked quietly.

His expression was of disbelief. He gave me a strange look.

"How should I know?" he replied.

"You don't know who I am?" I asked, eagerness welling up inside of me.

"I don't...I don't think so," said the custodian slowly. My eyes flickered over to the door, and he noticed. "There's nothing in there," he said quickly.

I looked up at him, and he looked right back at me.

"I think there is," I told him in almost a whisper.

The custodian began to get nervous. He wiped off his neck, glancing around to see if anyone could come to his aid.

"I told you," he said sternly, "there is nothing behind that door."

"But I feel something behind there," I said. "It's some kind of energy. What is it? Please, tell me."

The man's lip quivered, looking nervously between me and the door.

"I'm not telling you again," he said shakily. "There is *nothing* behind that door."

"Tell me what it is," I begged. "I have to know what it is. All this time, I could feel it inside me. The effects of Heartfire is—"

I shut up instantly. The man stared into my eyes with pure shock.

"How did you..." He looked right into my two blue eyes, studying them. Then I saw his expression change as something clicked inside of him. "This is impossible. I erased your memory!" Right then, he looked scared more than anything.

"Tell me about the experiment," I pleaded, advancing closer to the custodian.

"Stay away!" he said, stepping back. "That's an order!"

"I'm not mad at you!" I tried to explain. "Please, Thomas..."

"How do you know my name?" He backed away more, looking completely terrified. "You're not supposed to remember anything!"

"You know who I am!" I told him. "I won't hurt you."

"I'm sorry!" He was behaving like a sinner before an angry God. "I know what I did was wrong! Stay away!"

"Thomas..."

"I warned you!" He reached a shaking hand into his pocket and pulled out a remote control. After pushing a button on it, he thrust it back into his pocket. "The robots are coming to take you back. They'll erase your memory again, and everything will be back to normal, Kristy, I promise. It'll all be okay."

"No," I choked. "You can't erase my memory!"

"It's for you own good!" Thomas told me, trying to sound comforting despite his own discomfort. "Everything will be better soon."

"No!" I spun around and raced down the hallways at top speed. Everything blurred past me as I charged through the main lobby of the hospital and shot out the front doors. Looking around frantically, I quickly decided that I would have to lose the robots in a crowded area.

I raced down the streets, pushing and shoving about a dozen people a second. When I thought that I was in a big enough crowd, I began to walk casually with the flow of pedestrians. I walked a few blocks, skittishly glancing over my shoulder every now and then for any sign of the government's robots; for any sign of Jack and Laura. A few blocks down was the mall, and I decided to go inside. Surely there was a large enough crowd for me to blend into.

When I approached the automatic sliding doors I was met by the cool air conditioning as they slid open. Glancing behind me again, I walked casually inside the mall, pushed my hair out of my face, and immediately tried to mingle with a group of five or six people.

The mall was big. There were two levels packed with stores, meaning that I had a lot of space to hide out from the two robots. I followed my group up the escalator to the second floor. Trying to look as casual as possible, I went inside a store that sold movies and music CDs. Looking around, I realized that I was in a place full of younger adults, and that I'd be with other teenagers if it wasn't a school day. I just hoped Tyler was right when he said I could pass as being about five years older.

"Can I help you find anything?" an employee asked, coming out of nowhere. He was a tall, dorky-looking guy with slicked hair and glasses.

"No thanks," I said quietly. "Just looking."

"Alright," he replied. "If you need anything, just ask."

I hastily made my way to the back of the store, disappearing behind the racks. My eyes scanned over the different CDs to give the impression that I was looking for something, and occasionally picked one up and looked at it. After half an hour, I decided to leave the store and try to make my way back to Tyler's.

"Excuse me," I asked an employee. "What time is it?"

"Hmm," she said, looking at her watch, "It's almost ten o'clock now."

"Thanks," I said, taking off at a fast walk to the exit. Tyler wanted me back by eleven-thirty, and I had an hour and a half to make it.

I glanced quickly around as soon as I left the store. There was no sign of Jack and Laura, so I headed for the mall's exit, believing that I might have gotten away from them. I decided that as soon as I met back up with Gary and James that I would have to go live somewhere else. I felt my heart sink at the thought that I might never see them again. Feeling somewhat heartbroken, I walked over to the railing and looked down at the first floor. What would I do when it was time to go home?

"There you are, sweetie," said a woman's voice from behind me.

I whirled around and found Jack and Laura standing a few feet away.

"We've been looking all over for you," said Jack concernedly. "Come back with us, and we'll make everything all better."

"You're going to erase my memory," I said. "I'll forget everything about this place, won't I?"

"It's for your own good," said Jack. "Krystal, we understand how you feel—"

"You don't understand my feelings," I said dully. "You can't understand, because you're machines. You don't have feelings."

Jack and Laura looked at each other, then back to me.

"You know more than you'll be comfortable with," said Laura calmly. "If you let us rid you of all these painful memories, then you'll be happy again."

"No I won't," I told her, feeling my voice getting shaky. "If my memories are erased, then I'll still remember this place as a bunch of distorted visions that pop up at random times. I know what it's like not knowing what they mean, and now that I finally found out, I don't want to go through all of that again. I like it here. I like the friends I made, and I'm not going to let you take them away from me."

"Krystal," said Jack firmly, "remember those business trips that the two of us always went on? They were actually appointments to see Thomas so he could upgrade us and make us more efficient. It was also when we gave him our reports on you. He programmed us to possess special skills in case you would try to resist us. You wouldn't want us to use those skills, would you?"

By this time, a few people had gathered to see what was going on.

"I'll do whatever it takes to get out of this with my memories in tact," I said.

"How do you expect to resist us?" Laura asked, beginning to sound sinister. "You don't have a weapon of any kind."

"I don't need a weapon to fight you," I told her, getting into a fighting stance. "I have my power, and that's all I need."

"Do you even know what that power is?" said Jack, smirking. "You know it's not Soulpower, but you continue to use it without care?"

"I do what I must," I said.

"Then you leave us with no choice," said Jack. "We'll have to persuade you with force, and then you'll be a better person."

The two of them immediately leapt into the air like acrobats and landed on both sides of me. They started to use martial arts-style attacks, which I blocked. I jumped back, knowing that I was going to have a difficult time fighting them.

Their attacks were quick, and blocking them was painful. Jack grabbed me by the arm and tossed me onto the ground. I quickly rolled out of the way as he brought his foot down to stomp on me. As soon as I made it back onto my feet, Laura roundhouse kicked me in the back. Jack took the advantage to strike me in the back of my head, making me see stars for an instant.

I immediately retreated to the escalator. A little ways down, I was intercepted by Laura. The only thing I could do was block her attacks, owing to the fact that I didn't have any training in their fighting style. Seizing a quick opportunity, I kicked Laura in the stomach, and she rolled down the escalator. I jumped over her, and tried to make a dash for the exit.

Jack managed to get in front of me and punch me across the face. I staggered for a bit, and received a mighty blow to the stomach. Forcing myself not to double over in pain, I returned a quick punch, but Jack blocked it, grabbed my arm, and slammed me into the ground with a painful thud as my mouth hit. I bit open my lip, and blood gushed out onto the floor.

With no second thought, I leapt back to my feet and blocked more attacks from Jack. Laura joined in and both of them managed to easily overwhelm me with attacks, ending up with me stumbling back, wiping the blood off my face.

Not knowing where I was going, I ran down the mall and eventually into the food court. My power began to guide my actions, and I started lifting up tables and chairs with my mind and send them flying towards Jack and Laura. A chair collided with Jack and busted apart, slowing him down. Laura managed to jump over a chair aimed at her, but was hit with a table with food on it, which splattered everywhere on impact.

I continuously pummeled them with projectiles, pulling them out from underneath people who were using them, until there were no more tables and chairs. Seeing that I hadn't done anything more than slow the robots down and anger them further, I made a mad dash for the exit. As soon as I reached the doors with the huge glass windows, I remembered the attack that I had used against Night Stallion.

Concentrating my energy into my right hand (the one without the scar), I thrust it forward at Jack and Laura, sending a violent blast of wind towards them. The vacuum created by the wind blew the windows in, covering everything with glass. Anything that was standing in front of me was now on the floor. With nowhere else to go, the powerful gust of wind traveled down the mall like a wind tunnel. People were blown off their feet, and everything was knocked over.

Using this chaos to my advantage, I picked up a sharp piece of metal and looked for the two robots. As soon as I saw movement, I hurled the piece of metal like a javelin, piercing Laura through the chest. She flew back and was pinned against the wall. Electrical components sparked and popped as she hung motionless from the giant nail-like object.

"I see that you're not kidding," said Jack, getting up and dusting himself off. I stared at him, not daring to say anything. "It doesn't matter, because you still have to deal with me. I'll give you one last chance to come quietly."

"Not by your artificial life," I said stubbornly.

"Have it your way," he said, getting into his fighting stance. "Prepare yourself!"

With those words, I heard a crashing noise from above. To my shock and horror, I saw the demonic winged horse smash through the skylights, soar down, and land on Jack. Night Stallion immediately used its huge talons and sharp teeth to rip the robot apart until it was nothing but a pile of scrap.

I gasped and stumbled back, watching nervously as the demonic winged horse turned its head and looked straight at me, baring its teeth. Every part of my body trembled in fear as I desperately hoped that it would leave me alone. Suddenly, it spread its wings and took flight. I instantly prepared myself for it to attack, but it flew up and back out through the broken skylights.

My muscles relaxed so quickly that I almost collapsed. As I stared up through the skylights, I wondered what Night Stallion was doing out during the day. I automatically assumed that since it was Darknae, it wouldn't be able to come out any other time than night. The moon wasn't out during the day, so what was it doing? Why did it attack that robot, but not me?

Darknae does not kill when it is unnecessary. Zenox had said that. If that was true, then why did Night Stallion kill that robot? Or was this an exception, technically speaking that a robot is not a living creature? I looked through the mall at the wanton destruction that I created. Everything was a mess, and I quickly decided to get out of there as quickly as possible and make it back to Tyler's shop in time for lunch.

I hurried out of the mall and into the parking garage. My mind raced, trying to think of a way to get back to town. The bus would take me to the edge of the city, and then I'd have to use my own two feet on the way back. I rushed out of the parking garage and onto the sidewalk. I didn't know where the nearest bus stop was, so I started walking quickly, scanning the street for one.

A roaring engine from behind caught my attention. Turning to see what it was, a very beautiful black car approached me. The car was pure black and very futuristic-looking. It was the same car Zenox had given to Dexter, one of the Zoe cars. They had been designed at Base 15 as an SP weapon. I never knew what an SP weapon was, but I had heard about them a lot.

"Hello, Zoe," I said quietly.

The car pulled up next to me, it's door opening up by itself. I climbed into the driver's seat as the door closed. I had never driven before, but there was no better time to start learning than now.

My seatbelt buckled around me automatically. I put the car into drive and slammed on the gas. The wheels peeled out as I took off down the street, weaving in and out of traffic. I was living my dream of driving an awesome sports car. I was careening down a busy road in a strange vehicle without a license.

Oh well.

In no time, I made it to the long road that led back into town. Seizing the opportunity for a max speed test, I put the pedal to the metal. The engine kicked into high gear, and I was pressed back against the seat. All of the trees on both sides became a green blur. My heart pounded excitedly as I enjoyed the sound of the wind whipping past me. Just how fast I was going, I had to know. I looked down at the speedometer to see my speed.

The car slowed down by itself as if I had slammed on the brakes. The seatbelt locked and squeezed me tightly as the car screeched to a halt. Before I could figure out what had just happened, a dead branch fell out of a tree and landed in the middle of the road about a hundred yards in front of me. If the car hadn't stopped, I would've slammed into it.

I yanked off the seatbelt, flung the door open, and jumped out, looking frantically around to see what had stopped the car. There was nothing to be seen. I went back behind the car and looked around some more. When I didn't see anything, I noticed the back of the car was damaged. Curious, I took a closer look. It looked as if two clawed feet snagged the car and dragged it to a stop. They were about the same size and length apart as Night Stallion's front feet.

My eyes flickered up into the sky as I nervously scanned the area for the dark horse. Then I looked back at the branch that fell in the road a football field's length away from the car. Night Stallion had just saved me again.

Still looking around, I slowly got back into the car. This time, I drove carefully the rest of the way back to town. Just before I made it there, I stopped on the side of the road to push Zoe into the woods and out of sight, but the car started up and hid itself on its own.

It was getting close to Tyler's lunch break and I would have to hurry. I started running again, looking back up at the sky. Night Stallion was watching over me, but instead of feeling secure, I felt like I was being stalked. Why would Darknae protect me?

Deciding that it wasn't going to do me any good to stand around and wonder about stuff, I hurried back to the antique shop. Tyler was probably getting a little worried by now.

"I'm back, Tyler," I said, walking through the front door of the antique store. Tyler was dealing with a customer; an old man who looked older than Tyler was peering through the glass case at some old guns.

"Oh, there you are," said Tyler, looking at his watch. "I'll be taking my lunch break shortly. Just wait in the backroom for a bit longer."

"Okay," I replied tiredly, walking lazily to the backroom.

"Are you feeling all right?" he asked. "You look a little tired."

"I'm fine," I told him. "Yeah, I'm just a little worn out from everything."

"Better save your energy," Tyler replied. "Don't want to get sick, do you?"

I made it into the backroom and sat down in a chair. I felt a little tired, but I didn't know why. Running back shouldn't have drained that much energy, and I used Zoe more than half of the way.

Leaning back, I felt extremely terrible about Jack and Laura. I trusted them with everything, just to find out that they were just government machines made to watch over me. With a sickening jolt of realization, I then knew that I had no family and no home. There was nothing left for me.

Nothing, except for Gary and James.

Tyler took me to a local pizza parlor in town. As usual, I inhaled my food, and Tyler found it somewhat amusing. When we came back from lunch I went into the backroom again and rested my head on the table. I wanted to think about what I was going to do for a home, but I was too tired.

The rest of the time while I waited for Gary and James to get done with school was uneventful. I just stayed in the backroom of Tyler's antique store and doodled mindlessly. I couldn't help but think about Jack and Laura. There really was nowhere else for me to go. They'd probably just build new robots, wait to catch me off guard, erase my memory again, and then put me under the custody of the new androids.

Maybe it was for the best. Maybe if I let them erase my memory again I could start over. That way I would forget all about the painful experiences that happened to me in the past year. I gripped my pencil tightly as I looked at the picture I had drawn of Gary, James, and I.

No, I couldn't let them erase my memory. Sure, a lot of painful things had happened, but that would mean forgetting about the happiest moments of my life.

"Hey there!" Gary had come into the backroom with James right behind him.

"Hi," I said, standing up and hugging Gary.

"Nice drawing!" said James. "Is that us?"

"Yup," I replied.

"I like it," said Gary, picking it up and looking at it. "Hey, what happened to you? You have cuts and bruises all over you."

"Oh." I looked at the cuts on my arms from when I fought Jack and Laura. "It's a long story."

I had asked Gary and James to come back to my house so I

could tell them about Jack and Laura. We were just on our way out of town when we saw Brandon talking with Stephanie. Wondering what was going on, we went up to them to see what they were talking about.

"Oh, hi guys," said Stephanie when she saw us. She didn't sound very enthusiastic.

"Hey," said James, "what's going on here?"

"None of your business," Brandon mumbled.

"Brandon!" Stephanie gave him a mean look. "I just broke up with Patrick," she told us.

"I see how it is!" said James angrily to Brandon. "Trying to get back with her after a breakup. That's pretty low, even for you."

"Just go away," said Brandon. "It's not like that."

"Actually," said Stephanie, "I went back to Brandon. Not to get back with him, but just to talk to him. He's a really understanding person, and I thought he'd make me feel better."

Gary and James exchanged surprised looks.

"Okay...," said James after a while. "That wasn't expected."

"Yeah, alright," said Gary, accepting what Stephanie had just said. "Let's go, guys."

I looked at Stephanie and Brandon for a moment. Just as I was about to tell them good-bye, a horrible pain pierced my chest right where my heart was. I wanted to double over in pain, but it rendered me completely paralyzed. My head burned and throbbed ten times worse than it did after the truck hit me.

A vision of the angel repeatedly flashed in front of me, burning my eyes every time it did so. It felt as if I had swallowed lava, making it impossible to breathe. The pain in my chest raged, and I swore it was going to explode at any second. Right when I thought I was going to die, I felt the pain slowly disappear. Everything faded, leaving me in the dark. The angel was watching me. Her voice was cold and empty.

"It is time for me to awaken."

Thomas was in his secret laboratory in the hospital. He had built it years ago, shortly after assigning me to Jack and Laura. I had floated out of my body and was watching him. The large glass chamber that held his experiment was over in the corner. It was the same as the one in the old laboratory at Base 15. Nothing but a white cloud could be seen inside it, but it was releasing a substantial amount of energy. Undoubtedly, it was Heartfire, the same energy that removed my soul from my body. I could sense it. Whatever was in that chamber wanted me to see this.

A computer on one of the desks started to beep. Thomas looked up curiously, then slowly made his way over to view the results on the monitor. His face went from excited to concerned as he looked over the data.

"What is this?" he whispered to himself.

One by one, the other computers, devices, and machines began to make noise, warning Thomas of something he couldn't see. The energy in the glass chamber began to rise. Ice crusted over the glass chamber, making it nearly impossible to see what was inside. Thomas cautiously advanced closer to it, and then he scratched off some of the ice with this finger. Peering inside, Thomas gasped as a pair of pure white, hollow eyes opened up.

"Kristy," he choked.

The glass chamber exploded, sending Thomas flying back, killing him instantly. The computers and machines sparked and went out as the entire hospital shook. All power in the facility flickered for a few seconds. The empty part of my soul began to burn…and that was when that thing emerged from the shattered chamber.

It made its way out into the halls, instantly ripping apart the souls of anyone who saw it. Blue flares of Heartfire swept through the floors and walls. When the thing reached the reception desk, it blasted the entire front entrance of the hospital before it took to the streets of the city. Night had already fallen.

Metal, concrete, and asphalt warped and bent under the power of her Heartfire. Glass windows pulsed to the power, shattering and blowing out. Cars twisted as the people riding inside lost their souls. Electrical appliances and devices shorted out as she fluxed time and space around her. The blue halo of Heartfire above her head emitted powerful waves of soul-eating energy.

She made her way slowly through the city, destroying any souls that came near her. Her white, lifeless wings fanned out behind her. Her long, blonde hair masked her white, hollow eyes. She was the little twelve-year-old girl. She was the angel.

She was Kristy, and she looked just like me.

CHAPTER EIGHTEEN

I choked for air as I forced myself awake. Gary was sitting next to me, and seeing him instantly calmed me down.

"Krystal!" he said in shock. "It's all going to be okay. You're back home."

James, Stephanie, Brandon, and Abby were all standing around me in my living room. I was lying on the couch. Apparently they had brought me back after I had passed out. Strangely, I had no idea that I had even lost consciousness.

"How long was I asleep?" I asked timidly. It was hard to speak.

"For a while now," said Gary. "It's almost midnight."

I slowly sat up and looked around at everyone.

"Are you all here because of me?" I asked.

"That's right," said Abby. "James told me what happened when you all passed our house. Gary carried you all the way back here by himself."

"You were screaming like crazy again," said Brandon, "like that time in school when the ambulance came."

"Huh?" I thought about it for a little bit, but didn't remember screaming when I saw Kristy.

Kristy.

My chest began to hurt a little again, but only for a few seconds.

"What's wrong?" Gary asked concernedly.

"We have to stop her," I said shakily.

"Stop who?" Gary looked into my eyes. "You're really scared. What's wrong?"

Before I could answer, the sliding glass door to the pool exploded in. James, who was standing in front of it, was instantly thrown across the room. My heart filled with absolute fear as the angel hovered inside the house. Her slumped, broken posture looked like she was hanging from a noose. The long, white robes she was covered in swooped ominously a few inches off the floor. Her eyes were closed.

"*What the hell is that?*" Brandon shouted.

Stephanie and Abby both screamed in terror. The angel held out her hand and channeled a flare of Heartfire at Brandon.

Gary jumped in front of it and struggled to hold it back.

"Soulpower," said Kristy's cold, empty voice.

James pounced at the angel, wielding Flare Blade. Still holding back Gary, Kristy held out her other hand, grabbing James in midair with a claw of Heartfire.

"Luminae," she said with her ethereal voice.

She flung James aside, slamming him into the wall, then increased the power to the energy aimed at Gary, blowing him out of the way, leaving Brandon wide open. He attempted to get away, but was caught by Kristy's Heartfire. We all watched in horror his soul get ripped out and absorbed by the angel's blue halo.

I jumped to the floor and scrambled over to the corner. Gary managed to flame-punch the angel across her face. She appeared extremely rigid and somewhat rubbery when she was forced back. As Gary watched her for her next move, she unexpectedly teleported behind Gary and struck him with a ripple of shifted time, causing him to fly awkwardly back into James.

Kristy shot a flare of Heartfire at Abby and Stephanie, taking both of their souls simultaneously. Then she teleported and appeared directly in front of me. Reaching out with a cold hand, she grabbed me around the neck and lifted me into the air.

"Krystal," she said. Her voice was completely empty and emotionless.

"What do you want," I gasped. "Why do you look like me?"

"Because," she said, "you and I are connected."

Her white, empty eyes opened, staring directly into mine. My chest began to burn and my head throbbed. I felt Kristy's cold hand squeezing my throat. No matter how much I struggled to free myself, her grip was too strong.

"You are my opposite," said Kristy. "All you must do is die. Relinquish thyself."

"Those visions," I choked. "You caused them…"

"You were aware of my approaching awakening," said Kristy, tightening her grip on my throat. "If I had not awakened, you never would have had such visions."

Without warning, Kristy threw me aside. The loud crashing sound of shattering glass filled the room as Night Stallion pounced through the window of the living room right at Kristy. She held out both her hands and emitted a wave of energy at the horse, pushing it back outside. With a second wave of energy, Kristy blasted Night

Stallion back into the street.

"Darknae," she said, watching Night Stallion stagger back onto its feet. It was shocked at how powerful Kristy was.

"What's going on?" James choked. "How did she do that to Night Stallion?"

Gary rushed over to my side and helped me up. I was massaging my throat where Kristy had grasped me.

"We gotta go!" Gary ordered.

Taking my hand, he ran out the broken glass door with James. I looked back to see Kristy fending off Night Stallion. She threw it out the glass door and into the pool, splashing us with water.

"Man, let's get outta here!" James yelled. "C'mon!"

We leapt over the fence into another yard and kept moving as fast as we could to get away from the angel. My heart was pounding. I couldn't believe that my nightmares were coming true. The angel that haunted me all those years was real, and now it was after me. What did she want?

The three of us made it through several yards until we came to the street. As soon as my feet touched the asphalt, the sound of a roaring engine caught our attention. The Zoe car zoomed up to us and stopped. Its doors opened, apparently gesturing us to get in. Not pausing for another second, I jumped into the driver's seat. Gary took the passenger seat and James quickly squeezed into the small backseat. The doors closed and I took off in the direction of the city. My heart was telling me to go there.

"Oh my God," said James. "What's going on, man? Somebody, please tell me what's happening! This is crazy!"

"It's Kristy," I said quietly.

"Who is she, Krystal?" Gary demanded. "You know something, and you'd better tell us! That damn *thing* killed Abby! And Stephanie and Brandon, too!"

"She's my soul," I told him. My hands were gripping the wheel, but somehow the Zoe car seemed to be helping me guide it. "That experiment that Thomas had. Her power is called Heartfire, the energy used for soul surgery. Thomas told me it has time-shifting attributes or something."

"That's his experiment?" James asked in bewilderment. "What's that mean? It evolved or mutated into that angel thing? You've gotta be kidding…"

"How do you know her name?" Gary asked me. "You said

her name's Kristy."

"That's what my nickname was," I said. "Everyone at the labs called me that. She must've assumed that name."

Gary hung his head.

"Abby..."

I looked over at him and put my hand on his shoulder. He had just watched his sister get killed, which must have been devastating for him.

"There's too much going on!" James shouted angrily. "Why was she going after Krystal? And why did she attack Night Stallion? Man, nothing's ever simple anymore!"

"There's a lot we just don't understand," said Gary, "but we have to stop that thing. We have to stop Kristy."

"I think she's in the city," I said.

"Yeah," said James, "and it feels like Night Stallion is heading there too. It must be mad at Kristy for interfering with its Darknae plans."

The rest of the trip was in silence. I pushed the Zoe car to its limit, trying to get there as soon as possible. Gary stared out the window at the trees as they whipped by. Everything was coming to the end. I was going to end everything. Kristy was going to pay for what she had done.

When we finally arrived in the city, my heart skipped a beat at the sight that stretched before us. The entire city was empty of life. For the most part, the city looked intact with little damage. The streetlights were on so it wasn't completely dark. Dead bodies littered the streets where countless people lost their souls. Kristy had done a good job at sweeping through the city, taking as many souls as she could. I tried to think about why she needed so many souls.

I parked the Zoe car in the middle of the street in the heart of the city. The three of us climbed out and looked at the horror around us. We were in the middle of a ghost town. The moon was out, covering everything in its cold, silvery glow. However, it didn't seem ominous, but sad. There was nothing it could do.

"This is freaky," James whispered. "All those people...are all dead, aren't they?"

Gary looked around, holding back his fear and sadness.

"Yeah," he said. "This is..." His voice trailed off. He couldn't find the words to describe what we were seeing.

I heard the sound of large wings behind me. Whirling

around, I saw Night Stallion come down and land a few yards away from us. Its red eyes scanned the area around, growling at what it saw. Gary, James, and I watched it look at us. Slowly, the demonic horse walked over to James. They made eye contact for a few moments.

"It's talking to me," said James.

"What's it saying?" Gary asked.

"Uh," said James hesitantly, "I think it wants to work with us."

"Really?" Gary looked back at Night Stallion.

"It says Kristy is a lot stronger than us," said James, "and the only one who can stop her is Krystal."

"What?" Gary asked. "Why?"

"I don't know," I said.

"It says you have the power," James told me. "Your power is the opposite of Kristy's."

"My power?" It was true that my power was different from anyone else's. To think that it was actually the opposite power of Kristy's was unbelievable. Then again, she told me that I was her opposite.

"Night Stallion says it wanted to get closer to you," James told me. "It wanted to see if your power was a threat to Darknae. After seeing Kristy, it now knows what your power really is."

I couldn't believe what I was hearing.

"What is my power?" I asked.

"No idea," said James. "Darknae has never encountered anything like it. You're the first to ever have it."

"Exactly."

The empty voice echoed through us like a hundred daggers of ice. Kristy had appeared behind us. Night Stallion growled as she hovered closer to us.

"You!" James shouted. "You're part of Krystal's soul, aren't you!"

"That is correct," Kristy replied emotionlessly, "but that is also incorrect."

"What do you mean?" Gary asked nervously. "You were created when Thomas removed the emptiness from Krystal's soul."

"It is true that I was originally the emptiness in Krystal's soul caused by Darknae," said Kristy, "only I have evolved and grown into my sentience. I have become a force of the universe, much like Luminae and Darknae. However, Heartfire is a manmade force, not a natural one."

"Then how did I get my power?" I asked. My hands were shaking and sweat ran down my face.

"The universe thrives on balance," Kristy explained. "In response to Heartfire, it created your power and bestowed you with it. It is my eternal goal to destroy the power you possess."

"No," I told her. "This world belongs to Luminae and Darknae. It's none of our business to interfere with what they do."

"It matters not," said Kristy, advancing closer. "If you defeat me, your power will continue to exist and interfere with the natural forces. But I will not let that happen. I will crush you, Luminae, and Darknae. This will be a world filled with Heartfire. It will be my perfect world."

Night Stallion furiously charged at Kristy, baring its sharp fangs and claws. Kristy lazily lassoed it with a rope of Heartfire and whipped the horse into a building at blinding speeds. Night Stallion looked like it was in a lot of pain as it fell to the ground.

Gary, James, and I attacked Kristy all at once. All of her attacks were nonphysical and long range, and her ability to quickly teleport made it nearly impossible to touch her. All of the Luminae attacks from James were ineffective for the most part, and Gary's fireballs were easily neutralized. I tried using my special powers, but I didn't know how to do it. Maybe they weren't fully awakened.

The angel was at a clear advantage as she used her devastating energy against us. Night Stallion used its icy flame breath on her, but an invisible energy field protected her. The icy fire created a sphere of ice around the angel, then shattered with a flick of her wrist. A powerful shockwave channeled up Night Stallion's icy flame breath and exploded in its face, forcing it backwards.

"Let's end this!" Gary roared.

"We'll give you the signal, Krystal!" James shouted. "Then you give her your all, got it?"

"Okay!" I said.

Gary leapt at Kristy with his flaming fists, but she easily knocked him back. James aimed Flare Blade at the angel and fired a radiant beam of Luminae. Gary regained his balance and began pummeling her with a fury of fireballs as Night Stallion joined in with a stream of pure black energy. Darknae Sonata flooded the city as the moon sang its lullaby, firing its silvery energy at Kristy.

All of the energy converged into a single raging storm. Kristy created a protective barrier of Heartfire around her to hold it back. Everyone forced themselves to break her barrier, creating enormous shockwaves that slowly began to tear the city apart. The streets cracked as the ground shifted and ripped, buildings began to deteriorate and crumble, palm trees were being torn apart, glass cracked and shattered, and winds began to whirl and shred the streets. Cars were lifted by the waves of energy, sending them flying and crashing into everything.

Kristy emitted a powerful shockwave of energy, attempting to fight the tremendous energy being aimed at her. Gary, James, and Night Stallion staggered back a little, but never ceased their onslaught, pushing Kristy's energy back. She emitted another more powerful wave, but to no avail. She was actually being held back.

I waited for my cue, watching the angel struggle to restrain our attacks. Everything was beginning to appear distorted as the immense energy began to bend space and time. At long last, Kristy began to give under the pressure.

"*Now!*" Gary screamed.

Focusing all of my energy into my hands, I unleashed the strange attack I had previously used against Night Stallion and the androids, only this time I used both hands. A visible beam of energy shot out of my hands into the middle of the raging energy storm. There was an incredible fluctuation in energy, a small implosion, and then a massive explosion that sent everyone flying backwards. I was knocked unconscious by the intense concussion from the explosion as the city around us dissolved and evaporated.

CHAPTER NINETEEN

As I slowly regained consciousness, I could feel the wreckage on top of my body. Giving a painful heave, I pushed the debris off me. Luckily, it wasn't very much and it didn't crush or suffocate me.

My head spun as I stood up on my wobbly legs. Cuts covered me, but I didn't mind them. I looked around at the wrecked city. Most of the buildings were still standing, but they were stripped and wrecked. Dust and smoke choked out the morning sun that shone over the wrecked and twisted horizon.

Debris littered the streets as I made my way through the city, searching for the others. I shuddered when I thought about how much closer everyone else was to the explosion, and I prayed that they were all okay, even Night Stallion. Darknae murdered my parents, but Kristy was murdering my perfect world.

A glint of gold in the wreckage caught my eye. Flare Blade was laying in a pile of rubble. I looked around for James, but didn't see any sign of him. Picking up the sword, I decided I could give it back to him once I found him.

I spent what seemed like an eternity looking for the others. There was no sign of life anywhere. My wounds were beginning to hurt, but I ignored them and moved on. The piercing pain in my chest was coming back. Clutching my heart, I figured it must've been my power trying to awaken.

Just as I was about to give up looking, I saw a body laying facedown on the asphalt. There were tons of bodies strewn across the city, but this one looked promising. I slowly walked over to it, not looking away. At last I was close enough to see who it was.

"Gary," I said, rolling him over. "Gary, it's me."

His eyes were closed. The explosion must have knocked him out as well. He was covered with blood and deep wounds. I set down Flare Blade and rubbed his chest as I continued trying to wake him up.

"Hey," I said quietly, "wake up. It's me, Krystal."

That burst of uncontrollable rage surged through me again. My chest was pierced with pain, and my head throbbed. When it all went away, I looked back down at Gary as he lay motionless.

"Come on, Gary," I said, feeling myself choking up. "This

isn't funny. Wake up."

Another burst of rage. I grabbed Gary by his shoulders and shook him.

"Gary!" I shouted. "Get up, now! Come on!"

More bursts of rage filled me. I could feel the anger and fear building up inside me as the emptiness in my soul filled back up. My power was awakening, giving me back a complete soul.

Looking around frantically, I noticed Flare Blade resting next to me. Picking it up, I stood back on my feet. Its long, beautiful blade filled me with warmth. Maybe Luminae had restorative powers. Hopefully...

I raised the sword over my head and brought it down at Gary.

"Come on!" I demanded. "Wake up! Luminae! *Luminae!*"

Panic was growing inside me as my heart began to restore all of my emotions. Gary had to wake up. He just *had* to.

"Wake up, Gary!" I shouted desperately. Tears filled my eyes. "Come on, work you stupid sword!"

I dropped Flare Blade, which hit the ground with a clink. Falling to my knees, I burst into tears, bawling over Gary's lifeless body. My fingers tore into the street as I clutched my fists so tightly that they bled.

My perfect world...shattered.

The rage surged through me again, this time thousands of times more intense than ever. It filled every part of my body. Absolute hatred, pain, and despair coursed through my veins. Power radiated from my body. My soul became a ravaging torrent. It felt as if my chest was going to explode. A blinding pain throbbed in my head. I tried to scream from the torture...

Then it disappeared.

I turned around to find the angel staring at me. Her empty eyes looked directly into my soul.

"You have awaken," she said in her ethereal voice.

Enraged, I clenched my fists. Snatching Flare Blade, I furiously charged at Kristy.

"*You bitch!*"

Moving at incredible speeds, I attacked Kristy with Flare Blade. As if anticipating my move, she knocked me aside with a powerful blast of energy. Flare Blade fell out of my hand, and its warm energy stopped flowing through me. I immediately regained balance and returned fire with a huge storm of energy balls. Kristy spread her wings and took flight, avoiding my assault as she soared through the air at great speeds. In my failed attempt to knock her down, a large building was battered with my attacks and crumbled in a huge explosion.

A cloud of dust obscured my vision, forcing me to cease fire. I strained my eyes as I whirred around trying to find the faintest sign of the angel.

"Where are you?" I bellowed angrily.

I was answered by a painful blow to my back. Kristy slammed directly into me from behind, sending me flying through the air for several blocks. I was on a crash course with another building, so I quickly whipped myself around and jumped off it sideways, sending myself flying further into the air. Looking ahead of me, I saw Kristy flying directly at me for another attack.

My arm quickly filled with energy, which I used to grab the angel around the neck in midair with a powerful grip. I was going to throw her into the ground and hit her with a furious energy attack, but she quickly broke free from my grasp and did to me exactly what I was intending to do to her. I slammed facedown into the street and heard the sickening crack of my ribs breaking as a debilitating pain raced through me. Before I could even try to get back up, a huge explosion of Heartfire engulfed me, feeling as if someone had just poured boiling oil all over me.

When the energy had stopped raining on me, I forced myself to get back up. My ribs cracked some more, but I pushed myself as hard as I could to get back on my feet. Just I was almost to my knees, Kristy burst through the road from underneath me, knocking me into the air. She flew above me and knocked me right back down with a powerful attack. I could taste blood fill my mouth as I soared down toward the street.

I braced myself for impact, but Kristy used her mind to move a bus and intercept me before hitting the ground. The bus slammed me into a wall and crushed me, snapping my arm with a loud crunch. I cried in pain as I fell to the ground in a crumpled heap. Kristy appeared above me, grabbed my broken arm, and swung me around. She used my body to knock over streetlights, telephone poles, and just about everything else you can think of, and then finally tossed me onto the ground.

Lying on my back, I coughed up blood into my mouth. Kristy stood over me, staring at me with her white, empty eyes. She held her hand out at me and hit me with a powerful surge of energy.

I cringed in absolute pain as I felt my broken back push into the crushed street. Another pulse of energy hit me, pushing the blood out of my lungs.

Kristy used her mind to call over Flare Blade. I watched the beautiful, sparkling sword of Luminae hover above me; its sharp point aimed down at me.

With a swish of her hand, the angel speared me directly through the stomach. More pain surged through me. I desperately struggled to use my broken arms to pull the sword out of my body, but I slowly felt my body lose its abilities to move. Darkness filled my eyes as they grew too heavy to keep open.

The pain began to diminish. My mind was cleared of all negativity as I entered a dreamy state of weightlessness. Everything around me swirled and faded. With the last of my energy, my final breath was pushed out of my mouth.

"Gary…"

CHAPTER TWENTY

What was once a bustling city filled with thousands of people was now a destroyed heap of concrete and metal. The sun shone brightly in the Florida morning sky, but was blocked out by the cloud of dust and smoke from the disastrous battle. The hollow-eyed angel loomed over Krystal's bloodied, lifeless body in the middle of the wrecked city. Her wings fanned out, casting an angelic shadow on the ground. Heartfire's opposing force had been wiped out.

Miles away in another part of the city, Gary was also sleeping. He and Krystal were together in a better place, and Krystal was finally free of her pain. They were joined by James, who had also lost his life in the battle against the angel. Only where they could be together forever was their true perfect world.

Suddenly, Kristy sensed movement from behind. Before she could react, Shadow Blade skewered her through the back and out the chest. She turned around and came face-to-face with Night Stallion. It had been injured in the struggle against the angel, but still had the strength to move. Filled with hate for what Kristy had tried to do, it was determined to end everything itself.

Using its mind, the horse ripped the sword out of the angel's chest, who flinched slightly with pain before receiving another debilitating stab to the chest. The blue halo of Heartfire over her head began to fade. Night Stallion tore the sword from Kristy's body again to deal the final blow, piercing Kristy directly through the heart. The halo burned out, her wings went limp, and then the angel fell to the ground right beside Krystal.

Night Stallion walked over to where Kristy laid. It removed Shadow Blade from her with its teeth, then absorbed the sword into its body. The absorption of Shadow Blade restored the demonic horse's strength, healing its wounds completely.

The horse looked over at Krystal, the girl Darknae had tried to protect for those past few years. Darknae had finally learned what her true power was, and now that Krystal and her mutated soul had been eliminated, Night Stallion could resume its eternal battle against Luminae.

Flare Blade began to glow warmly with a brilliant light. Night Stallion watched the sword rise out of Krystal's body and into the air. Turning upwards, Flare Blade emitted a bright beam of light into the sky. All of the smoke and dust was blown away as the sky lit up. The heavens opened up, and the great bird awoke from its long sleep. Its body glowed like a meteor as it soared down from the realm of Luminae. With its long, sharp talons, the mighty creature swooped down and gripped the crumbled pavement. Its feathers were made from white fire, and its beautiful blue eyes moved across the ground. It looked down at Krystal with pity before turning its attention at the demonic horse.

White Phoenix and Night Stallion. Both were the ultimate forms of their powers, and each wanted a perfect world for itself. Now they were without Rionahs, making them both vulnerable to each other.

They stared at each other for a few moments. Never had both physical beings confronted each other directly, and both were taking the time to get a good look at their sworn enemy. With the blink of an eye, the mighty beings spread their wings and engaged in the battle that determined the fate of the world.

More dilapidated buildings crumbled under the explosive shockwaves of Luminae and Darknae. White Phoenix and Night Stallion forcefully clawed at each other while moving at blinding speeds through the devastated city. Beams of incredible energy ripped through the concrete remains as the divine bird and demonic horse swooped under broken bypasses and through collapsed subway tunnels. The destructive results of their battle meant nothing to them, and they would stop at nothing to make the world their own.

Black wings appeared on the edge of the bird's vision. Reacting quickly, White Phoenix fended off a powerful attack from Night Stallion. Their talons lashed at each other as they moved at nearly impossible speeds through the sky.

Night Stallion used its front claws to clutch the phoenix around the neck. Spinning around, the horse let go of the divine bird and sent it crashing through the side of the large office building. White Phoenix instantly regained its balance and soared through the building's halls and corridors and crashed through a window on the other side and immediately embraced Night Stallion again.

The opposite beings were in the midst of a midair struggle miles over the city when Night Stallion accidentally let its guard down for a split second. Seizing the opportunity, White Phoenix dug its sharp claws into Night Stallion's back and heaved the horse straight towards the ground with tremendous energy and speed. The sonic boom rippled through the city as the horse slammed into the ground, creating a massive crater that tore up the sewage lines.

Holding its position in the air, White Phoenix gazed down at the cloud of dust and debris that was made from Night Stallion's impact. The demonic horse was fast, so every fraction of a second had to be watched carefully. Searching for any sign of movement, the bird continued to scan the ground for a black figure creeping through the dust.

The ground shook and ruptured as an explosion tore through the city and dug miles into the ground. Darknae channeled itself into the earth before beginning an upward shift of energy that rattled the very foundations of the planet. In the center of it all, Night Stallion charged straight into the sky directly at White Phoenix. The horse was engulfed by the flames of the underworld, focusing the entirety of its Darknae power on the Luminae bird.

Preparing itself for the ultimate power of Night Stallion, White Phoenix spread its wings upward at the sky and called upon the power of the heavens. The sky opened up, revealing the pure divine light of Luminae. Stars poured their cleansing fires into the bird's flaming feathers as White Phoenix began its downward attack aimed directly at Night Stallion. The sounds of trumpets blared through the phoenix's body as it pinpointed its assault directly at the demonic horse.

As the two deities grew nearer, their apocalyptic energies ripped at each other and split the universe in half. White Phoenix and Night Stallion collided just before the universe shattered from the polar opposites converging. Luminae and Darknae fused and cancelled each other out, resulting in both creatures falling from the sky, nearly unconscious from using their ultimate powers.

White Phoenix became empowered just before impact with the ground, spread its wings, and took flight without taking any further damage. However, Night Stallion remained immobilized and slammed into what was left of the asphalt. The bird remained in the air, looking down into the debris for any indication of Night Stallion.

Suddenly, the sound of the air being sliced came from behind. White Phoenix had no time to react before Shadow Blade pierced its back. The divine bird squawked in pain as it looked down at the sharp sword sticking out of its chest. The combination of the wound and incredible amount of Darknae from the sword overwhelmed the bird, draining its energy.

As White Phoenix began its helpless descent from the sky, it saw Night Stallion staring down at it from above.

CHAPTER TWENTY-ONE

The air began to grow cold as the sun's light slowly darkened. Around the world, billions of people heard the beautiful lullaby of the moon before they felt the life get sucked out of them as Luminae's presence faded. Lakes, rivers, and oceans dried up as forests and jungles shriveled and turned to dust. As White Phoenix crashed through the mosaic roof of the downtown cathedral, the last remaining life on the planet disappeared.

Night Stallion burst through the doors of the cathedral as lightning cracked the sky. White Phoenix writhed in pain as its flames faded and died, leaving nothing but a skeleton on the floor.

The horse made its way over to the deceased phoenix and used its sharp teeth to remove Shadow Blade from the skeleton's ribs. Upon absorbing the sword again, Night Stallion grew to full strength.

Miles away on the other side of the city, the moon shone down upon James. His light brown hair laid messily upon his face. The youth and joyfulness that once filled him no longer existed.

Not too far from that spot was the resting place for Gary. The moon shone down upon him as he slept amid the destruction. His kind face was covered in dried blood. The gentleness and gratuity that once filled him disappeared from the world.

And in the heart of the ended world was Krystal. Her long blonde hair was strewn across the ground as the moon's silver glow shone on it. Behind closed eyelids were her beautiful blue eyes, staring into the emptiness. The innocence and affection that once filled her faded into nothingness.

The moon's lullaby covered the world, spreading Darknae to every corner of the earth. It moved across the sky until it eclipsed the sun, putting it out with a final glint of light, and everything was then covered with the moon's cold silver glow. Night Stallion stepped out of the cathedral. It looked around at its perfect world. Above, the moon sang its lullaby.

"Unacceptable."

Night Stallion whirled around and came face-to-face with the hollowed eyed angel. Her lifeless wings fanned out behind her; the blue halo above her head glowed brightly. The horse growled angrily, wondering how she didn't die.

"It seems as if I was not powerful enough," said Kristy, looking around at the world consumed by Darknae. "You look surprised. It should come as no surprise to you that I am still alive. A force can only be stopped by its opposite, and she is dead."

Night Stallion couldn't believe what it was hearing. It bared its teeth threateningly, but it had no effect on the angel.

"Unfortunately for you," said Kristy, "the only person who can stop me thrived in the world of Luminae and can not survive without it because her powers were not fully awaken."

Kristy looked up at the moon as it shown darkly in the sky.

"However," she said, "although I can no longer be destroyed, you have grown too strong for me to take over. My only option is to exercise my ability of time manipulation and go back to the point before my awakening. I will then continue to wait and evolve into a more powerful being. I may not be able to destroy Luminae and Darknae, but if I grow stronger I will be able to overpower them and cover the world with Heartfire."

With no intentions on letting Kristy go through with her plan, Night Stallion lunged at her. Kristy teleported out of the way and charged all of her Heartfire energy. With its true power, Night Stallion was barely effected by the tremendous amount of Heartfire, but was too slow to prevent Kristy from using it.

In the flash of an instant, the hollow-eyed angel unleashed her ultimate power. All time in the universe froze as the very fabrics of space-time began to rearrange. All events after Kristy's awakening were completely erased. Everything continued as normal without the interference of Heartfire.

Krystal, Gary, and James continued their pursuit against Night Stallion. Krystal hadn't had any visions since they defeated Zenox as there was no threat in the near future she was unaware of. Jack and Laura were still able to keep a close watch on her as they reported everything back to the lab.

Thomas was in his secret laboratory at the hospital when he heard one of his computers beep. He examined it, but the beeping quickly stopped and all energy levels returned to normal. Discouraged, Thomas went back to his desk and began calculating again. His experiment on Krystal's soul was still not complete…

To be continued…